D1079715

Blood
Moon

ALSO BY ALYXANDRA HARVEY

The Drake Chronicles in reading order:
My Love Lies Bleeding
Blood Feud
Out for Blood
Bleeding Hearts

◆ ◆ ◆

Haunting Violet

◆ ◆ ◆

Stolen Away

Blood
Moon

ALYXANDRA HARVEY

BLOOMSBURY

LONDON NEW DELHI NEW YORK SYDNEY

Bloomsbury Publishing, London, New Delhi, New York and Sydney

First published in Great Britain in July 2012 by Bloomsbury Publishing Plc
50 Bedford Square, London, WC1B 3DP

First published in the USA in June 2012 by Walker Publishing Company, Inc.
175 Fifth Avenue, New York, NY 10010

Text copyright © Alexandra Harvey 2012

The moral right of the author has been asserted

All rights reserved
No part of this publication may be reproduced or
transmitted by any means, electronic, mechanical, photocopying
or otherwise, without the prior permission of the publisher

A CIP catalogue record for this book is available from the British Library

ISBN 978 1 4088 3190 8

MIX
Paper from
responsible sources
FSC® C018072

Printed in Great Britain by Clays Ltd, St Ives Plc, Bungay, Suffolk

1 3 5 7 9 10 8 6 4 2

www.bloomsbury.com

In the violet hills,
the moon's bloodshot eye sees all.

THE DRAKE FAMILY TREE

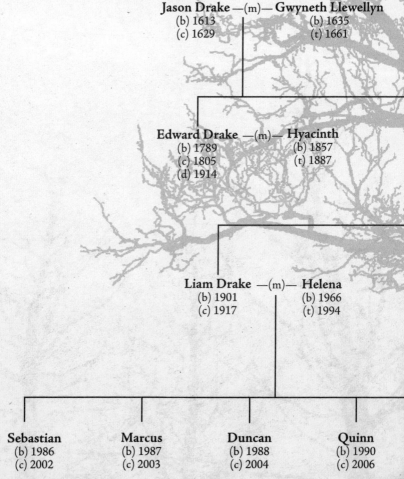

Jason Drake —(m)— **Gwyneth Llewellyn**
(b) 1613   (b) 1635
(c) 1629   (t) 1661

Edward Drake —(m)— **Hyacinth**
(b) 1789   (b) 1857
(c) 1805   (t) 1887
(d) 1914

Liam Drake —(m)— **Helena**
(b) 1901   (b) 1966
(c) 1917   (t) 1994

Sebastian   **Marcus**   **Duncan**   **Quinn**
(b) 1986   (b) 1987   (b) 1988   (b) 1990
(c) 2002   (c) 2003   (c) 2004   (c) 2006

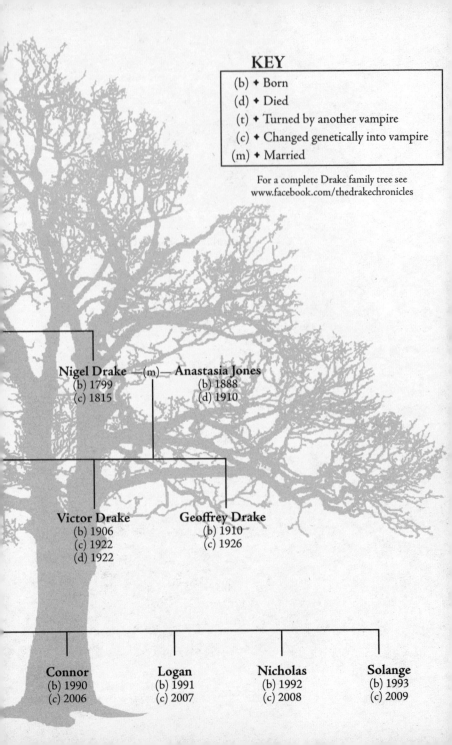

KEY

(b) ✦ Born
(d) ✦ Died
(t) ✦ Turned by another vampire
(c) ✦ Changed genetically into vampire
(m) ✦ Married

For a complete Drake family tree see
www.facebook.com/thedrakechronicles

Nigel Drake —(m)— **Anastasia Jones**
(b) 1799   (b) 1888
(c) 1815   (d) 1910

Victor Drake   **Geoffrey Drake**
(b) 1906   (b) 1910
(c) 1922   (c) 1926
(d) 1922

Connor   **Logan**   **Nicholas**   **Solange**
(b) 1990   (b) 1991   (b) 1992   (b) 1993
(c) 2006   (c) 2007   (c) 2008   (c) 2009

Chapter I

Lucy

Saturday night

"You tried to eat your boyfriend's *face?*"

Okay, so it wasn't the most sympathetic response I could have come up with, but I couldn't help it. I was punchy from fatigue and had what felt like an adrenaline hangover. And not only was I covered in ashes and bruises from fighting feral *Hel-Blar* vampires and blowing up a ghost town, but I was sure there was some kind of mistake.

Solange didn't do stuff like this.

Well, usually.

She looked so wispy and pale she was practically translucent, except for the blue veins that traced her collarbone. Her fangs were out, all three sets. She held up a hand when I stepped closer. The light glinted off the personalized royal medallion around her neck. "Stay downwind," she said tightly.

I frowned. "Are you telling me I stink?"

She nodded once, pained. "Blood."

"Oh." I'd been fighting *Hel-Blar* all night so she was probably right. Only clearly she didn't mind the smell.

She frowned. "And gunpowder? Why do—" Solange shook her head. "Never mind, you have to help Kieran. *Now.*"

"That's really his blood?" When she looked at me as if she was about to burst into tears, I swore. "Shit. Where is he? What happened?" She pointed to the line of pine trees behind the oak, the tall grass shivering around the exposed roots. I thought I saw a black combat boot. I broke into a run. "Kieran!"

He moaned, propped up against a tree, blood running down his neck and arm. There was a bite mark just above his collar, the flesh ragged. Under all the red, he was the color of boiled mushrooms.

"Kieran, can you hear me?"

He swallowed, trying to speak. The movement made the blood run faster, soaking his shirt. "Solange," he croaked. "Help Sol—"

"She's fine," I assured him. I took the bandanna I knew was in his cargo pants pocket above his knee. It was standard issue for a Helios-Ra agent. I wadded it up and pressed it over his wound, trying not to feel nauseated. "Can you press here?" I asked him. "As hard as you can." I glanced over my shoulder. "What the hell happened to you two?" I slipped my arm under Kieran's shoulder on his good side and tried to lift him. He weighed a ton.

"Don't just stand there!" I shouted at Solange. "Help me!"

She stayed where she was.

"Solange!"

"I don't know if I can!" she shouted back frantically.

"Then call 911. What's the matter with you? He needs an ambulance."

"You know they can't come here," Solange said.

"Can't tell anyone," Kieran agreed, moaning. "They'd hunt her."

While I certainly wasn't going to let anyone hunt my best friend—even if she had turned my own boyfriend against me just last week—I wasn't going to let *her* boyfriend bleed to death in the woods either.

"We'll take you to the school infirmary, then." I grunted, trying to haul him to his feet. He stumbled, sliding up the trunk. He was clammy and shivering. "We can tell them it was a random attack. But we need to get you there *now*. You need stitches." I tried not to think about Solange's teeth as the weapon that had gouged him. At least she hadn't gone for the jugular. Small comfort. Blood was sticky on my hands. "Solange, I can't get him to the van by myself. I'm not the one with vampire strength."

"I can still taste his blood, Lucy." Her hands were clenched so tight the knuckles looked as if they were outside her delicate skin. "I can smell it everywhere. It's in the grass, in the air, on me. I'm not safe."

I swore again, viciously enough to have made the proverbial

sailor proud. I fumbled for the nose plugs around Kieran's neck and tossed them at her, grateful that Kieran was still a vampire hunter to his core, even if he was dating a vampire princess. "Put these on."

I was a student at the Helios-Ra Academy now too but I wasn't in regulation uniform, just my usual embroidered peasant blouse and crystal beads. I hadn't even started classes yet; I'd been too busy killing monsters.

Solange clipped them on her nose, closing her nostrils tight against the violent scents drenching the woods. Even I could smell the coppery tang of blood, but it was making me queasy, not hungry. The nose plugs gave her a momentary reprieve, and she was at Kieran's side so fast the wildflowers flattened around her. She looked awful, but she took Kieran's weight, and we dragged him to the van. I opened the side door, and we slid him half onto a seat, his feet still dangling out of the open door. I was panting and sweating from the exertion. I couldn't remember the last time I'd slept. But I didn't have time to stop, not yet.

Not even for my best friend, who was suddenly licking her lips, her teeth faintly pink, smeared with Kieran's blood, her eyes red veined and fierce. I heard the dry rasp of bat wings, felt the shadows of them moving toward us even if I couldn't see them clearly in the dark.

We were in so much trouble I nearly gave up right then and there.

"Solange!" I tried to snap her out of the bloodlust. "Remember who you are!"

"I think I finally am." She was practically purring.

I'd known she was in a bad way when Nicholas and I found her a few days ago, drunk on human blood, a willing donor passed out at her feet. And then she'd attacked me for making comments about the mysterious vampire Constantine, whom I'd never met but did *not* like. I especially didn't like the way she said his name, as if he were hotter than Johnny Depp.

"Get in the van, Kieran," I said, moving very slowly to stand in front of him while he struggled to lift his heavy feet all the way in. He pushed something at me, hiding it in the small of my back. It was too square to be either a knife or a stake.

Taser.

"No, don't go," Solange said, pulling off the nose clips and tossing them aside. "I'm still hungry."

Apparently adrenaline, fear, panic, and guilt could only hold out for so long against bloodlust.

Solange was gone.

I wasn't sure who was standing in front of me. She might have Solange's ethereal beauty and her ballerina grace, but she wasn't Solange.

Oblivious, Kieran leaned toward her, as if I weren't in his way.

Vampire pheromones.

Without his nose plugs, he was vulnerable. I'd grown up with Solange and her brothers so I was mostly immune. Theoretically.

Because, lately, Solange was breaking all of our theories.

Kieran didn't even notice the bats swarming above us. I ducked my head a little, trying not to scream like a child in a Halloween haunted house. "Crap," I said darkly, shoving him down into his seat. "Solange, back off."

"No."

Kieran leaned farther forward, his blood dripping on the car mat and out into the grass. He tried to shove me aside so that Solange could finish her dinner. I shoved back without turning around, making sure to poke him hard in his wound. The flesh was warm and ragged and sticky under my finger. I decided I might just throw up later. It was worth it though, as Kieran recoiled, hissing through his teeth. The pain broke the lure of Solange's pheromones, if only for a moment. I elbowed him savagely so that he fell back completely into the van, and then I slammed the door shut on him.

Solange only smiled. Her eyes were veined in red, like an autumn leaf. "I'm still thirsty," she murmured.

I scowled, trying to remember the Solange I knew, covered in clay and only wanting to be left alone. "Too bad," I said through my teeth, which weren't nearly as impressive as hers. Her fangs gleamed when her smile widened. Bats flew in a whirlwind over her head. "Go away, Sol."

"Mmm, I don't think so." She shrugged one shoulder. "You can run if you like. I'm going to start with Kieran first. You'd only taste like lemons and ash. I can smell your anger." She wrinkled her nose as if I were spoiled meat. "It doesn't enhance you, not like the others."

"Gee, I'm so sorry that the fact that I want to punch you right in your princess nose might ruin your palate. We're not bottles of wine."

She just shrugged again.

And then she was pressing me into the van, so close I could see the blue under her skin, hear the flap of bat wings and the crackle they left in the air. I couldn't be sure she wouldn't snap my neck just to get to Kieran, slowly bleeding himself into a coma behind me.

So I did the only thing I could think to do.

I Tasered my best friend.

I wasn't sure if it was the jolts of electricity running through her or the proximity of the dawn, but she fell backward onto the grass. I didn't even have time to make sure she was all right. Technically, she was already dead, so a little shock wouldn't hurt her for long. Okay, 1500 volts, whatever. She'd survive, but Kieran needed help now.

I paused.

She'd survive being Tasered, but not the dawn.

I'd have to bring her with me.

"Shit," I said. "This is just the worst night ever."

I approached her carefully, nudging her with the toe of my boot. She lay still, pale and slight. "If you bite me, I'm biting you back," I muttered, crouching down to lift her up. When she didn't open her eyes and try to eat me, I felt marginally better. I dragged her awkwardly toward the van and stuffed her into the front seat. "If you wake up cranky, I'm so Tasering you again." I ran around to the driver's seat. "I've already blown up a town tonight, so don't think I won't."

The bats, angered, dive-bombed me. I tucked my head into my collar and ran faster, hollering. The screaming didn't scare the bats off but it made me feel better. I felt one catch in my hair, then bounce off my shoulder.

"I really hate everybody right now," I said, diving into the front seat. I yanked the door handle just as another bat hit the glass. Solange was slumped next to me. I kept the Taser in my right hand, contorting to start the van with my left. Kieran shifted in the backseat. "Don't die," I told him sternly.

He tried to chuckle but it turned into a wet gurgle. I hit the gas pedal and peeled out of the field, kicking up clods of dirt and grass.

"Don't wake up," I chanted at Solange. "Don't wake up."

The bats followed us like a black, leathery cloud. Their eyes were red when they dipped down into the spear of the headlights.

"Don't wake up," I said again. "And don't be such a stereotype. *Bats*. God."

They were so thick now, it was hard to see. I prayed really hard that I wouldn't drive us right into a tree. I craned my neck. The Taser was heavy, making my wrist ache. A bat hit the windshield, cracking it like a rock. Blood smeared the glass.

"I'm sorry!" I yelled. "Get out of my way, you stupid flying rodents."

Another hit, and another. A crack snaked through the windshield. Fur and blood matted in the fissure. Bile burned the back of my throat.

Solange stirred.

I jabbed the Taser at her but she was faster. She dodged out of the way. The van wobbled precariously as I fought to keep hold of the steering wheel. Kieran was passed out in his own blood. Solange glanced back at him and licked her lips. It was a tiny moment of distraction and likely the last one I'd get. I stabbed the Taser at her again. It glanced off her shoulder, but it was enough to freeze her, her face contorting.

"I'm sorry, I'm sorry, I'm sorry," I repeated over and over as I slammed on the brakes. She flew into the dashboard. I reached over her while she was still stunned and opened the passenger door.

Then I shoved her out as hard as I could into the grass.

She sprawled, bats circling overhead like vultures. I sped away with the door still open, banging against tree branches. The smell of pine and cedar mixed with Kieran's blood. I looked into the rearview mirror. Solange sat up slowly.

I hit the gas harder.

CHAPTER 2

Solange

I ran because I could, because dawn was coming, because I didn't
know what else I should do.

I knew what I *wanted* to do.

Lucy might have dropped me with her Taser but I was still
burning with Kieran's blood, nearly dizzy with it. I could feel it
coursing through my veins, making me feel invincible, making me
feel alive again. I wanted more. More than I had ever wanted chocolate, more than Lucy wanted Johnny Depp.

The gray van sped away, gleaming like a tin can. I could peel
the roof off like it was the lid. The 1500 volts of electricity Lucy
shot through me might have killed me when I was human, but now
it only made me pause, was merely a choke chain on the hunger.
I could have snapped the chain if I'd wanted to.

Yes, let's.

I stopped running. I didn't actually *want* to eat my boyfriend or my best friend. It wasn't their fault they smelled like food.

I wasn't sure it was my fault either, though. I felt like an addict. Or maybe it was only that I was finally getting what I needed, as if I'd been anemic and hadn't even realized it. I was a vampire. It's not like it was wrong for me to drink blood. It was natural, necessary. Vital.

I nearly turned around then, to chase Lucy and Kieran down like rabbits.

The thought made me gag.

I went back to running, this time in the opposite direction. Kieran's blood was on my shirt. I needed the cool wind, the pounding of my feet in the loam, the push of muscle and bones, to distract me. I wasn't sure if he could forgive me for what I'd nearly done. I wasn't sure I could forgive myself. I was at war inside my own skin, hunger and honor, nature and nurture, need and repulsion.

The light in the forest was changing slowly, so slowly that only another nocturnal creature would have noticed. The owls and badgers would be scurrying off to their nests as the light turned luminous. The bats that were still following me drifted away.

As the sun rose inexorably behind the trees, my steps became heavier. I was too far from any of our safe houses underground, too far from the farmhouse, which I didn't want to return to anyway. I couldn't bear to look at my family right now, to give them proof that I was weaker than they were. The Blood Moon encampment was closer. I'd be safe there.

I forced myself to keep running. A pine branch scraped across my cheek. The sun was like a boulder on my back. I might as well have been Sisyphus, condemned to roll a huge rock uphill every day in Tartarus as punishment for his sins. Logan had gone through a Greek myth phase, and he'd read me a new one every night the summer I was ten.

Screw Sisyphus.

I wasn't going to just lie down and die. My family and friends had fought too hard so I could survive. Aunt Hyacinth still wore the scars on her face.

Dawn wouldn't have me, not today.

I tripped over a root, any natural grace fleeing under the laborious heaviness of my limbs, but I wouldn't let it stop me. I wasn't quite fast enough to catch my balance or my footing. I fell.

Right into Constantine's arms.

He twisted so he was dipping me, as if we were dancing in some fancy ballroom. He should have been wearing an embroidered frock coat and a velvet hair ribbon, not a plain leather coat. My hair dragged the ground. I knew the moment he saw the blood staining my shirt and dried on my chin. His fangs lengthened, his eyes gleamed violet, like amethyst beads. He bent forward, dragging the tip of his nose along my exposed throat, tickling. I should have been frightened or disgusted. Instead I just dangled there, comforted. He licked my collarbone.

"Mmm, fresh," he murmured, his British accent thicker than usual.

He was licking Kieran's blood off me.

I used his hand on my lower back to stabilize myself, and pushed my feet up into the air, vaulting into a backflip. I landed in the bushes a few feet away, berries scattering around me, hands clenched.

Constantine just raised his eyebrow at me, unflappable as always. I'd never seen him wear any expression except dry amusement. "Whose blood are you wearing that you won't share, beloved?"

"My—never mind," I said.

"It's fresh." He licked a drop off his left fang. I swallowed hard. He shook his head. "You're entirely too hard on yourself. This isn't some movie where you have to suffer and gnash your teeth to prove your goodness. You are who you are. It's to be celebrated."

"I drank from an unwilling . . . friend." Could I call Kieran my boyfriend after tonight? Did I have that right? Didn't he deserve a girlfriend who wouldn't attack him? Someone like him, full of honor and ready to die to do the right thing. Someone Helios-Ra. Not a vampire like me.

And I was feeling feral. I was the only Drake I knew of who was having this much trouble with the bloodchange. It had only been a couple of months, but by now I should only be dangerous right at dusk or if I was left to starve. I shouldn't be dangerous to kiss.

I tried very hard not to think about the *Hel-Blar*, who attacked anything that moved, even one another. I might have more fangs than other vampires, even more than the Hounds who were ostracized for their double set, but I still had fewer than the *Hel-Blar*. And I wasn't blue like they were, and I didn't smell like mushrooms and stagnant water. Anyway, weren't we still finding that there were undiscovered vampire races, since Lucy's cousin Christabel was turned?

Constantine's mouth quirked. "I can't tell if you're about to cry or let out a battle yell, love."

"Neither," I said quietly, forcing myself out of the bushes. "I'm just going to walk." Which at the moment was a battle in itself.

"I could carry you," he suggested.

I shook my head grimly. I'd been carried once before, had lain unconscious in Montmartre's arms when he'd thought to trade my family's safety for me. I wasn't going to be that Solange anymore. I didn't want to be rescued. I'd get to safety myself or die trying.

"I'll walk," I said again.

"You're ruining my very romantic gesture, Solange," he said. Despite the circumstances, I couldn't help but love the way he said my name. His voice was like smoke, dangerous as a forest fire and comforting as a beach bonfire all at the same time.

I was feeling tingly over a vampire not an hour after trying to drain my boyfriend and being Tasered by my best friend. Clearly, I was going to hell. I limped along, gritting my back teeth. *Don't be such a martyr.*

I frowned, glancing around. "Did you hear that?"

Constantine raised his eyebrows. "No, what?"

I shook my head. I must be more tired than I thought. "Nothing."

"We're still rather far from camp," he said. "I assume that's where you're going?"

I nodded. He walked easily beside me, unfazed by the sun. I didn't know how old he was or how long he'd been a vampire, but it was long enough that he could fight the approach of the dawn. I was still so newly turned I dropped before everyone, even Nicholas, who had only just turned the year before. It made me vulnerable. And it made me stupid to have been out so close to sunrise. My mother was going to kill me.

Constantine pulled a glass vial out of the inside pocket of his coat and handed it to me. I didn't take it right away. It dangled from his fingers, and in the dark it looked more black than red. "This will give you strength."

"I don't want it," I lied. My fingers were literally trembling with the need to snatch the vial away from him. I bit down hard on my lower lip to distract myself.

"You're making me feel like a drug pusher in one of those old after-school specials," he remarked wryly. "It's just blood, Solange. Food. Without it you die."

"I'm not . . . thirsty."

His smile was crooked and sardonic. "You've just turned. You're *always* thirsty."

He was right.

"Drink it if you want to make it to camp. Otherwise you'll have to let me carry you." He shrugged one shoulder. "I don't mind, but you seem to."

Being brought in unconscious. My family would freak right out.

I took the vial and wrenched off the silver-topped cork. I tilted it, letting the blood slide down my throat, swallowing greedily. It sparkled through me as if it were made of stars and lightning. I laughed. Constantine's gaze raked me from head to toe and he smiled slowly, hungrily. I would have blushed if I were still human. I picked up my pace. "Let's go," I said.

"Of course, princess." He gave a short bow.

I frowned at him. "I told you to stop calling me that."

"And I told you to stop being ashamed of who you are. Most would kill, literally, to be a vampire and a princess, never mind both at once."

"I'm not a princess." I rolled my eyes. "And the last guy who gave me a tiara wore it through his chest."

"You *are* a princess," he said sharply, ignoring my reference to Montmartre's untimely end by my mother's hand. And mine. I'd been the one to shove the tiara but had needed Mom's strength to get it through his heart. I wasn't going to be anyone's vampire bride. "You might wish otherwise, but lying to yourself won't change the facts. You should be proud, love."

It wasn't the first time he'd said that to me. But he didn't get it. The fact that I was a princess had nearly killed Aunt Hyacinth, had Lucy thrown in a dungeon, had assassins tracking my mother. And my being a vampire had nearly killed Kieran.

I wanted to call Lucy to see how Kieran was, but there was no cell-phone coverage whatsoever this deep into the mountain forests. I wouldn't know until well after sunset tomorrow. The worry dimmed the fire of the blood in my system, the sweet metallic taste on my tongue. We made it to the outskirts of the camp as the mist rose off the river and trailed between the pine trees. A guard nodded to us once and let us pass.

The field that usually hosted wildflowers and bumblebees now bristled with huge canvas tents and swarms of vampires wearing such an odd combination of historical costumes it was as if we'd stumbled onto a circus. In private and for formal vampire occasions we tended to revert back to the clothing of our bloodchange. Even this close to dawn with the mists thick around our ankles and the call of the first birds in the treetops, I could see Victorian bustles, Celtic tattoos, medieval tunics, a 1920s beaded flapper dress, a woman dressed like a very pale Marie Antoinette.

A dog barked from the caves set back into the mountains. The Hounds slept there, and the rest of us had canvas tents like the kind I imagined littered medieval jousting tournaments. There were few humans allowed, mostly personal guards and bloodslaves who traveled with specific tribes. I couldn't stand the word "bloodslave," but Constantine only laughed and called me colonial when I mentioned it. He hadn't met Lucy yet. She'd punch him right in the nose if he called her a bloodslave.

Still, for all its flaws, there was a sharp, delicate beauty to the encampment, like a honed sword. It was silver and filigrees and handcrafted art. And it was blood and death and teeth. No amount of silks and velvets could hide the undercurrents. There were secrets here, and hunger and passionate affairs and bitter feuds. It was like living in a boiling iron cauldron set over a raging fire.

Sometimes the steam had to escape or the whole pot would explode.

Like right now.

I don't know who started it. I only saw a vampire, his blond-white hair straight and pale as moonlight, on the path where it branches into a crossroad. He was from the Joiik family, one of the oldest vampire lineages on the Raktapa Council. Coming from the other direction was a vampire I didn't recognize, dressed in a prim tweed skirt and a white blouse. She spat out a curse and launched at his head, fangs flashing.

She never made contact.

A crossbow bolt split the air and cleaved her heart, turning her to ash. A second bolt caught the Joiik, because he'd reached for his weapon. If he'd stayed still and trusted the Blood Moon secret guard to protect him, he wouldn't have been hit. Now he was dust.

It happened so fast, I barely had time to squeak. Constantine gripped my elbow, fingers digging painfully into my skin. He was holding me back, protecting me. And I was suddenly remembering that hundreds of years ago, Blood Moons were places of trials by combat and executions.

"Don't move," he murmured.

There were vampire tribes here from all over the world, each with its own customs and traditions and histories. Not to mention feuds. It took a special kind of guard to keep order in a place like this; a guard no one had ever seen and couldn't accurately describe. Even Madame Veronique, who was nearly a thousand years old, couldn't tell us who they were or even what they looked like. We only knew some of them must be human since the crossbow bolts apparently came during the day as well. They kept to the trees and the shadows, constantly circling, constantly watching. No one was exempt from their justice. Not princess, not council; only the queen.

The back of my neck prickled. "Are they gone?"

Constantine's violet eyes flickered back and forth. "Never, but the danger's past I think."

A Joiik woman with long blond braids rushed to the ashes under the leather tunic, marked with a Thor's hammer design. She keened loudly, brokenly. The sounds made the back of my throat hurt.

Constantine's hand nudged me and we moved backward, out of the way. "Best get you home," he said.

We weren't far when Bruno stepped in front of me. "The Chandramaa guard?"

I nodded mutely.

"Are you all right?"

I nodded again. "Yes."

He gave Constantine a long, hard look. Bruno looked just like the old biker he was: bald, covered in tattoos, and burly as an oak tree. Nothing intimidated him. He scowled at me. "Lass, do you have any idea how much trouble you're in?"

They knew about Kieran. And if they knew about him, then he must be in serious condition. I hadn't meant to drink so near his jugular. He was dying. The guy who'd saved my life was dying. My *boyfriend* was dying. "I—"

"Your parents are worried sick," Bruno continued, oblivious to my inner nervous breakdown. "This isn't the time to be breaking curfew." He spoke softly into his walkie-talkie, then pointed to the blue tent painted with the Drake silver dragon and the Latin motto underneath: "*Nox noctis, nostra domina*," which translated roughly to "Night, our mistress."

"On with ye," Bruno directed.

I turned to Constantine, slightly embarrassed that I was being treated like a naughty child. I was a vampire princess, as everyone insisted on reminding me. So shouldn't I have a little power over my own life? I bristled. Constantine winked as if he knew what I was thinking, as if it was our own private joke.

Dawn hadn't arrived yet but the darkness was going gray, glinting on silver paint on the tents and on the gold banners. I felt like water, uncontainable, soft, and everywhere at once, as if even my skin couldn't hold me in. My eyelids fluttered, closed. Constantine took a step closer, and Bruno elbowed him back.

"I've got her," he said, his Scottish brogue thicker than usual. He picked me up and carried me into the family tent muttering, "Bloody English."

CHAPTER 3

Nicholas

We were cutting it close.

We would have gone back to the farmhouse but dawn was unfolding and we were already in the mountains, running from the smoke and rubble of a collapsed ghost town and a breed of vampire we'd had no idea even existed. Quinn and Connor were slowing down, each holding up Lucy's cousin Christabel, who was dragging her feet so heavily she left a trail in the dirt. She'd been a vampire for barely a week, and she was already embroiled in politics and assassinations. I'd been a vampire for a year and a half now, and I wasn't much better equipped. My boots felt as if they were weighed down with rocks. I nearly tripped on a tree root.

Quinn glanced at me. "Gonna make it?"

"Yeah, yeah," I answered. "Though what's the point? Mom's going to kill us anyway."

"True."

"If that thing doesn't kill us first," I added when the stench of rot and mushrooms hit us. Cracking twigs and clacking jaws followed. *Hel-Blar* weren't exactly subtle. They didn't so much hunt as attack, but what they lacked in finesse they made up for in numbers and sheer savagery.

And the three streaming between the pine trees and down the hill toward us weren't tired like we were. They hadn't been fighting all night. They were drawn out of their nests by the smell of blood and battle. I didn't know if they'd followed us from the ghost town, but it seemed unlikely. They probably caught wind of the fire and fight, and bad luck had them stumbling on us.

"Shit," I muttered. "You guys better run."

Quinn snorted. "We're not leaving you alone, you idiot."

"Christa's barely able to stand," I argued. "And she doesn't have any battle training, so get out of here already."

Christabel propped herself up on Connor's shoulder. "I'm fine," she said thickly, too sleepy to enunciate. "Give me a stake."

"You're lisping," I pointed out.

"So maybe I have a lisp," she insisted. "It's rude of you to make fun of me."

I exchanged a glance with Connor. "Definitely related to Lucy," we said in unison.

I reached for a stake as the *Hel-Blar* descended. "Just go, damn it."

"I'll stay," Quinn said, his hands full of stakes. "Connor, you take Christa and go."

"Too late," Connor snapped. He hauled Christabel over his

shoulder and scaled the nearest tree, depositing her in the crook of a huge willow branch. He handed her a stake. "Don't fall on this."

"What?" she asked, befuddled. It was like that for the newborn vampires. Dawn made them stupid.

"*I'll come to thee by moonlight,*" Connor said, quoting her favorite poem. "*Though hell should bar the way.*" He kissed her quickly. "And don't fall out," he added.

"Don't die," she replied sleepily.

"Dude," Quinn grinned. "Did you just recite poetry?"

"Shut it," Connor shot back amiably. He dropped down to the ground just as the *Hel-Blar* reached us. We automatically circled the tree, protecting Christabel. She lay in the cup of branches in her military jacket and combat boots, her long reddish hair trailing between the silvery willow branches.

The weight of the approaching sunrise fought with a surge of adrenaline in my system. It felt like I'd been awake for days, drinking gallons of coffee. Quinn let out a holler and leaped on the closest *Hel-Blar*, attacking before he could be attacked. He'd always been that way. Luckily, he was a good fighter and his hands were covered with ash before Connor finished cursing at him. I took out the next vampire with my last stake.

A second wave of *Hel-Blar* came snarling through the woods. When it became apparent that we were about to be dangerously outnumbered, I did the only thing I could do.

I ran.

I didn't give my brothers a chance to stop me, just drove my stake into the chest of the *Hel-Blar* blocking me, then leapfrogged over him as he crumbled to ash. Quinn gave a shout when he real-ized what I was doing, but it was too late. The two *Hel-Blar* closest to Quinn and Connor stayed where they were, gnashing their teeth—but the others changed their course.

Because if there was one thing besides blood that a vampire, *Hel-Blar* or otherwise, couldn't resist, it was the chase.

The *Hel-Blar* pursued me because they couldn't *not* chase me. Some of us could chain the predator, even if it hurt like hell, but the *Hel-Blar* were feral to begin with. Self-control was not among their attributes. And prey that ran away was all the sweeter. It awoke something primal inside us all, even my dad, who was the most civilized of us.

I ran fast enough that for a while I left behind the stagnant pond stench, trading it for pine needles and frost.

But it didn't last.

Dawn was too close, and I was too slow. I couldn't run any-more, not with any kind of real speed. When the trees stopped blurring around me, I stopped altogether. Better to preserve my faltering strength for battle. At least the *Hel-Blar* were far enough away from Quinn, Connor, and Christabel. I stood my ground at the edge of a patch of frostbitten grass, under a tree glittering with gold-dust lichen. The ground was liberally strewn with broken branches. They would have to do as makeshift stakes if worse came to worst.

And in our family, lately, worse *always* came to worst.

Case in point, the *Hel-Blar* currently closing in on me. There were at least five that I could see. At the clacking of jaws, I raised my stake.

The first *Hel-Blar* leaped at my throat, maddened with thirst. He was clumsy with need, which gave me the chance to dodge out of the way and spin around to stake him from behind. Ash settled on the grass at my feet. The second *Hel-Blar* wasn't nearly as animal in his thirst, and there was a gleam of intelligence in his bloodshot eyes. It was like that with some of them: they were present and clever enough to be conscious in their feeding.

Not good.

Saliva spattered over my boot.

Not good at all.

I jerked back, using the tree to stabilize me so I could kick out with force. The *Hel-Blar* hissed as my heel caught him in the sternum. He stumbled back against another vampire, and they both staggered. The third darted around their flailing limbs, snarling. I couldn't see the fourth at all.

I jabbed forward with a branch, but he reared back up, snapping it out of my hand. I grabbed another branch but only managed to stab him in the collarbone.

"Shit," I had time to mutter disgustedly before he went for my throat again. I got him in the knees that time and had to bend backward so he wouldn't head butt me as he doubled over.

When the others closed in, I leaped up to grab hold of the branch above my head and swung into the tree. I jumped to the next tree and the next, trying to gain ground. Two followed me up the trees like homicidal squirrels, and the other two tracked me from the undergrowth. If they'd had stakes I'd have been dead already. I ran along cedar boughs and oak limbs until the trees thinned out to a meadow. I teetered on the last branch, cursing.

I didn't have anywhere left to go.

And I was nearly too tired to care.

I propped myself up against the trunk and waited for the *Hel-Blar* to reach me. The rotten stench of them hung in the cold air. They crashed through the leaves, teeth snapping, jaws cracking. The sound skittered over me like poisonous spiders. I was trying to decide whether to climb higher or take my chances on the ground when a new sound wrapped around us, a soft growl that shivered through the grass.

It was the best sound in the world.

Motorcycles.

My brother Duncan screeched into view, circling my tree and sliding sideways as the bike dipped. He lifted one hand and shot a miniature crossbow, catching one of the *Hel-Blar* in the chest. She hissed, grasped at the bolt, and then drifted into ashes, like snow. The *Hel-Blar* on the branch beside me was momentarily distracted. I didn't have the energy to grapple with him so I just leaned over and shoved him right out of the tree. He fell, screaming, and by the time he hit the ground, Duncan's backup had arrived and dispatched him.

Duncan stopped the motorcycle, glancing up at me, his jeans smeared with engine grease as usual. "Okay, little brother?"

I lowered into a crouch. "Connor, Quinn, and Christabel are still back there." I pointed and the guards behind him took off in that direction. I slid to the ground, wiping ash and dirt off my face. "Thanks."

Duncan took a plastic water bottle filled with blood out of his bike satchel and tossed it to me. "Don't thank me yet. Mom and Dad got your message about the ghost town and Saga. They sent me to get you."

I winced and took a long pull off the bottle. "How mad are they?"

Duncan snorted. "Dad broke a chair."

"Crap." Mom broke furniture all the time, but Dad prided himself on his control and even temper. I felt a kind of fear that not even a feral *Hel-Blar* trying to kill me could engender. I drained the bottle and felt like I could at least make it to the camp on my own two feet, even if what I actually wanted to do was hunker down in a safe house until my parents cooled off.

Duncan and I waited until our brothers and Christabel came toward us through the trees, looking pale but grateful.

Quinn slapped me on the shoulder affectionately, then scowled. "Don't ever do that again."

I just snorted. We martyred ourselves for each other all the time. It was genetic.

Duncan gave another bottle to Christabel.

She grimaced. "No way."

"You're a *vampire*, kid," Duncan told her. "Drink up."

She looked at the blood through the thin plastic and gagged.

Connor slipped his arm around her shoulder, holding her up. "Uncle G. will come hook you up in the morning," he said encouragingly. Christabel still couldn't stomach the idea of drinking blood, even though her body not only craved it but required it for survival. Uncle Geoffrey had to give her a transfusion every time she woke up. Connor took the bottle from her and drained it himself, wiping his mouth with the back of his hand.

One of the handful of guards Duncan had brought with him nodded a greeting. He wore the mark of the royal house on his shirt. He was old enough that the dawn wasn't even fazing him. His two companions were human, lean and lethal as swords. "We'll take rear guard," he said. "And we'll leave you two of the bikes."

"Thanks." Quinn took the keys from him before I could and climbed on the bike. He glanced at me. "Get on."

I hopped on behind him, grumbling but too tired to argue who got to drive. Connor helped Christabel up on the bike in front of him and she sat backward, looping her arms around his neck. If she passed out before we got there, he'd have a better chance of catching her so she didn't fall off completely. We passed another unit of royal guards before we reached the camp.

We left the motorcycles in the narrow field beside Duncan's minigarage tent. He spent most of his time there with the tools, equipment, and jerricans. The encampment was too crowded for him, and he only joined us at dawn or for family meetings. While Connor might not like crowds, Duncan was downright antisocial. We walked into the torch-lit encampment.

Right into a cluster of belly dancers.

They shimmied around us, wearing tarnished silver coins and tribal tassels. Musicians stood in a half-moon to the side playing drums. All of a sudden it felt as if we were in some kind of ancient desert caravan. I half expected to see a camel.

"Pirates, Huron warriors, and belly dancers in one night," I muttered. "My head hurts."

Christabel blinked, her words slurring. "Is that real?"

One of the dancers shimmied her hips.

"Hell, yeah," Quinn answered reverently.

Vampires gathered along the tents, watching the show. The dancers' bare feet whispered over the grass-flattened ground. One of them began to whirl, her braided hair falls lifting in the air. She spun and spun until she was a blur of colors and textures. The drumbeat struggled to keep up. The other dancers shimmied on the spot until their coins scattered like shooting stars.

"Um, what the hell?" Connor wondered.

"Compliments of one of the Egyptian tribes," a girl answered. She wore paint-splattered overalls and looked more like a university art student than a vampire. Her hair was a cloud of dark brown curls, her skin like milk chocolate. "This place is like an arts and culture expo. Totally awesome."

Christabel was weaving on her feet. "'Sometimes a troop of damsels glad . . . ,'" she quoted.

The girl beamed at her. "*The Lady of Shalott*! That's my favorite painting by Waterhouse."

Christabel was momentarily distracted from her faint. "You know 'The Lady of Shalott'?"

"I'm Sky." The girl introduced herself, grinning. "And we should definitely hang out."

"Totally. Anyone who—" Christabel passed out midsentence. Connor caught her.

Sky shook her head sympathetically. "Newly turned?"

"Very new," Connor said, carrying Christabel through the crowd toward the Drake tent.

The drums reached a peak, and the belly dancers circled us in their embroidered choli blouses and beaded skirts, smelling like sandalwood incense and amber perfume. One of them flashed her fangs at me before the drums stopped suddenly and the girls dispersed into the appreciative audience.

"She was flirting with you, little brother." Duncan grinned at me.

"She was not," I muttered. "Give me a break."

Sky laughed. "She totally was. She has a thing for Drake boys."

I've said it before and I'll say it again.

Girls are weird.

"Ready?" Quinn asked when Sky wandered off and we couldn't avoid the family tent anymore.

"Hell, no."

"Me neither."

Mom and Dad waited just inside the tent flap. The light from the oil lamps glinted off fangs, narrowed eyes, and Mom's weapon collection.

"Congratulations." Dad spoke first, his voice soft as smoke before it fills your lungs. "I honestly don't know which of my children I'm angriest with right now."

CHAPTER 4

Lucy

"What, are all the crazies out tonight? Moon's not even full yet."

Theo, the head nurse in the school infirmary, looked competent, calm, and thoroughly disgusted. Since he was still dealing with the fallout of the ghost town I helped blow up just a few hours ago, I couldn't blame him. He eyed me sternly. "Didn't you already blow up a bunch of people tonight?"

I nodded sheepishly. Kieran was already sprawled on a gurney. I helped Theo push him inside. He was even paler in the bright infirmary lights. There was no one in the waiting room, only empty coffee cups. The green curtains were drawn around all of the emergency beds. My nose burned with the sharp smell of antiseptic.

Kieran moaned, blood soaking through the makeshift bandage. Theo cursed. "What the hell happened to him?"

"Vampire."

"I can see that." He lifted Kieran's eyelids and made a sound in the back of his throat that I couldn't interpret.

My palms started to sweat all over again. "He's going to be okay, right?"

Another nurse rushed over from one of the back rooms, her uniform askew, muttering. "That old hunter they brought in from the ghost town? The one who thinks he's all tough?" She shook her head. "Big baby." Her eyes widened when she saw Kieran. "Isn't that Hart's nephew?" Hart was the leader of the Helios-Ra and everyone's boss. Technically, I guess he was my boss now too. Hah. The only person I'd take orders from was Helena Drake.

"*Hel-Blar?*" Theo asked me.

I shook my head quickly. "No."

"Are you sure?"

"Yes."

Kieran coughed weakly. "Not *Hel-Blar*," he confirmed.

Theo nodded to the other nurse. "Get him on saline, and have the doctor check him out."

"Right away." She pushed Kieran behind one of the curtains.

I went to follow but Theo stopped me. "We got him," he said. "He might not even need a transfusion, just rest. Like you."

I blinked because there were two of him. Relief made my muscles weak, and the fatigue I'd been holding off rushed in. I wobbled. Theo frowned. "Go to bed, Lucy. Now."

"I'll just nap in the chair until the doctor's checked Kieran out."

He pushed me toward the door. "Go to bed," he repeated. "I promise I'll call if anything changes."

"But . . ."

He closed the glass door in my face and locked it.

Rude.

I went back to the dorm because I was too tired to do anything else. Birds sang from the rooftops. Hanging out with vampires was hell on a girl's sleeping patterns.

I dragged my feet along the path as the sun rose just enough to light the mist off the pond and snaking between the trees. I was glad campus was deserted so no one saw my pathetic shuffle-walk. I yawned so widely a bear could've mistaken my mouth for a cave and crawled in to hibernate for the winter. The grass glittered with dew and made the metal handle of the dormitory door slick and cold. There'd be frost in the mountains, settling over the embers and ashes of the ghost town where my cousin had been imprisoned.

I hauled myself up the stairs and down the hall to my new room. My roommate, Sarita, didn't even stir when I came in, sleeping with her blankets tucked perfectly around her. She even slept neatly. I fell into bed still wearing my soot- and blood-stained clothes and muddy shoes. I should call Hunter and tell her Kieran was in the infir—

I fell asleep reaching for the phone.

I would have slept straight through dinner if Sarita hadn't kept waking me up.

Clearly no one had told her it's not smart to wake up a sleeping girl covered in weapons and mud. Seems basic to me, but then, I'd grown up with the Drakes.

"What?" I grumbled when I opened one eye to find her just standing by my bed. I slept better in a house full of vampires. This whole roommate thing wasn't off to a great start.

"Are you sick?"

"Yes," I mumbled, hoping it would make her go away. I pulled the pillow over my head.

"It's not that flu, is it? Students died from that, you know."

"That wasn't a flu," I said through my pillow. "That was some weird pill one of your teachers was slipping students." Students with ties to vampires, to be precise. So, said vampires would drink from them, get sick, and die. Hunter discovered the secret plot and saved the school. And then Quinn saved her, so it all worked out in the end. I was still getting a kick out of seeing him so into a girl. Just one girl. He'd even erased the other numbers on his phone. In Quinn's world that was cataclysmic. He may as well have sere-naded her on the front lawn of the school for all to see.

"How do you know that?" Sarita asked.

The explanation would make her head hurt.

"And do you always sleep this late? It's five thirty."

I groaned. "Sarita?"

"Yes?"

Everything I wanted to say was rude or violent.

I bit my tongue. See, I was learning stuff already at this school. "Never mind." I got up and went down the hall to the bathroom. I wasn't awake enough to remember the events of last night until I was back in my room. I got dressed quickly so I could get to the infirmary to check on Kieran. The sun was already fading. It would be dusk soon. I texted Solange and then Nicholas.

"We studied the historic vampire clans of the Raktapa Council last year," Sarita interrupted me, peering closer at the cameo I always wore. "Isn't that the Drake family insignia?"

I touched the pendant protectively. "Yes." Nicholas gave it to me over the summer. I'd switched out the velvet ribbon for a more durable chain when it became obvious that velvet was too delicate for my present circumstances.

"I don't think you're allowed to wear vampire crests at school." She was aghast.

I stared at her for a full ten seconds before answering, "*Om Namah Shivaya.*"

She blinked. "Huh?"

How to explain that my mother taught me Vedic mantras as a way to deal with stress and the imminent loss of my temper. Especially when punching someone in the nose was inappropriate. I speared her with my best Helena Drake glare instead. We were saved by a sharp knock on the door.

Hunter was on the other side, eyes wide. "Kieran's in the infirmary." Her blond ponytail swung anxiously.

"I know. I brought him there."

Seeing Hunter, Sarita stood at attention as if this were a military school and Hunter a general. "Hi, Hunter."

Hunter threw her a distracted smile then frowned at me. "I'd ask you why you didn't come tell me, but you look like shit."

"Gee, thanks," I said drily. I grabbed my sweater. "Let's go check on him."

We hurried out of the dorm and into the cold late-autumn evening. My breath misted in the air. Winter was definitely on its way. The trees shivered, scattering the last of their leaves. Students hurried to the dining hall and down from the gym, bundled in thick sweaters.

"What happened?" Hunter asked. "And can I tell you how sick I am of this place?" she added as we neared the infirmary. The fluorescent lights made squares of white on the grass.

I didn't know what Quinn had told her about Solange and her struggle. Or if Kieran had mentioned it. "It was a vampire," I said. "I went to meet Solange last night and we found him like that." Lie. Big fat lie.

Hunter paled. "*Hel-Blar?*"

I shook my head. "No, he was lucid. It was just a vampire bite. He lost some blood. Theo didn't look freaked out or anything."

"Theo never looks freaked out."

"Did he call you? What did he say?"

"Kieran's mom called," Hunter replied as we stepped into the bright, medicinal cleaner–scented room. "She won't come to campus. She's not . . . Well, she's fragile."

"She is?" Kieran never mentioned his family, beyond his dad, whom he'd once thought the Drakes had murdered. It had been Hope actually, the Helios-Ra agent who'd taken over the society along with Kieran's uncle. She'd tried to kill Solange too.

Even dead, I did *not* like her.

Theo came around one of the curtains and eyed me critically. "Better. But you need more sleep. And protein."

"How's Kieran?" Hunter and I asked together.

"He's got a few stitches, lost some blood. Probably have a scar. Could have been worse."

"Can we see him?" Hunter asked. "And the answer to that question is 'yes,' Theo. He's my best friend."

Theo just snorted. "You need more sleep too, Hunter. You lost more blood than he did, and it wasn't that long ago."

"Yeah, yeah. Where is he?"

"He went home."

"He did?" She sounded surprised. "His mom didn't . . ."

"No, his friend Eric picked him up."

"Kieran has friends?" It was a stupid question. Of course he had friends. I was just used to seeing him as Solange's boyfriend, or before that, as the annoying agent from the annoying secret society. Which I was now a member of. When, exactly, had life become so ridiculously complicated?

Oh yeah, when I'd had to Taser my best friend.

"Lucy, are you coming?" Hunter was waiting for me by the door. "Theo's right, you need dinner. Cafeteria's that way."

"Aren't you eating?"

She shook her head. "I want to call Kieran, then I need to put in some time at the gym."

"I hate you."

"Why does everyone say that when I mention going to the gym?" she muttered as she walked away.

When I got to the cafeteria I felt lost in a way I hadn't felt in a long time. I'd gone to the same school and had the same friends and driven down the same country road to see them nearly every day for years. I never really noticed that until now. But recent events had kicked me out of my safe cocoon. In the past few months alone I'd been captured by hostile vampires, been held in a dungeon, gotten stitches in the back of my head, and electrocuted my best friend. None of those things made me feel as awkward or helpless as this tidy cafeteria with its antique floors and stained glass windows and the pause in the hum of conversations as everyone stopped to watch me in the doorway.

I wasn't used to being the one who hesitated uncertainly.

No way in hell I was going to be that girl now.

I forced myself to step forward, trying to smile with a breezy nonchalance I was nowhere near feeling. I struggled to ignore the itchy weight of so many eyeballs tracking my every move. The Helios-Ra student body wasn't exactly large—there were only about thirty students per grade—but most of them were here right now, whispering about me between mouthfuls of meatloaf and mashed potatoes.

Even though I was starving, I suddenly couldn't stand the thought of bringing my plastic tray to an empty table and pretending I didn't notice all the staring. Ordinarily, I would have just introduced myself to the first friendly looking group, but I didn't have it in me yet. Tomorrow. After I talked to Solange and Nicholas and Kieran.

I grabbed a protein bar and a banana for later and decided to text Solange again. I knew she must be fine, since no one had called to tell me otherwise. But I should probably apologize for the Taser thing. And let her apologize for trying to bite me.

"God, you're still here?" someone sneered. It was a girl who'd given me attitude the first day I'd moved into the dorms, only she was with two guys this time. I could practically smell the testosterone and it wasn't coming off them. I nearly groaned out loud. I so wasn't in the mood for this. And I'd watched enough 1980s John Hughes movies to know this wasn't going to go well.

"I can't believe they'd let a vampire spy in here," she said. There were a lot of stakes on her belt. "You know you don't belong here, right? I mean, you're not stupid enough to think this is normal? Especially with all of the agents coming in to protect the town from all of your friends."

The other students fell silent around us, openly eavesdropping.

"You know what? I'm a little tired from beating people up all night to deal with your issues." I wondered how much detention I'd get for starting a brawl in the cafeteria.

"We'll be watching you," one of the guys warned, looming.

"I've been loomed over by the best," I informed him. "You need to practice."

"Oh yeah?" He stepped up closer, purposefully bumping me back.

I had a lovely daydream of breaking his nose.

In fact, I was making a fist before I'd even realized it.

"Whoa." Hunter's friend Jenna was suddenly beside me. "Ben's an ass but he's not worth scrubbing toilets for a month."

I paused. "Detention is toilet duty?"

"For hitting another student, yeah."

I lowered my fist reluctantly. "Gross."

"She's a traitor, Jenna," Ben insisted, looking vaguely surprised that she wasn't automatically on his side.

"And you're being a Neanderthal." She narrowed her eyes warningly at him. The freckles on her nose didn't make her look any less intimidating. She turned to me, ignoring them. "Want to go for a run?"

"Yes."

And that was scarier than any bully.

◆

I was sweaty and panting painfully at the end of the track when one of the teachers pointed at me.

"Lucky Hamilton?"

"Close enough," I sighed. Clearly, I was going to have to reeducate everyone on campus. I hadn't gone by Lucky since my first day of regular school.

"The headmistress wants to see you."

I winced. "I didn't do it."

He quirked a smile. "Her office is on the ground floor, the brick building there."

Jenna wiped her face with a towel. "Tough luck, Hamilton."

"Shit," I grumbled. "Classes haven't even started yet."

"She probably just wants to warn you that Hunter and I are bad influences." She grinned.

I snorted. "Please, Hunter gets straight As."

"And she's dating a vampire."

"Details."

"Just watch your back. School's tense right now," Jenna added.

I thought about Ben and his cronies. "I'm getting that."

"Even Hunter's getting crap from Ben and Jody," Jenna said, reading my expression. At least I finally knew the girl's name. "And after that doctor changed Spencer to save him, everyone's been extra jumpy. She was fired."

"But Spencer would have died."

Jenna shrugged one shoulder. "Better dead than undead." She smiled apologetically. "Old Helios-Ra motto."

I ground my teeth. "Racist. Or specie-ist, whatever."

She held up a hand in defense. "Hey, I like Spencer, fangs or not."

"I know. Sorry. It makes me cranky."

"Makes Hunter cranky too. Should've heard the mouth on her. I had no idea she knew words like that." She grabbed a bottle of water from her gym bag. "Anyway, just be polite and Bellwood shouldn't come down on you too hard. She's kinda mean but she's fair." She nodded toward the office. "Don't keep her waiting though."

I glanced at my watch and forced my rubbery legs into a jog. I had to make this fast if I wanted enough time to meet Nicholas before campus curfew. I'd break it if I had to, but I'd rather not. I was already on the school radar as it was.

Bellwood's office was at the end of a row of empty classrooms. It was ruthlessly organized and neat, almost as ruthlessly organized and neat as Bellwood herself. Sarita must just worship her. I waited in the doorway for her to acknowledge me. She didn't glance from her computer screen. "Sit."

I only barely resisted the urge to bark like a dog.

Instead I sat down, wondering which of my many infractions I was about to be busted over. She finally looked at me after a squirming moment of awkwardness. There were laugh lines at the corner of her mouth, implying she must at least know *how* to smile. You wouldn't know it to look at her now. I reminded myself that I'd survived Lady Natasha and countless vampires, not to mention Solange's mother. I could survive a high school principal.

"You did very well on your placement tests," she began without preamble. "Which is why you were put in eleventh grade despite your admitted inexperience with the League. Your grasp of vampire customs is impressive, Lucky, but your knowledge of the Helios-Ra is considerably less impressive. You've been assigned a private tutor to help you catch up. You'll have to work hard if you intend to graduate with the others."

"Yes, Ms. Bellwood." Should I have called her Headmistress Bellwood? It sounded like something out of a Victorian boarding school.

She looked at me finally, stern but not unkind. "I know this must be a big adjustment for you."

"I guess so." Understatement.

"It's an adjustment for our students as well." Had she already heard about my run-in with Jody and Ben? Impressive. "Which is part of the reason I agreed to this transfer when Hart requested it. He runs the League, Lucky, but he does not run this school."

"Um, thanks?"

"If the events of the last few months have taught us anything, it's that the world is clearly changing and we need to be strong enough to adapt if we want to endure. My sole purpose at this school is to train my students in the best way possible so they'll survive. I don't need to tell you a vampire hunter's life can be abbreviated."

I nodded.

"I understand you have special allowances because of your association with Hart, but that will only get you so far."

I hadn't even taken advantage of any special allowances yet. I wasn't even sure what they were.

"I'm trying to say that taking out seasoned hunters who were technically doing their job by attacking a vampire nest is frowned upon," she continued. "But since you also saved Hart's nephew by bringing him to the infirmary last night, you've already managed to balance out your transgressions. Which is fairly impressive in itself. However," she added sharply, "I would greatly prefer for your name not to come up with such frequency."

Me too. It was hardly stealthy.

"We'll be watching you."

"'Cause that's not ominous," I muttered. "Yes, ma'am," I added out loud.

I didn't bother telling her she wasn't the first person to say that to me today.

CHAPTER 5

Solange

Sunday, sunset

The first thing I heard when I woke up was my mother's voice.

I hadn't noticed her at first, waking with the fiery hunger that blurred my vision red and made all of my senses too sharp. I drained two bottles of blood before I could remember who I was. I wiped my mouth clean and felt better. Then I thought about Kieran and felt worse.

"Solange Rosamund Drake."

Mom's voice reverberated down the metal stairs into the underground safe house. Her tone could've been used as a rapier, and my head already hurt, but I couldn't tell her that. She'd know I drank fresh human blood last night, to wake up with what I considered a blood hangover. Constantine assured me it was normal. It took some time for vampires to process so much blood, and live blood from the vein was so much more potent than blood bottled and refrigerated. You needed less, but wanted more.

"Solange, get up here. Now."

I sighed and climbed up the metal ladder reluctantly. The tents were guarded day and night, but they were still vulnerable. Sunlight couldn't be staked; the wind might blow a ceiling off and we'd be weak as kittens. So we slept underground during the day, and gathered as a family in the evenings in the tent. The tunnels under the mountains and under the forest were currently crowded with vampire families.

The inside of our tent was lit with oil lamps, the grass was covered with thick Persian rugs, and Madame Veronique's hand-embroidered tapestry of the Drake insignia hung on one wall. There were couches, wooden tables, carved benches, and a long medieval-style table.

I pushed my tangled hair off my face and tried not to look guilty. "Hi, Mom."

"Don't you 'Hi, Mom' me," she returned sharply. "You were brought in unconscious at dawn." She was wearing her black battle leathers. Queen or not, Blood Moon or not, Mom was Mom.

"I just lost my way in the woods."

"Which is why you should have had a guard with you," Dad interjected smoothly. His calm disappointment was every bit as bad as Mom's temper. "I'm sure we talked about this."

I swallowed a retort, which would've had me grounded, vampire princess or not.

"I'm a vampire," I said. "It's not like I'm defenseless."

"You're also sixteen years old, young lady," Mom snapped. "And you have a curfew for a damn good reason."

"I know," I said quietly. "I'm sorry." I needed to get out of here. I had to find out if Kieran was okay. I glanced at the door. Torches flickered on the other side of the painted canvas. I shifted toward it.

"Where do you think you're going? We're not done here."

"Mom, I said I was sorry." I was having flashbacks to this summer, when everyone hovered around me and worried. I literally itched under my skin. I wasn't going to be the princess in the tower anymore. Not for anyone. "I have to go."

"Where?"

"To see Kieran."

She shook her head. "He can wait."

But that was the thing. I didn't know if he could.

"I'm going."

"Solange." Dad rose to his feet. He looked worried. "It's not safe. For either of you."

"And we'll be going on lockdown in a couple of days," Mom added.

"I know," I said. "All the more reason you should let me go tonight before the Blood Moon starts. It's not like I can call him from here."

Dad looked briefly proud. He always preened a little when one of us won an argument using plain, calm logic. It was the same pride Mom felt when we could hit a moving target with a throwing knife. Mom saw the look and sighed. "Fine. Back by 3:00 a.m.," she told me sternly. "And take someone with you."

I grabbed my leather jacket off the coat tree. The inside pockets were heavy with stakes, daggers, and assorted weaponry. I stopped under the overhang, and I would've taken a deep breath of the cold mountain air if I still breathed. The weight of the past few months and the memory of Kieran's blood on my lips made me shudder.

"Are you sick?" Nicholas asked, coming out of the shadows. "You look weird."

"I'm fine." I eyed him warningly. "I wish people would stop asking me that."

"Okay." He shrugged. "So long as you don't throw up on my shoes."

"Deal." I half smiled. "I have to go to town."

"Does Mom know?"

"Shut up."

"Cranky."

I wrinkled my nose. "A little. Will you come with me?"

"Sure."

We stepped out into the bustle of the fields, the stars so crisp overhead you could see the Milky Way. There was a path already worn through the grass, torches flickering where it branched out. Guards stood at the front and back of every tent. The ones with royal crests on their shirts dipped their heads when they saw us.

"That's still weird," Nicholas muttered.

The one I'd lulled to sleep last week with my pheromones watched me warily. I tried an apologetic smile. Heads turned curiously when my extra fangs caught the light. I let my hair screen my face. "Damn it." Constantine would've told me to flash them proudly. I couldn't see him anywhere. Whispers rolled in our wake, like ripples behind a boat on a clear pond.

"It's just a couple of teeth." I hunched my shoulders. "What's the big damn deal?" I asked, even though those same teeth had me in a panic a few days ago. The extra fangs weren't normal; neither was the keen bloodlust or the fact that my pheromones worked on other vampires. We were still trying to keep that last part a secret.

"It's not that," Nicholas replied grimly.

"What then?" He was suddenly so close to my side, I stumbled when his elbow knocked me off balance. "What are you doing?"

"It's the Furies."

I blinked. "Who?"

"Sebastian told me about them. They used to serve Lady Natasha."

I went cold at the mention of her name. She might be dead, on the tip of my mother's stake to be exact, but she'd also tried to kill me and eat my heart. It wasn't something you forgot.

And apparently I wasn't the only one who remembered.

There were seven Furies: three vampires and four human blood-slaves, all women. They had dyed their hair the same white as Lady Natasha. They even wore it in the exact same style, bone straight with severe bangs. They wore elaborate white dresses, just like she had the night she tried to kill me. They looked exactly like her except that they each had the mark of her house tattooed on their faces: three black raven feathers. The feathers they wore in their hair were bleached white.

It was creepy.

"London's not with them, is she?" We hadn't seen our cousin since before my birthday. Even her parents couldn't find her. She'd sent them an e-mail to let them know she was okay, but she'd essentially run away after I turned.

"No, she's not." Nicholas angled himself between me and the Furies when they began to hiss.

"Usurper," one of them spat. "Murderer."

Technically, Mom was the usurper, but I didn't say it out loud. I had a feeling semantics weren't exactly important right now. I was a figurehead to them, a scapegoat. That damn prophecy again.

The Furies approached, like the spores of a poisonous white mushroom drifting dangerously close. My neck prickled. Nicholas tensed, about to reach for a weapon. I grabbed his arm, remembering the Joiik woman weeping over the ashes of her loved one at her feet and the red-tipped arrows of the Chandramaa.

"Don't," I told him. "Just back up and keep your hands visible." I held mine up as if we were at gunpoint.

"I don't trust them."

"Then trust the Chandramaa." He hadn't seen them in action yet, hadn't seen Constantine's cheeks go so pale they looked like bone knives. And I was sure he didn't frighten easily. My fangs elongated, making my gums feel raw and itchy. My lips lifted of their own accord.

I tramped down the surge of adrenaline and the need to fight back. No wonder Mom was so cranky. This kind of thing was her worst nightmare.

I wasn't loving it either.

"Let's get out of here."

◆

We were being tailed.

It wasn't surprising; our parents had put guards on us the minute the tribes starting arriving from around the world. I'd been compelling them to leave me alone. I'd also compelled them to wait for me and not tell anyone so that I always returned with them. I felt a little guilty about it but they were driving me nuts.

And tonight, I didn't even feel guilty.

I just wanted them gone.

I pulled a U-turn, tires skidding and black marks burning into the street. The guards screeched to a halt, confusion plain on their faces even under their helmets. They lifted their visors.

"Is there trouble, my lady?"

I blinked, distracted. "Did you just 'my lady' me?"

It's only proper.

I shook my head. "Never mind." I slipped off my motorcycle and stood between them, close enough to see their pale eyes, close enough that I could affect them with my pheromones. I didn't actually need the eye contact, but it helped.

"Go away, please." I didn't bother telling them to wait for us. I just wanted to get to Kieran.

They nodded in unison and then turned their bikes around and drove away. Nicholas yelled something at me, but I pretended not to hear him over the engine of the motorcycles. I kept going and he had no choice but to follow.

Lucy and I had driven by Kieran's house once before, late at night when we were sure we wouldn't be caught, but I'd never been inside. I stopped a few houses down and walked my bike to the maple tree in front of his house. I leaned it on its kickstand and stared at the tidy garden full of icicle pansies and at the warm light at the windows. It looked so normal.

Nicholas came up beside me. "Damn it, Sol. Ever heard of the speed limit?"

"Oh, right, coming from the guy who got three speeding tickets the first week he had his license."

"That's different." At least he had the grace to look sheepish. "And what the hell was that with the guards?"

"I just asked them to give me a little privacy."

"Uh-huh." He didn't sound the least bit convinced. After a moment he leaned against a low-hanging branch. "Sol?"

"Yeah?"

"Why are we lurking?"

"I'm not lurking," I said a little defensively. "I was just waiting for you. Thought you got lost."

I turned back to the house. I could see a leather couch through the living room window and the corner of a coffee table with a candle and a jar of roses. I should knock on the door. Or at least text Kieran to let him know I was standing in his garden. I knew he was all right; Lucy had left me a voice mail while Nicholas and I were on our way to town. But what if he didn't want to see me? What if he hated me now? Or worse, what if he was scared of me?

I was scared of me.

"Did you guys have a fight or something?" Nicholas asked quizzically.

I shook my head. "Will you come with me?"

"To the front door?" He frowned. "Seriously, Solange, what's going on?"

I flashed my fangs at him. "What if his mom opens the door?" Even if I kept my mouth closed she'd take one look at my bloodshot eyes and assume I was on drugs. Neither of which was the first impression I was keen to make. Nicholas, at least, could pass for human.

"Oh." He ambled ahead of me and rapped on the door. I hovered nervously behind him, pulling up the hood of my hoodie from under my jacket.

Kieran's mom opened the door, just as I'd feared. She was more fragile looking than I'd thought she would be. I'd assumed she'd be muscular and tough like my mom, or earthy like Lucy's mom. She'd been married to a vampire hunter after all, before Hope murdered him. But she seemed frail, her hair wispy and soft around her face, which was so thin it was nearly gaunt. Even the pearls around her neck looked too heavy for her.

"Yes?"

"Sorry to bother you, Mrs. Black," Nicholas said politely. "We're friends of Kieran's."

She smiled, her hands fluttering at her throat. I tried not to stare at the blue veins pulsing there. "Oh, are you from the school as well?"

"Um, no."

She peered over his shoulder and saw me. "You must be Solange," she said softly. "You're just as pretty as Kieran said." Her eyes were moist, as if she might start weeping. I shifted nervously from foot to foot and tried to smile without showing even a hint of teeth.

"Mom, who's at—" Kieran cut himself off as he came around the corner and saw us on the porch. "Solange." I pursed my lips. I couldn't even say hi or ask how he was. There was a bandage around his neck and shadows under his eyes. I could see the mark on the back of his hand from where the IV drip had been attached. "Mom, I got this," he said gently. "Why don't you go back inside."

She fussed shyly. "You should invite your friends in."

"I will."

She smiled at me again and went to the kitchen, where a kettle was soon whistling.

"We should stay out here," Kieran said when he was sure she was out of earshot. "She doesn't know you're a vampire."

"How is that even possible?" I asked.

"She was never part of the Helios-Ra, even when Dad was alive. And now she rarely leaves the house." He shrugged and then winced when the movement pulled at his wound. "Hunter's the only one from the League she'll even talk to, and I asked her not to say anything."

Nicholas raised an eyebrow. "Dude, what happened to you?"

"Vampire," he answered, not looking away from me. "They kept me at the school infirmary for the day but I'm okay now. Lucy brought me in."

Nicholas stilled. "Lucy found you?"

Kieran nodded, not catching the sinister edge to Nicholas's too-calm and too-polite voice. "Yeah, in the woods."

"Alone?" Nicholas prodded. "She was *alone* and she found you during a vampire attack?"

Kieran glanced at him when the grinding of Nicholas's teeth alerted him. He tried an easy smile. "Afterward," he assured Nicholas. "When it was all perfectly safe."

He was lying to protect me.

Again.

Because I hadn't been perfectly safe.

Not even close.

"It's like she does it on purpose." Nicholas reached for his cell phone, muttering under his breath as he dialed Lucy's number. He stalked to the maple tree and hauled himself up onto the lowest branch so we could all have a little privacy.

Kieran leaned in the doorway as if he was still too weak to hold himself up. Guilt tore through me like fire in a dry field.

"I'm sorry." I stuck my hands in my pockets because I didn't know what else to do with them. "I'm so sorry."

"Are you okay?"

I nodded. "Yes. Do you need to sit down?"

"I'm fine." He rubbed a hand over his face. "What happened, Solange?"

"I don't know," I said miserably. I couldn't stop seeing the way he'd slumped against the tree, his blood on my clothes, the taste of it in my mouth. "I didn't mean to. I just . . . it's animal." I didn't know how else to describe it. I didn't mention the voice whispering to me. He'd really think I was crazy then. "I thought I was stronger. I'm sorry," I said again. He'd saved me from the rogue Helios-Ra unit who'd tried to abduct me, and he'd been the one to give me his own blood so I could survive the bloodchange. I'd be dead right now if it weren't for him. Maybe that's why he was so hard to resist. His blood had brought me back from death.

"Does anyone else know?" he asked.

"I made it back to the camp and went straight to sleep." I didn't tell him about Constantine. Why make things worse? My eyes burned. "It's all such a mess."

Kieran reached out to touch my hair, brushing it off my cheek. I could smell the warmth of his skin, the blood just under his wrist. "It'll be okay."

"You don't know that." I turned my head away.

He didn't say anything. He knew I was right.

"We're going on lockdown soon at the camp," I added. "No Internet, no cell phone reception, no humans past the guards." Well, no humans who weren't bloodslaves, anyway. I didn't need to explain that; he already knew. I could tell by the clenching of his jaw. "So I probably won't see you for a while."

He stepped up close to me, tipping my chin up with his hand. He lowered his head until his mouth brushed mine, softly, tenderly. I tasted his lips, trying to memorize his smell of mint and cedar. I kissed him until we forgot where we were, forgot that he was injured, that I was sorry, that anyone could walk by and see us there. He kissed me back until my veins burned under my skin. I wanted more. He wanted more. His lips brushed my ear and all I could hear was his breath, like the ocean. It made me dizzy, hungry, wild. I would have swallowed him whole if I could have.

When my arms slid around his waist, my fingers brushed the unmistakable shape of a wooden stake tucked into his belt at his lower back.

You can't protect him. And you can't trust him.

I stilled, pulling away just enough to speak, but not enough that my lips didn't touch his even as I formed the words. "Is that a stake?" I asked. "Were you going to stake me?"

He tilted my head farther back so my fangs were visible. "Were you going to go for my jugular?"

We stared at each other for a long, hot moment that burned through me.

"Are you still going to college in Scotland?" I finally asked.

"Yes," he said quietly.

"When?"

"Not until after New Year's. I can't leave my mom alone for Christmas; she's always worse then."

"Maybe it's for the best." I couldn't believe I was saying that, even as I was still recovering from his kisses.

"Maybe it is." And I really couldn't believe he was agreeing with me.

"It could be pheromones, or just everything that's happened," I said, desperately trying not to feel the pain I was feeling. Why couldn't we just lose ourselves in the fire again? When passion was enough, and the questions didn't matter. "We don't really know each other that well, technically."

But I was lying to myself. My chest felt hollow, and I was aware of my heart in a way I hadn't been since it had stopped beating. I hurt everywhere. We'd been each other's bridge. We'd survived treachery, vendettas, and bounties.

But we couldn't seem to survive each other.

I didn't want to say good-bye but I didn't know how else to protect him. I was no good for him. The next time I lost control, I might actually kill him.

"Good-bye, Kieran."

His voice was husky, as if he were just waking up. "Good-bye, Solange."

I choked back a sob. I wouldn't cry. I turned on my heel and stumbled down the porch steps. The night was full of town noises: cars, dogs, radios. The wind scattered dried leaves across the empty road.

"Solange?"

I stopped but didn't turn around. I knew we had to let each other go. But I also knew if I saw those patient dark eyes, the sun tattoo on his bicep, the regulation cargo pants, I'd throw myself at him. I only had the strength to leave if I didn't look at him.

"You know the safe house we hid in when Hope's unit had you?"

I nodded.

"There was an old tree there with exposed roots. Do you remember it?"

"Yes."

"Those roots make great little hiding spots. If you ever need to send me a message," he said, "if you need me, I'll be there. You know that, right?"

I nodded again, my throat aching.

"I love you, Solange."

"You don't even know me anymore," I said, because I barely knew myself. "I'm a vampire."

"You were human when I met you," he reminded me. "And you were brave and beautiful. You're still brave and beautiful."

I felt like crying. "I have to go."

I ran to my bike, kicking it into gear even before I was perched on the seat.

Nicholas frowned at me, scrambling out of the tree. "What's the matter?"

"Nothing. I need to be alone."

"I can't leave you, Sol," he said, jumping on his motorcycle and pulling up beside me. "You know that. Mom would kill us both."

I leaned over, close enough that I could see his pupils even in the shadows. I concentrated as hard as I could, willing him to obey me. A bat dove down from the roof of Kieran's house. The front door closed. "Leave me alone, Nicholas."

He recoiled as if I'd slapped him. "Sol, don't."

Anger and confusion and hurt boiled inside me. "Just go away! Leave me alone!"

"Shit," Nicholas croaked painfully. His eyes were furious and hurt. "You promised you wouldn't ever do this to me again." I could tell my pheromones were repelling him, as if we were oppositely charged magnets. He'd let me be tonight. He didn't have a choice. His hands clenched, his shoulders tensed. "What the hell's wrong with you? Where's Kieran?"

I tossed him a fierce look before taking off down the street.

"We just broke up."

CHAPTER 6

Nicholas

It was entirely possible that my baby sister was turning into a monster.

If anyone else had been doing this to her, I'd have staked them. But she was doing it to herself, which made it so much worse.

Because I couldn't even stop her.

We'd been raised not only to protect each other but to protect her especially. I wasn't just letting her down, but my entire family. The buzz of pheromones and adrenaline tingled through me, like a rash just under my skin. I wanted to go after her and shake some sense into her, but even taking a single step in the direction she'd fled made me feel as if there were spiders inside my veins. I couldn't believe she'd done this to me.

Again.

Since I couldn't go after her, I went back to Kieran's. He opened the door before I'd even knocked.

"Maybe you didn't hear," he said bitterly. "We just broke up."

"Yeah, what, three minutes ago? You stop loving her yet?" I knew damn well if Lucy broke up with me I'd still love her until I turned to dust.

Kieran sighed. "What do you want, Drake?"

"You know this is only going to get worse."

He touched the bandage on his throat. "No shit."

"Can I count on you? Even now?"

He paused, watched me carefully. "For what?"

"I don't know yet," I said, frustrated. "But Solange isn't well." I took a small box out of my pocket and shoved it at him. "Take this. Just in case."

He frowned at the package. "What is it?"

"You'll know if you need to use it," I said quickly, glancing behind me. "Someone's coming." I took off before he could answer. I checked my watch. Lucy wouldn't be able to sneak out for a while yet. I put my bike into gear and took off down the road, the cold slap of the wind in my face soothing. I figured I may as well go back to the farmhouse and get some of my stuff. Music, earphones, and my laptop for movies were the only things that would keep me sane for two weeks in the tunnels and the Drake tent. And Connor, Quinn, and I were on family lockdown after tonight for at least the next few days, because of the ghost-town thing. I was surprised Mom didn't drive right over to the academy to lecture Lucy and Hunter as well.

I remember when my life used to be boring.

Vampire or not, I'd had a pretty normal life. Despite our liquid diet, we still had chores and homework, music to listen to, dogs to walk, parents to navigate.

And then Lucy happened.

Never mind prophecies and bounty hunters, she was the one who'd really turned my life upside down. And it was worth it to have her finally see me as me and not just as Solange's older brother. She made everything better. But the thought of losing her to vampires or vampire hunters made everything gray, as if even the trees and stars were made of ash.

She was necessary.

And infuriating.

I was glad she'd saved Kieran, but I still couldn't believe, after everything that had happened, that she'd been out in the woods alone. *After* blowing up a town.

Actually, I could totally believe it.

I was still grumbling to myself when I pulled up the driveway and left my bike by the cedar trees. Since I was home anyway, I may as well take advantage of it and stop by Solange's shed. I didn't know what I was looking for exactly, only that there had to be something somewhere to explain the stranger she was becoming.

Broken pottery shards skittered under my boots, like beetles under a disturbed rock. Solange was ordinarily neat about her workspace. Her tools and any broken pieces were usually piled in a large bin to be reworked, but right now they were scattered on the floor, and the wall was dented and dusty, as if she'd thrown most of her work at it. The shelves were nearly bare. Something about that made my belly go cold, even more than the way she'd compelled me.

There was a guard waiting on the front porch when I headed up to the house to search Solange's bedroom. She'd kill me if she ever found out about this.

The guard nodded politely. "Your Highness," she said.

I missed Bruno and the way he called me "ijit."

I smiled awkwardly at her and closed the front door.

And nearly lost an eye to an antique ivory stake when I turned around.

A woman swathed in thick black veils stood on the bottom step of the staircase, the chandelier glittering above her head. "Nicholas, is that you, dear?"

I stared at her. "Aunt Hyacinth, the hell!"

"Language." She clucked her tongue. "Honestly, your manners are becoming positively savage. I was only gone a few weeks."

"Is that any reason to try and stake me?"

"It's these veils," she admitted. "It's a little difficult to see properly, and everyone smells mostly the same in the house if I'm not paying attention."

"Then take them off," I suggested quietly, while surreptitiously tensing to leap out of the way of another projectile. You developed pretty good reflexes when you grew up around Drake women. Not to mention Lucy Hamilton.

"Well." She tilted her head, and I could feel the glitter of her eyes even through the lace. "Perhaps I could shorten them." They were long enough to touch her fingertips. She'd taken to wearing them after a hunter had scarred her face with holy water. Vampires generally healed quickly and completely, but sometimes holy water was just stronger. And I hadn't thought anything could be stronger than Aunt Hyacinth, not really. It made me even more scared for Solange and my mother.

I shoved my hands in my pockets. "Is it safe to come in?"

She laughed. "Yes, it's safe." She shook her head before drifting away. "I've never known the house to be so empty. It's rather disconcerting."

She was right. Even the dogs were in the woods. Only guards were here patrolling with any reliability.

I stopped by my room first to get my stuff, then headed to Solange's room. The curtains were pulled tight, the hand-embroidered coverlet was neatly tucked in, and nothing was out of place. I went through her desk first, then checked under the bed and in her closet.

I was so going to get my ass kicked for this.

And I had nothing to show for it. No diary, no weird drugs, no secret blueprints to some nefarious plot, nothing. I kicked the dresser, cursing. A bowl of the silver thimbles Aunt Hyacinth used to collect as a girl and passed on to Solange tumbled to the floor. I cursed again.

"What's going on, miscreant?" Logan stood in the doorway, wearing his favorite frock coat as usual, but there were rips in his jeans.

I lifted my eyebrows at his pants. "Holes?" He was impeccable about his fancy goth clothes.

"Isabeau," he admitted ruefully. "The Hounds are a great tribe, but they have no sense of fashion."

"So she tore your jeans?"

He grinned. "No, she tore at a *Hel-Blar*. I just happened to get in the way."

I grinned back at him. "Cool." Have I mentioned? Our girlfriends are fierce.

"What are you doing in here?" Logan asked.

"I don't know," I admitted.

"You don't know?" he repeated, confused.

I sighed. "It's complicated."

He snorted. "It always is. Solange or Lucy?"

"Solange." I shook my head. "Let's get out of here."

He followed me down the stairs. "What's going on, Nicholas?"

I nodded to his guard on the other side of the door. "Wait," I mouthed.

We went out to the porch and Logan smiled easily at her. "We're going to walk back," he said. "To patrol. And to talk about girls," he lied. "Can you hang back, Grace? My brother here's a little shy."

She smiled back at him. "Sure."

"You can take my bike," I added, tossing her the keys.

"Sweet." The silver studs on the leather strap across her chest glinted in the light as she turned toward my motorcycle. She had a dozen stakes easy on that strap and a sword strapped to her back.

Logan looked down the lane and frowned. "Where's your guard?"

I waited until we were crossing the field to the forest to tell him the rest. The growl of the motorcycle behind us helped cover our voices. I told about Solange compelling our guards, even the part about finding her in the woods drunk on a bloodslave.

"Our Solange? Really?" Logan scrubbed his face. "Have you told Mom and Dad?"

I shook my head. "No. It's been a bad day already."

It got worse.

Of *course*, it got worse.

The woods were crawling with *Hel-Blar*, vampires from around the world, and vampire hunters. We passed a broken stake stuck in a birch tree, a clump of ferns covered in what looked like ash, and several trails of blood.

"Remember when no one ever came here?" Logan asked. The moon scattered light between the branches and turned the river to pewter.

"Yeah, I kind of miss being in shameful exile," I agreed.

And then we heard it, even over the rumble of the motorcycle pacing us.

Battle.

Logan and I glanced at each other and then launched into a run, the trees a blur of green and gray around us. The sounds of a struggle, cursing, the distinctive quiet whoosh of a vampire turning to dust. We skidded to a stop under a huge ponderosa pine tree.

It looked like the fight was down to three vampire hunters and a vampire girl in black pleather pants out of the Matrix movies. I recognized the short black hair and the sneer, instantly.

She was family. And though she might have accidentally almost gotten Solange killed this summer, she still needed our help. Because she was clearly losing.

Grace sped up and cut us off, sliding the bike between us and the fight. "Stay back," she ordered, drawing a sword, slender as an ice pick.

We diverted around her, leaping into the air and landing in unison on the other side.

"That's our cousin," I tossed back at her, still running. "London! Hang on!"

Grace tossed back a few words that weren't anatomically possible. Logan pulled the nearest hunter out of the melee and threw him into a clump of purple monkshood. He landed on his arm and there was an audible crack.

"Is it broken?" his partner shouted.

"Dislocated," he grunted.

I jumped over him and grabbed his partner. She whirled, snarling, and tried to bite me. And she wasn't even a vampire. I dodged a punch and then a stake, but only just barely. I used vampire speed to pop from one side of her to the other, until she was frustrated and dizzy. Then I threw her at the first hunter just scrambling to his feet.

London used her elbow on the third hunter's nose, and blood sprayed into the grass. He didn't fall, only staggered and grabbed for another stake. There was a cut on London's cheek and a gash under her knee.

"Nick, behind you!"

I reacted to Logan's shout before thinking. I dropped and rolled toward the attack instead of away, which was expected. I caught the hunter in the ankles and knocked her down. Her stake still flew true enough to pin my sleeve to a tree root. I yanked free just as the wounded hunter also threw a stake, this one at London. She yelled and toppled. I smelled blood but couldn't see if she was badly hurt.

Logan bent his body forward as if he'd been doing yoga with Lucy, and then he kicked backward at the last second and caught the female hunter in the hip. Grace flew off the motorcycle, fists flying, and knocked her out to finish the job.

Logan reached London just as her eyes rolled back in her head and she slumped down into the pine needles. "Stakes are soaked in holy water!" he yelled. "She's down."

It distracted me just long enough to get caught by the hunter with the beard. He lashed out at a brutal angle, catching my knee-cap. I fell, screaming, my fangs biting through my gums. He kicked my shoulder as I bent to grab my knee, rolling me slightly into a nest of withered ferns, keeping me pinned. His boot ground down on my neck. Pain choked me. He was stronger than he looked, with scars on his throat and a rattling necklace of vampire fangs.

Logan was bent over London and didn't see me.

Grace was busy trying not to get killed herself.

The stake descended.

And then Solange was suddenly there.

She dropped down from a tree so quickly the hunter must have thought she could fly. I barely saw her, just a wash of pale skin, a battle yell, and a frenzy of bats in the air. The hunter fell back just enough that I could break free of his boot. I yanked on his foot and he fell to one knee. I pushed up, coughing.

Solange was a good fighter, and stronger, but he'd had more years to practice. He wasn't easy to best. I limped forward but I was too slow. He punched Solange with a fist the size of a bread box, as if he was a retired wrestler turned hunter. He got her in the cheek close enough that her fangs cut her lip open. Blood spattered like a fine mist. It hit the hunter in the left eye, over his nose, and across his mouth.

I saw the exact moment he tasted Solange's blood on his tongue.

The moon was bright enough that she looked like pale porcelain, except for the veins prominent at her wrists and throat. The blue was like the center of a flame, like the sky before a storm. And I knew what he saw when he looked at that blue.

Hel-Blar.

His partners stirred, the unconscious woman sitting up blearily, the other man snapping his shoulder back into the right place. They saw Solange the same way. The woman shouted. The bearded hunter wiped his face and started at the blood on his fingertips for a moment. He reached for another stake, this one stainless steel and made with such lethal precision it would pierce flesh and slide through bone with little effort.

He didn't aim it at Solange.

He just spat the blood out of his mouth and then stabbed himself with the stake, right in the heart.

Time slowed down. The other hunters froze, looking sad and furious.

But not surprised.

He gurgled and fell, making wheezing sounds of undiluted pain. He had just enough strength left to pull out the stake. Blood pooled out of the wound, stained his shirt, and dripped into grass. Solange turned away. The rest of us stared, unable to do anything else. He jerked once, his eyes rolling back in his head. The smell of his blood and sweat and fear was rancid in my nostrils. It galvanized me into action.

"We need something to press on the wound and stop the bleeding. He needs a hospit—"

He died before I could finish my sentence.

"He killed himself," Solange croaked in disbelief. "He just . . . killed himself."

"Better dead than undead," the woman hunter said viciously, coldly. "He did right."

Solange whirled, her eyes flaring, her fangs elongated. "I'm not *Hel-Blar*, you idiots."

Grace stepped between them. "Don't bother, princess."

The male hunter's gaze snapped on her. "Princess?" He reached for another stake.

"We're losing her!" Logan yelled, lifting London into his arms. She was pale and limp, the wound in her shoulder blistering. "There's no time for this!"

The hunters looked grim and exhausted and utterly unwilling to back down. Solange lifted her hand, and then brought it down again, pointing at them.

Bats dove out of the branches. They attacked the hunters, nipping at their eyes, but avoided the rest of us entirely. The hunters punched and swatted frantically but there were too many bats, too many teeth and leathery wings. The sound they made was unholy.

"Run," Solange suggested darkly.

The hunters ran. Logan did the same, in the opposite direction, with London. Grace stood over the body of the dead hunter. He was human and didn't conveniently blow away like vampire ashes did.

"Call Bruno," I told her, jerking a hand through my hair. The bruises on my throat were already fading but my knee still throbbed. "He'll know what to do, and if he doesn't, Hart will."

"I can't leave Logan."

"You don't have to, he just left *you*."

Grace hesitated. "Still, my orders . . ."

Solange put her hand on Grace's arm. "Grace, look at me."

She was going to use her pheromones and compel her. I shoved between them.

"Solange, no." I glanced over my shoulder at Grace. "Just make the call. We'll go with Logan."

Then I pushed Solange into a run. We followed the trail of London's blood until we caught up with Logan. London should be healing enough by now not to drip blood over the forest floor. She didn't look right, too pale and too gray. I dialed Uncle Geoffrey's cell phone as we paced like wolves between the pine trees. We'd be out of range soon, and we needed to know if we should take London to the farm or the camp. He wasn't answering.

"Damn it," I snapped. Both the caves and the royal courts had dodgy reception. We didn't have the time to run around searching him out. *London* didn't have the time.

"Call Mom," I told Solange as I called Dad. No reply. Solange shook her head as well.

"Where the hell is everyone?" I tried Aunt Hyacinth on the off chance she actually bothered to answer her phone.

"Hello?"

"Thank God. Where's Uncle Geoffrey?"

"He's at the cam—" I hung up before she could finish. "Camp," I said to Logan. We turned left at the river, ran at full speed for another ten minutes, then charged past the guards and the vampires milling about under the torchlight. We burst into the family tent, Logan carrying London's arms and me holding up her legs.

Dad rose from his chair. "What—" He cut himself off. "Find Geoffrey," he said to the courtier he'd been talking to. I recognized her from the royal caves.

We lay London down on a sofa. Dad crouched beside her. "London? Can you hear me?" She didn't make a sound. That was unusual in itself; she was usually all bluster and bravado. He peeled her shirt away from the festering wound. It was raw, as if acid had eaten through her skin.

"Holy water," I confirmed as Logan dropped into a chair. Solange started to pace. "There were three hunters. I didn't see who she was with; they turned to ash as we got there."

"You saved her," Dad said firmly. He pulled a bottle of blood out of the cooler stored inside the wooden chest by the couch and tipped it up to London's lips. "Geoffrey will get her well."

"Solange saved me," I said. "Where did you come from anyway?"

"Smelled the blood," she said tightly.

"Since when do Helios-Ra just wander around attacking us?" I asked. "I thought we had treaties, and Hart was on board and all that." And my girlfriend was currently trapped in their school. Every muscle in my body throbbed to run out and find her.

"They don't," Dad said thoughtfully. "Are you sure they were Helios-Ra?"

"Who else would they be?"

"Huntsmen."

"What's the difference?"

"Huntsmen are vampire hunters, just not League. They haven't come to Violet Hill since before any of you were even born. No point with all the Helios-Ra about."

"Do they wear fang trophy necklaces?"

He nodded grimly.

"And commit suicide if they think they've been infected?" Solange asked quietly.

Dad nodded again. "Did one of them . . . ?"

"Yes."

Dad winced. "In front of you?"

London started to whimper. She wasn't conscious but she was thrashing on the sofa. I helped Dad hold her down. Her skin was hot, feverish. Vampires didn't run hot. We just didn't.

Uncle Geoffrey finally arrived, toting his medical case. He went straight to London, the pleasant, slightly befuddled scientist replaced with clinical precision. He went tight-lipped when he saw the wound.

"Stake soaked in holy water," Dad said. "Huntsman's weapon."

Uncle Geoffrey looked even grimmer. "Who knows what other

tricks they have," he said. He hooked London up to a blood bag to give her a transfusion since she didn't appear to be swallowing. Vampires needed blood to heal. Lots of blood. And sleep.

"She'll be okay, right?" Solange asked. "I mean, Aunt Hyacinth survived holy water." Scarred, but survived. And vampires didn't scar easily.

"Hyacinth had Madame Veronique's blood," Geoffrey said, rummaging through his case. "That's what saved her. And I have none."

Vampires didn't drink other vampire blood as a rule. It served no nutritional purpose. Unless it was the blood of an ancient from your own lineage—then it could heal you. Madame Veronique was the oldest living Drake, according to all the family stories. Her twins, born in 1162, were our first direct ancestors and the reason our particular branch of the family tree turned into vampires on our sixteenth birthdays.

"Well, where is she?" Logan asked. "Can we bring her here?"

"Would she even help?" I asked. "She's not exactly puppies and rainbows. And you know how she feels about London's side of the family." London had served Lady Natasha, not believing that she'd wanted Solange dead. She'd nearly handed us all over into a trap.

"I have her blood," Solange announced softly. We turned to stare at her. "Well, don't I?" she asked Uncle Geoffrey. "I drank that tiny bit to heal me through my bloodchange. Is it still inside me?"

Uncle Geoffrey blinked. "I honestly wouldn't know. But it's worth a try."

Solange approached the sofa. There was enough blood being

pumped into London's veins that she was lucid, her eyes half-open. But her lips were already dry and cracked, as if she'd been ill for weeks and was severely dehydrated. Before Uncle Geoffrey could pass Solange a lancet, she'd already sliced her wrist open with her triple fangs. A trickle of blood moved down her arm and she hurried to press the cut over London's mouth. London swallowed thickly, painfully; once, twice, three times. Bats whispered at the tent ceiling, their shadows huge and distorted by the torchlight.

At Uncle Geoffrey's nod, Solange pulled back, pressing the edges of her cut together to help it heal faster. London's gaping wound didn't magically heal but it did look slightly less angry. Geoffrey fussed over her for a few moments then nodded, satisfied. "Well done, Sol," he said proudly. "I think she'll be fine, eventually." He pulled empty test tubes out of his case. "Fascinating. If I could get more blood from you . . . I never thought to test—"

"No." Solange backed away. "No more tests, Uncle Geoffrey." She fled the tent before anyone could stop her.

CHAPTER 7

Lucy

Sunday night

I snuck off campus using the route Hunter showed me earlier. Between her and Quinn, they kept it free of school surveillance, and it was the best way for me to see Nicholas. It was getting darker so much earlier now that winter was approaching; we had more hours available to us before my new school curfew, which, despite Bellwood's warnings, I had to ignore tonight. I waited until I was securely hidden inside the forest before taking out my cell phone. Nathan, a friend of mine from my old school, answered on the first ring.

"I'm still mad at you," he informed me in lieu of a hello.

"I know," I said. "If it makes you feel any better, there are way more mean kids here."

I could practically hear him frowning. "I thought art school kids were supposed to be cooler than the rest of us."

"So did I." I'd lied to him about my new school. Nathan was strictly a civilian and knew nothing about vampires or vampire hunters. The only thing he knew about Nicholas was that he was hot. And it had seemed the most believable excuse to have my parents send me off to some artsy alternative school in the mountains. "I miss you guys."

"You wouldn't miss us if you came back," he grumbled. "Tell your mom that school's bad for your chi or whatever."

"Can't. Nonrefundable deposit."

"That bites."

I snorted a laugh. "You have no idea."

"There's a party in Megan's backfield Saturday night. Last one before the snow hits. You're coming."

"It's cold."

"So what, Grandma? Too busy hanging out with guys in black turtlenecks talking about Picasso?"

"Picasso?"

"Isn't that what art students do? And I've seen you draw, Hamilton. I can't believe they even let you through the front door."

He wasn't wrong. "I'm on the music track."

"That makes more sense. Anyway, the party. If you bail on me I will never forgive you. And Linnet will cry. You want that on your conscience?"

"Oh, please. Linnet won't cry. But I won't bail," I promised.

"You better not. So, any cute boys at that school?"

I thought about Hunter's friend Jason. I'd have to ask around if he had a boyfriend. "Some."

"Good. Bring them." Nathan hung up.

I switched on my flashlight as I tramped deeper into the woods. Most of the moonlight was blocked by thick spruce and pine. Since I didn't have vampiric eyesight, I'd walk into a tree if I wasn't careful. The trail was barely a suggestion, but there were white ribbons tied around branches to mark the way. The path ended abruptly in a small clearing thick with late-blooming goldenrod. I thought I might still be technically on school property. No wonder Hunter had commandeered this spot for her secret tryst. The wind was frigid and nibbled hungrily at my fingers and the tip of my nose. I slipped on the stripy mittens my mom made for me. Like everything else she touched, it still smelled faintly of Nag Champa incense. I felt vaguely homesick.

And then Nicholas came toward me through the field, the tall yellow flowers bending around him, and the stone of worry lodged in my throat loosened. He was sleek and dark and beautiful, the way thunderstorms are beautiful. I never got tired of the way he smiled at me, both solemn and wicked. Even if he wasn't exactly smiling right now.

The goldenrod brushed my shoulders and I slapped it out of the way. Nicholas didn't speak, just pulled me up against him, holding me pressed to his chest, his face buried in my wind-tangled hair. I stroked his back, the muscles cool and hard even through his shirt.

"What is it?" I whispered. "What's wrong?"

"Everything but you," he said hoarsely. Even though I'd known him most of my life, had seen him fall out of trees and trip over his own feet when we were growing up, even though we'd played countless pranks and honed our sarcasm on each other, he could still make me melt. And that still took me by surprise sometimes.

When he finally looked at me, his features were calm but fierce in their stillness. He was suddenly all predator, that beauty sharpened and deadly. I shivered, not afraid of him but afraid *for* him. There was something stark in his gray eyes, glinting in the moonlight.

"Let me guess," I said. "Apocalypse, disaster, blah blah blah. I feel like we're constantly living out a season ender of *Buffy*."

"With any luck this won't be that bad."

"Notice your luck lately?" I asked. "A hundred rabbit's-foot charms wouldn't help you." Not that I'd ever do that. I happen to like bunnies and cutting off their feet is barbaric.

"True. You know, you could've been attacked by the same vampire that got Kieran last night," he said, and I knew that wasn't what he was really upset about. "What if it was an ambush?"

"It was," I snorted. "But I handled it. Solange didn't tell you?"

"Tell me what? Wait, she was there?"

I stepped back. It was hard to think when he was standing that close to me. Embarrassing but true. "Hell yeah, she was there. I Tasered her."

He blinked. "You used a stun gun on my baby sister?"

"Right after she tried to eat Kieran and then have me for dessert."

Nicholas just blinked at me again. It was rare that I could surprise him into speechlessness. He lowered himself slowly down to the ground as if he were suddenly an old man too weak to stand. The weeds and grass swallowed him up. "She could have killed you."

I sat too. "But she didn't. And she didn't *want* to, that much was obvious."

"Still."

"Yeah. Still."

"I can't believe she didn't say anything," he added tightly. "And I just went with her to see Kieran."

"He's okay?"

"Yeah, he's fine. Except they broke up."

"They *broke up*?" I reached for my phone. No voice mails except the one Nicholas had sent earlier and no texts. I switched it on. The dial tone chirped in my ear. "It's not broken." I scowled. "She didn't even call me! Is she all right? Does she need ice cream?" Not that she really ate anymore, but some rituals were sacred.

"She used her pheromones," he said, his fangs poking out. "She compelled me to back off and leave her alone. She's getting stronger, Lucy."

I stared at him. "Again? She did that to you again?" Just last week she'd forced him to kick me out of the farmhouse because I'd mouthed off about the annoyingly mysterious Constantine.

Nicholas just sat there looking shell-shocked and hurt. Fury sizzled inside me. It was bad enough she'd attacked me, but now she was messing with my boyfriend.

And that just would not do.

Fury turned to rage, burning like an ember inside my chest.

Nicholas winced. "You're mad."

"You think?"

"No, I mean you're *mad*." He licked his lips.

"Oh, right. Sorry." I took a few deep breaths, and added a few *Om Namah Shivayas* for good measure. When Nicholas stopped looking like he was in pain, I let out one last long breath. It went to mist in the cold air, like dragon's breath, which was apt as I felt angry enough to breathe fire.

Oops. Another deep breath.

"We have to tell your parents," I said when I was calm enough to unclench my fists. "We can't keep covering for her. Not now." A part of me felt like a traitor. My job as best friend was to cover for Solange. But we were in way over our heads. We couldn't save her from herself without help.

And fast.

"I know," he said, sounding just as conflicted. "But she saved me tonight too."

I went cold. "What?"

"London was attacked. I got caught by a Huntsman, and he would have had me too, if it weren't for her. They're worse than Helios-Ra hunters."

"Are you okay?" I catalogued the mud and grass stains on his clothes, the tear in his shirt collar, the blood I hadn't noticed on the cuff of his left sleeve.

"I'm fine," he assured me.

"You and I know her better than anyone else. What do you think she'll do?"

"I don't know," he admitted. "That's what scares me." He shook his head. "I don't want to talk about it right now. We don't have much time as it is." He handed me a set of car keys.

I frowned at them. "Aren't those mine?"

"Yeah. Duncan got your car from the garage and fixed it himself. It's parked on the road outside your school."

I smiled brightly. "I love your brother."

"Hey, now."

"It's okay, I love you more."

"Good, because he said not to drive it in the rain. Once he's done with Aunt Ruby's Mustang and the Blood Moon stuff, he'll fix it up right." His hands closed around my elbows and lifted me right off the ground.

I squeaked. Then flushed. "I never made that sound," I informed him loftily, as he pulled me over to sit in his lap. "And hi."

"Hi." He grinned crookedly, brushing his hand along my jaw and into the hair at the nape of my neck. "I'm calling a time-out on all the worrying."

I linked my hands together around his neck. "Okay."

"The Blood Moon starts soon."

I wrinkled my nose. "I know." I didn't want to admit how weird I felt about not being able to contact him or Solange or their brothers. Or any of the Drakes for that matter. I even missed their dogs.

He shrugged out of his jacket, pulling something out of the

inside pocket. I was confused at first; it wasn't a stake or a dagger or a weapon of any kind.

"It's a CD," he said, giving it to me. "I made you a mix. For when we're apart." I knew if he'd still been human he would have been blushing. Back then I would have teased him mercilessly about it. But now I just wanted the CD.

"You made me a mix?" I was dangerously close to simpering. I straightened my spine. "Thanks," I added. "What's on it?"

"Listen to it and find out." His thumb brushed over my mouth. "I kind of miss you already," he said softly, leaning in to nip at my lower lip.

I nipped back, and the kiss fell with dizzying speed into need and want until even the back of my knees tingled. He kissed me as if we had all the time in the world, as if it weren't cold outside, as if winter weren't coming, or the dawn, or any of the dangers that waited for us outside this field. I kissed him back as if he were right, as if there were only the two of us, as if the only worry we had were my curfew. He fell back, bringing me with him. We reclined in our own little world of grass and clover with only the stars to see us. Kissing him was addictive; it was breath and blood and chocolate.

And then reality came crashing down around us.

"Hey, vamp lover, we know you're out there."

"You've got to be kidding me." I lifted my head, recognizing Ben's voice. I was still sprawled on Nicholas. "They *followed* me?"

He shifted so I was sitting on the ground and he was in a crouch, balanced on the balls of his feet.

"Go away!" I yelled, jumping up.

"We're just doing our duty," Jody shouted back. I could make out her outline by the cedars, if I squinted. "You know, *killing* vampires instead of kissing them."

I turned on one heel and glared at her. "Bite me, Jody."

Nicholas stood slowly, unfurling like deadly smoke. I knew what they saw: pale skin, gleaming eyes, sharp fangs. I just saw someone worth protecting.

"I mean it, you guys," I added fiercely. "Back off."

The first stake would have caught me in the shoulder if Nicholas hadn't shoved me out of the way.

"Hey! Watch it!" If punching other students was against school policy, I was pretty sure we weren't allowed to stake them either. And I'd dropped my CD and nearly stepped on it. Now I was really cranky.

"Friends of yours?" Nicholas asked drily.

"Yeah, they're thinking of making me prom queen," I shot back. I stepped in front of him to shield him. He cursed and nudged me back, trying to block me.

"Stop it."

"You stop it!"

I tripped him. Then he hooked his leg behind my knees and dropped me. I flailed and landed on a lump of wilted wildflowers. I scowled at him. So much for romance.

"Excuse me, but they can't stake me," I reminded him. "It's illegal. And it would get them expelled." They seemed the type to care about that.

"They can still hurt you," Nicholas insisted stubbornly.

"Yeah, but they can *kill* you. So stop being a hero."

"You first," he snorted. "Can I hurt them just a little?"

I sighed, thinking of treaties and detention. "Probably not." I had stakes but they were useless right now. "Wait," I said, smiling slowly. I still had pepper eggs in the pouch at my belt. They looked like silly putty but they were filled with cayenne pepper. The blue one was full of Hypnos powder, but I wasn't about to waste it on a few idiots. Hunter gave me the casings, but Marcus helped me make the mixture to put inside. It was a Helios-Ra invention based on some old ninja weapon, but Marcus was already working on a new recipe. He was the brother who worked with Uncle Geoffrey the most, so he had access to supplies the rest didn't have.

I hurled one, still grinning. It exploded and one of the students, Ben I thought, yelled.

"Ha," I said. "That'll teach you to bully me."

"Nice shot." Nicholas approved.

"Thanks. Go home now."

"Yeah, right."

"Seriously. They won't stop until you're gone. I can handle them," I reminded him.

"But—" He paused, tilting his head slightly. His nostrils flared. And then he cursed, very softly. Too softly.

I swallowed nervously. "What now?"

"Not sure." He took my hand and we ran, hunched over in the tall grass. We stopped under a tall maple tree. Nicholas scaled it quickly while I waited on the ground, keeping an eye on the bullies still throwing out taunts. Nicholas dropped beside me so suddenly

I jumped a foot in the air. I was swinging my fist before it registered that it was just him. He bent back just enough that I missed his nose.

"Bounty hunters," he replied grimly.

I frowned. "But there's no bounty on the Drakes anymore," I said. "Right? So why are there vampires after you now?"

"These aren't vampires."

"They're not?"

"No, they're vampire hunters."

I goggled. "*What?*"

He nodded sharply. "Loners. Huntsmen, like the ones who attacked London. Apparently not everyone wants to toe the Helios-Ra line. Some hunt on their own. No rules."

"Well, shit." Not that I loved rules, but I loved them more than vampire hunters without any restrictions or treaties.

"Pretty much," Nicholas agreed.

I craned my head, searching through the undergrowth. "I can't see them."

"They usually wear trophy necklaces of vampire fangs."

"That's gross."

He sniffed the air. "I think there's two, maybe three." He cursed. "Same ones that got London. Son of a bitch."

"Can we beat them?"

"Probably not."

I was afraid of that. "Bullies and murderers," I said. "Not our best date, Drake."

He snorted. "Not our worst either." Then he kissed me quickly, fiercely. "Just stay low."

I grabbed his sleeve as he turned away. "Not so fast."

"No time to argue, Lucy."

"Then don't argue," I shot back. "You just said we can't take them."

"So?"

"So, don't be dumb. I like you better undead than dead." I made a fist on his sleeve and dug my heels in the dirt to keep him from bolting heroically. "I can distract them while you run."

His fangs poked out of his gums. "No."

I just raised an eyebrow at him. "Yes."

"They're getting closer. From the east, from behind those cedars, I think."

I pressed on. "So I'll throw the rest of my eggs at them while you take off in the opposite direction."

"I don't like it."

"You don't have to. But the fact is, I'm not in danger. You are. So don't piss me off, Nicky."

He nearly grinned. I could see his lips twitching. "Don't push it, *Lucky*."

I let go of his shirt and filled my hands with my last two eggs. "Ready?"

"Not quite."

He whirled me around and bent me backward over his arm, kissing me until I felt too hot to be inside my skin. "I'll see you after the Blood Moon."

And then he was gone.

I had to remind myself that it was only for a few weeks and it was stupid to feel like crying.

Better to kick some ass.

I waited until I was sure Nicholas was well away before I shouted, "Vampire!"

When the first bounty hunter charged out of the bushes, a pepper egg hit him square on the forehead. He sneezed and cursed, blindly throwing a stake in my direction. I had to dive out of the way. I landed hard, spitting dandelions and mud out of my mouth.

The next one was smarter, not leaving the cover of leaves and darkness. The moonlight showed barely a glimpse of a tooth necklace and then nothing at all. I crawled through the brush, being poked by dried grass, tickled by dried Queen Anne's lace, and pinched by burrs. "Just once I'd like to go out without someone flinging stakes about," I muttered, crawling faster. "I'm going to get a complex at this rate." I stopped behind a half-naked dogwood, using it for as much cover as I could.

"He went south!" I called out, knowing Nicholas had gone north.

"No," Jody shouted. "He went west!"

Since she was wrong and actually helping to add to the confusion that would protect Nicholas, I didn't throw my last pepper egg at her.

Even though I really wanted to.

"We're Helios-Ra," I shouted, not wanting them to start hunting us too.

There was a loud sigh from the bounty hunter still in the bushes. "Then go home, children."

I might have bristled at that if I didn't want to get out of here as much as they wanted us to. I peeked out slowly. "Don't shoot!"

The bounty hunter I'd attacked was still rubbing his eyes. "Get out of here before you really piss me off."

I ran. So did the others.

"This isn't over," Jody hissed as we burst out of the woods and back onto the campus lawns.

I rolled my eyes. "Oh, shut up."

CHAPTER 8

Solange

No matter how well I hid, Constantine always seemed to find me.

He was leaning against a huge boulder that had fallen off the mountain over a century ago. It was soft with moss and lichen. His eyes were violet, even in the darkness. "There you are, princess."

"Hi." He made me feel like I was ten years old and a thousand years old at the same time. It was confusing.

"What's the matter here?" He pushed away from the rock and approached me slowly, languidly, as if the air were honey. "You've been crying."

I didn't say anything.

"That bad?" he pressed.

"My cousin nearly died. I had a fight with my best friend. I . . . almost attacked her."

"And did she deserve it?"

"She used a stun gun on me."

"She deserved it, then," he said dismissively. He was close enough that I could see the flecks of gray in his irises and my own face reflected in his pupils. I looked pale and pathetic.

I lifted my chin. "And I broke up with my boyfriend."

He looked almost satisfied. I must have imagined that. All he said in a husky voice was, "The human boy?"

For some reason I didn't like hearing Kieran referred to as a boy. "He's a hunter."

"Worse and worse."

I frowned. "Could you not gloat?"

His smile was quick and unapologetic. "Why mourn the inevitable? A vampire princess and a vampire hunter. The basic mathematics of it was flawed, pet."

I thought of Lucy and Nicholas and Quinn and Hunter. "I don't believe that."

But he's right, you know. You have to be careful. You have to be strong.

He shrugged one shoulder. "And yet you've broken up with him."

"Not because he's a hunter." Because he was human. I didn't want Constantine to be right. And I didn't want to feel this way. I didn't want to think or wonder or worry. I just wanted it to stop. But it wasn't.

It was getting worse.

I couldn't pretend otherwise, not anymore. Not to myself, anyway. I'd go on pretending to my family for as long as I possibly could. They spent enough time worrying about me as it was. And I certainly couldn't admit to them that it gave me a kind of rush to use my pheromones, to know I was powerful all by myself, without the sword of the Drake name.

But the truth was, it made me feel like more than the overprotected, prophesied daughter born to a royal family. More than the girl other vampires only wanted for politics or greed or delusions of rare vampire babies. I *liked* that feeling. I liked knowing I could keep people away without lifting a hand, without a weapon of any kind, without even the help of my infamous brothers.

Only Constantine understood. I didn't scare him. And lately, I scared everyone, even Lucy.

Because she's human. They don't understand you, not like I do.

"What is it?" Constantine asked.

I realized I was rubbing my ear. My hand dropped. "Nothing." This voice seemed different, like it was not my own anymore.

"Are there other side effects if you drink from the vein?" I asked. "Ones that I don't know about?"

"Being strong, healthy. Nothing you can't handle, love."

Everyone else wanted to keep me safe, and I appreciated it, don't get me wrong, but Constantine just wanted to make me powerful. His death wouldn't be on my hands; I wouldn't have to carry the burden that at any time he could be staked just for knowing me or for trying to protect me. He trusted I could take care of myself. There was something seductive in that. Well, for me anyway.

Besides, being with Constantine stopped me from obsessing over Kieran.

I missed him already. I could feel the grief howling inside my chest, like a wolf on the tundra. And I already knew I'd be checking the tree for messages even as I told myself I shouldn't. He'd taken on the League, and his entire belief system, to be with me.

And then I'd tried to eat him.

Girlfriend of the Year, that's me.

"You look positively maudlin," Constantine said, slipping his arm over my shoulders. It sent a tickle through my throat. He leaned down so that his mouth was very close to my ear. "What you need is distraction. And I have just the thing, love."

I knew exactly what Lucy would have done. She would have scoffed at what was an obvious line, would have elbowed him in the stomach and flounced away, secure in her disdain. That was, no doubt, the smart thing to do.

But she'd never met Constantine.

She didn't know the way his dark voice sent shivers over the back of my neck, the way he was impossibly beautiful, all dark colors and romantic shadows.

And I was tired of doing the smart, responsible thing.

I wanted to have fun. Uncomplicated, unpolitical fun.

I smiled back at him, leaning in closer. "Let's go."

◆

It was like a fairy tale.

And for once, *not* the kind where someone wanted to eat my heart.

The meadow was circled with willow trees, and a narrow creek cut through one side, edged with silver pebbles and frost. The grass was flattened under several thick Persian rugs in ruby reds and ink blues, all piled over each other. Candles burned in iron lanterns dangling from the trees and in standing candelabras. A table spanned the narrowest part of the river, and there were several chairs on either side, moth-eaten brocade armchairs with scarred armrests and cobwebbed feet. There were several chests and benches and thick incense smoke hanging like scented mist.

"It's beautiful," I murmured. It was like all the best parts of a storybook. If Constantine had traded in his jacket for a suit of armor I wouldn't even have blinked. In fact, I felt as if I should be wearing velvet and lace-trimmed butterfly sleeves. Something in me sighed. I couldn't tell if it was me or the strange inner voice I couldn't seem to silence.

"This isn't Chandramaa territory," Constantine warned me as the other vampires turned to stare at us. "We're on the other side of the boundaries here."

Vampires lounged, drinking from old-fashioned wine bottles. A bloodslave sat on an overstuffed cushion with a smile of welcome. I looked away.

"Princess," a girl about my age said in a thick Irish accent. She wore a long skirt with raggedy tulle at the hem and a tight, faded T-shirt. Her feet were bare, her toes painted turquoise and resting across the legs of another vampire with blond dreads. "You finally broke free of the gilded cage. Fight the man, Drake, even if you're the man."

"Marigold is our little anarchist," Constantine drawled affectionately. "Don't let her scare you away."

Marigold grinned at me. I couldn't help but grin back. It was hard not to like a girl with a name like Marigold who wore a candy ring on a chain as a necklace. Constantine's hand smoothed down my shoulder, resting on my lower back. It was distracting, as if all of my nerve endings congregated under his palm and sparked. I had to force myself to concentrate on what he was saying.

"That's Toby and Elijah, and, over there, Ianthe. There are others lurking about." Toby abandoned a purple velvet couch, which Constantine led me to. "I don't know that one; he's new."

The guy with dreads smiled easily. "I'm Spencer."

The name sounded vaguely familiar. When I stared at him, he added, "Hunter's friend."

He'd been turned by one of the doctors at the Helios-Ra Academy after being infected with *Hel-Blar* saliva in the infirmary. He might be a vampire now, but he still looked like a surfer. And his friend Hunter was dating my brother. Neither of us mentioned any of the above.

"What is this place?" I asked, sitting down. A broken cushion spring poked me in the hip.

"We call it the Bower," Marigold explained. "When we get tired of the bleeding royalists—no offense—and the Chandramaa breathing down our necks, we come here."

"Think of it as an exchange of ideas and customs," Constantine added smoothly. "A safe place. The people here have traveled far to be a part of the Blood Moon. Marigold is from County Clare, Elijah is from Morocco."

"We don't know where Toby's from," Marigold said, grinning. "He doesn't speak a lick of English."

"I'm Solange," I introduced myself, although Marigold had already outed me as a princess.

"You are *dhampir*," Ianthe said in a thick Greek accent. I blinked at her matter-of-fact tone. "Vampire father and human mother, yes?"

"Originally, yes."

She shrugged. "It is not so uncommon." The ancient families of the Raktapa Council usually garnered respect or suspicion, usually both.

"Oh." I could have kissed her. I was *common*. I grinned. Constantine chuckled.

"I told you, you're hopelessly colonial. There are lineages far rarer than yours in the world."

"Watch out for Sarabeth though," Marigold said. "She's a right nasty piece of work. Easy to recognize too, with those goat legs."

I blinked. "Sarabeth has goat legs?"

"Yeah and if you stare, she'll kick you with them." She rubbed her knee. "Hurts like a bitch."

Ianthe nodded. "Very rare, the Baobhan-Sith."

"And don't offer her whiskey because she's Scottish and you think she'll like it. That pisses her off too. Just ask Jude." Marigold rolled her eyes. "Never mind her, we've bigger problems, apparently."

"What?" I wondered.

"One of ours has gone missing, likely dead," Elijah said softly. "A vampire."

"Really?" I asked, surprised. "Even with the Chandramaa around?"

"This wasn't a vampire dispute," Ianthe explained. "It was a human kill."

Elijah spat. "Hunters."

I felt my eyes widen. I tried not to look at Spencer and give him away. "Helios-Ra?"

"We don't know that," Jude interjected. "Could've been anyone."

"Huntsmen, Helios-Ra, they're all the same. Human."

I swallowed. "But how do you know it wasn't another vampire?"

"Smell of human all over the bloody murder site, wasn't there?" Elijah looked at me speculatively. "This conversation's too gory for a pretty girl like you." He had no idea I'd just watched a Huntsman commit suicide. He smiled at me, fangs poking out from under his top lip.

Pheromones. Oops. I shifted closer to Constantine.

"Thanks for bringing me here," I said to him softly, as Spencer and Ianthe argued over whether or not vampires were intrinsically magical. Ianthe said they performed magic, while Spencer said they *were* magic. Elijah said he didn't believe in magic and could we please discuss the vampire penal codes instead.

"You're very welcome." Constantine bent his head toward me as bats filled the sky over us. "You can make your own destiny, Solange. You just have to look a little farther than your front door."

I could love this Bower. Everyone looked so comfortable, drinking blood out of wine bottles and talking. Even Spencer sprawled with Marigold, drinking from a glass.

I shook my head. "How are you so well-adjusted?" I asked Spencer. "You've only been a vampire for what, a month?"

He shrugged. "Better than the alternative. Besides, I can still surf at night." He winked at Marigold. "And there are perks."

She winked and pulled him to his feet. "Let's go explore those perks, shall we, boyo?"

They vanished into the quiet, cold forest. It wasn't long before the others wandered away as well, Ianthe with the giggling blood-slave. Some of the candles guttered out and the shadows wrapped around me like a thick shawl. Frost glittered on the willow leaves.

"Pass me the bottle, would you?" Constantine asked, pulling a clean wooden cup out of a basket next to the sofa. I was handing him the bottle when it broke in my hand, glass shards dropping to the carpet. One of them dug into the pad of my thumb and stuck there. Blood and wine dripped down my arm. My fangs lengthened.

Constantine didn't say a word, just brushed the rest of the glass off my leg and then pulled the sliver out. Blood immediately trickled out of the cut. His eyes flared, the blues and purples of a summer twilight. His fangs gleamed as he leaned into me, crowding me back against the velvet sofa. I didn't stop him. He was so close, pressing me into the cushions. I didn't know if he was going to kiss me.

And then he just lifted my hand to his mouth, slowly. He still didn't speak, didn't look away, just closed his mouth over my wound. He sucked at the blood. I blushed but I didn't pull away. The cut stopped bleeding; it was so small a nick that I could feel it healing already. Constantine dragged his lips over my inner wrist, pressing such a soft, hungry kiss over my blue veins that I nearly sighed.

Then he rose and walked away, leaving me lying on a couch in the middle of the forest, feeling more like the princess in a fairy story than I ever had before.

◆

Constantine was right.

I needed to take control of my own destiny.

And Isabeau was the only person I knew who might be able to help me. She also knew what it was like to have a prophecy hanging over your head. Of course, hers had said she'd hook up with one of my brothers and she'd done just that. My prophecy was slightly more sinister.

At least, that's what I assumed.

No one actually knew the exact words of the stupid thing. They'd been muttered one night by a crazy lady in sixteenth-century Scotland. Someone must have overheard her, since the story had spread, but no one had ever written it down. 'Cause that would be, you know, *helpful*.

Instead, my very existence was bandied about like a vampire bogeyman to scare monarchs and rebels alike. And I was starting to worry that the vampire lore might be right. So I'd do what Dad had always taught us to do when we were scared or confused: I'd get more information.

We'd never believed in magic before, and because of that, and the fact that we'd been expelled from court for so many centuries, we didn't know as much as we could. But maybe I could fix that. And show my family that I wasn't made of sugar and moonbeams.

Because after a moment on a velvet sofa with Constantine I felt wicked, made of pepper and fire and wine.

Leave it. You can't trust magic. But you can trust me.

And there was that voice. I shuddered. I really needed answers.

I finally tracked down Isabeau at the camp outskirts, on the path toward the mountain caves where the Hound delegation was staying. The tattoos and scars on her arms and neck were visible in the flickering torchlight. So were the other three vampires standing in a half-moon around her.

They had no idea what she could do to them.

Aside from my mother, Isabeau was the best fighter I'd ever seen. She was quick and vicious and could work magic to confound you. But she couldn't do any of that here, not in the Chandramaa's territory. They circled her, snarling. I couldn't help but compare them to Marigold and Spencer and even Toby, who hadn't said a single word.

"We hear you've got double fangs, like the Host."

Isabeau stiffened. "I have never belonged to Montmartre." She put a hand on her wolfhound's neck when he growled. "*Non, Charlemagne. Attend.*"

I rushed forward, flashing my triple set of fangs on purpose for the first time.

It felt good.

The vampires froze, staring at me. "Princess."

I leaned closer, smiling savagely. "Go away."

Their pupils dilated and they nodded mechanically.

"And be grateful I don't make you bark like a dog," I added.

"Yes, princess."

They wandered away, looking confused.

Isabeau tilted her head consideringly. "This is new, *n'est-ce pas?*"

I nodded. "Kind of. Can I talk to you?"

"*Bien sûr.*"

"In private?"

"Yes, come this way." I followed her away from the camp, toward the caves. The hundred tiny sounds of the tribes coexisting trickled away under the wind and the smell of approaching snow. I could hear dogs padding toward us and a drum from somewhere deep in the mountain. We stopped on an outcropping, high enough to see the stars over the treetops. I felt nervous, but in a good way. Like I might actually have control over my own future.

"I want to know more about the prophecy," I said. "About me." Snow drifted between us, melting when it touched the stones. Charlemagne barked and tried to bite the flakes out of the air. "Is there any way to magically see the prophecy? Or hear it? Logan told me you did that with one of the paintings in the royal caves. You made him see the moment it was painted."

She frowned. "I suppose there must be."

"But you don't know how?"

She looked intrigued. "I can think of a few spells that might help, but not as clearly as you might like. And it would take some time for me to gather the ingredients. Two weeks at least."

"I don't have two weeks!" I said pleadingly. "Isn't there another spell?"

"I suppose we could ask Kala," she said. "She can do it."

"She can?" I said eagerly.

"I say she can, not that she *will*."

"Can we ask her now? Please?"

She blinked at my impatience. "I suppose so."

I spun on my heel and darted into the nearest cave. She didn't follow. I poked my head back out. "Well?"

She was smiling. "That cave leads nowhere." She pointed to another cave farther down. "This way."

If these were only the Hounds' temporary caves I could only imagine how incredible their permanent space was. The walls were studded with torches, and the entrance was already painted with reddish ocher and decorated with dog bones hung with beads. Logan told me that after a dog died (of natural causes), their bones were turned into holy objects. I remembered finding a dogs-paw death mark, which we'd thought meant that Logan was dead.

A dozen dogs greeted us with wagging tails and the odd growl. Isabeau made a sharp hand movement and the growls died. We climbed down farther into the labyrinthine caves, into the smell of wet rock and incense. Tattooed Hounds with bone beads in their hair went still and silent at our arrival. Even the drumbeat stopped before I could see who was playing it.

Isabeau kept walking, looking the most comfortable I'd ever seen her, inside the quiet mountain with dogs crowding at her knees. She led us down rough-hewn steps into a deep crevice hung with beads. We had to squeeze into the damp darkness, rock scraping my shoulders and my hands until they bled. Then the crevice opened abruptly into another cave, lit with a single candle burning in a tin lantern dangling from the ceiling.

A woman I assumed was Kala, the Hounds' Shamanka, waited for us on a fur pelt, a painted drum in her lap. Her hair was long and braided, and hung with so many bone beads that she clacked and clattered when she moved. Blue spirals were tattooed on the left side of her face and all the way down her arm. It was the same color blue of the dog-and-knot-work tattoo Isabeau had on her arm and the fleur-de-lis, on the side of her neck.

"Finally," Kala said. "You've come."

I blinked, startled. "You were expecting me?"

Isabeau smiled gently. "It's difficult to surprise Kala."

"Sit!" Kala barked at me. I was sitting on furs before I'd even registered the command. Isabeau slipped away before I could ask her to stay. Kala bared her fangs at me in what I hoped was a smile. "You've come to see, have you, my girl?"

I nodded. "To see the prophecy."

She cackled. There was no other word for it. "Hope for you yet, then." She shook a seed rattle hung with dog teeth before I could ask her what she meant by that. The sound bounced off the walls and reverberated off my bones. Even my fangs felt as if they were vibrating inside my head. With her other hand she used a fan of cedar branches to waft smoke from a small fire set in a circle of white stones. I coughed and my eyes burned. The smoke was thick and green and tasted odd, coppery. She chanted in a language I didn't recognize until I felt dizzy and disoriented. The smoke clung to my hair, to my eyelashes, inside my nostrils. The chanting and the rattling stopped abruptly, and the silence was so sudden I flinched.

Kala reached over just as suddenly, and drilled the tip of her index finger very hard into the spot between my eyes. "See."

Everything went black.

CHAPTER 9

Nicholas

"What happened to you?" Marcus asked when I ducked into the barn that doubled as Uncle Geoffrey's laboratory. Acres of scrupulously clean tables gleamed under track lighting. There were microscopes, an ultrasound machine, even an X-ray machine, not to mention shelves of machinery whose purposes were unknown to me. Marcus stood in front of a row of test tubes filled with blood. He wore a white lab coat and his hair was disheveled, as if he'd been running his hand through it.

Christabel sat on a recliner in one corner, near a small television and a wooden chest filled with DVDs. She was staring at a box of pizza on her lap, frowning.

"What's with you?" I asked.

She glanced up, blinking. "I used to love pizza." She sounded bewildered.

"And now you don't?"

She shook her head. "It tastes like cardboard." She sniffed deeply. "I can smell it but I can barely taste it."

Marcus nodded sadly. "I still mourn coffee."

"But it's weird." She stuck out her tongue and went cross-eyed looking at it. "I still have taste buds. I should be able to *taste* it."

Marcus smiled sympathetically. "It's because your brain can't handle the thought of drinking blood," he explained. "But your body's smarter. It makes it so that nothing else is as tasty as blood. Because you need it to survive. That's Uncle Geoffrey's current theory anyway. And I'm inclined to agree." He raised an eyebrow at my pants as Christabel pushed the pizza away with a sigh. "So, what's with you?"

I looked down at my ripped jeans streaked with mud and bristling with burrs. "Date with Lucy."

"Is she mad at you?"

I snorted. "No. I'm still standing, aren't I? We ran into Huntsmen."

Marcus whistled. "As bad as they say?"

"Ask London."

"Is she okay?"

"Uncle Geoffrey seems to think she'll be fine." I leaned against the wall, exhausted. "Solange offered her blood, seeing as she drank from Madame Veronique once, and it helped."

Marcus looked interested. "Really?"

I couldn't help but grin. "Yeah, Uncle G. wanted to run some tests, but Sol wouldn't let him."

"It's all right, we still have a few tubes of her blood left," he said, motioning to the tray in front of him. "I'll keep working on it."

"Have you found anything?"

"No," he answered, disgusted. "It's blood. It's Drake DNA. It reacts curiously to different additives and stimuli, but never consistently." He gritted his back teeth. "It's damned annoying."

"Is she sick? Is it dangerous?"

"She's not sick."

"But it's dangerous?" I pressed.

Marcus sighed. "I wish I knew."

CHAPTER 10

Lucy

Sunday night, later still

I pushed open Hunter's door without knocking.

"There are vampire hunters outside!" I announced. "Did you know that?"

Chloe didn't even look up from her laptop. "She keeps forgetting she's at a vampire hunter high school," she said to Hunter. Soda cans littered the ground around her chair.

Hunter was sitting on her bed, reading a novel. "Why are you covered in burrs?" she asked, unconcerned.

"Vampire hunters," I explained impatiently. "Like I said."

She put the book down, her blond ponytail swinging behind her. "Students attacked you?"

"No. Well yes, but I'm not talking about them. I'm talking about old guys wearing fangs as jewelry. Huntsmen." I brushed burrs and leaves off my sweater. The knees of my jeans were stained with mud.

Chloe finally looked over, interested. Her hair was a mass of dark curls springing every which way, as usual. "Really?"

"Yes," I said, rereading my texts just to remind myself that Nicholas was safely the hell away from this weird-ass school. "And they did *not* like my boyfriend."

Hunter frowned. "Huntsmen? Here? Are you sure?"

"Hello?" I spread my arms out, twigs and leaves drifting to the carpet. "I'm sure. And I have the bruises to prove it."

Chloe's fingers flew over her keyboard. I raised an eyebrow at Hunter. "Is she Googling hunter-assholes? I doubt they have their own Web page."

Chloe snorted. "You'd be surprised."

"She's hacking the school files," Hunter said. "She does it all the time."

"Don't they have security for that kind of thing?"

Chloe snorted again. "Please." I knew that tone. Connor used it whenever someone called his computer mojo into question.

I sat on Hunter's bed, rubbing my elbow. It was sore now that the adrenaline was diluted in my system. I must have landed on it harder than I thought. "Ouch."

"I can't believe you saw a Huntsman."

"That's a stupid name," I grumbled.

She just smiled. "I know, but you've seen the handbook. We're big on old words and medieval oaths and secret symbols. Anyway, Huntsmen almost never come to Violet Hill. There's no point with the academy here and everything."

"How are they different from the other hunters? Besides their barbaric fashion sense?"

"They're not Helios-Ra," Hunter explained. "They do their own thing."

"That's pretty much what Nicholas said," I admitted.

"Drives the teachers nuts," Chloe said smugly. "Whenever they threaten to fail us, we threaten to become Huntsmen."

"*You* threaten that," Hunter said drily. "The rest of us just do our homework."

"Ha. Also? I rock." She sat back and smirked at her screen, then at us. "Just what I thought. A staff alert went out about Huntsmen in the area." She scowled. "Wait a minute. They were *invited*."

Hunter straightened. "That's really rare," she explained, for my benefit. "Helios-Ra and Huntsmen get along better when we don't share territory."

"Like vampires," I said.

"I want to see York's face when you say something like that in class," Hunter grinned. York was her least favorite teacher. She turned back to Chloe. "So I assume they were invited because of the Blood Moon?"

Chloe nodded. "Increased patrols to protect us and the town, I guess."

"Figures," I muttered, a knee-jerk reaction to what I considered rampant vampire racism.

"You can't be telling me that you think all vampires are as hot as your boyfriend, Hamilton," Chloe said incredulously, swiveling around. The wheels of her chair squeaked. "Or as hot as Hunter's boyfriend. Which is not possible by the way," she interrupted herself. "Anyway, some vampires do kill, you know."

I thought of Lady Natasha and Montmartre. "Trust me, I know."

Hunter's phone interrupted us with a discreet trilling, like a baby bird. I just looked at her. "It's stuck on that ring," she admitted, reaching to grab it from her nightstand.

"It gave me nightmares right out of that Hitchcock movie *The Birds* last night when it went off at three in the morning." Chloe raised her eyebrows at me. "Then she *giggled*."

"I did not," Hunter shot back, but she was blushing just a little.

I grinned. "Quinn Drake."

She blushed harder. "Both of you shut up. Now." She frowned at her phone. "Uh-oh."

Chloe groaned. "No uh-ohs. I still have a paper to finish for tomorrow morning and it's nearly 2:00 a.m. already."

"Quinn?" I asked. "Is everyone okay?" I checked my phone again but there was no warning from Nicholas or Solange.

"Not Quinn." She got to her feet. "Lia."

"Who's Lia?" I asked as Chloe and I followed her into the deserted hall. The lights were low.

"She's a first year," Hunter whispered. "I'm one of her floor monitors."

"And?"

"And she's sneakier than she looks." Hunter paused on the bottom step. "Stay between Chloe and me, and only step where I step."

I stared at her. "Why? Are there bombs?" You just never knew with this school.

"Just don't want to get caught roaming after hours," Hunter explained. She darted nimbly up the staircase, avoiding certain steps.

"School's bugged," Chloe whispered from behind me.

"Is that even legal?"

"Who would we tell?"

I flashed her a grin. "My mom. She could picket and protest this school into a mass of quivering fear."

"Cool."

Hunter ducked under a camera I never would have even guessed was there. I was impressed despite myself. We reached the top floor and went down the hall, past the bathrooms. Lia's door was cracked open. Hunter slipped in with Chloe and me on her heels.

Two girls were crammed into the corner of an unmade bed, noses pressed to the window. They wore their pajamas and the lights were out. Only the moon showed their silhouettes. The one with glasses turned around. "You got my text," the one I assumed was Lia said. "Come see, quick!"

The three of us hopped on the bed so suddenly Lia's roommate was squashed in the corner. She squeaked, twisted, and fell right off the bed.

"Sorry, Savannah," Hunter said, but she didn't move and she

didn't look away from the view out the window. She was so close her ponytail tickled the side of my face.

"What are we looking at?" I asked. All I could see was the shadowy quad, a streetlight hitting the gym windows, and the outline of trees.

"There," Lia pointed. "I saw a van pull up without its headlights on and Theo ran out of the infirmary."

"Ask her what she was looking for," Savannah snickered.

Lia flushed. "That's not important."

"Where's your kit?" Hunter asked sharply. Lia grabbed it off the floor and practically threw it at her. Night-vision goggles, binoculars, stakes, and other contraptions spilled out over the blanket.

"Hey, I never got a kit," I muttered. "I totally want night-vision goggles." Hunter already had them in her hand so I reached for the binoculars.

We all bent our necks at an angle guaranteed to give us arthritis when we got old. Assuming we actually got a chance to *get* old, of course. If I crossed my left eye slightly I could just see the infirmary door. The path was easier once you knew what you were looking for. There was a flurry of movement behind the van door, but we couldn't make out what they were doing.

"So what were you looking for that had you wedged back here?" Chloe asked Lia, while we waited impatiently for something to happen.

"Nothing."

"Liar." Savannah grinned. "She heard Kieran was in the infirmary and she wanted a look."

Lia pinched her roommate. "You suck, Savannah."

Savannah just shrugged, unrepentant.

Hunter smiled briefly. "Kieran's already gone home," she said gently.

"Oh." Lia tried not to sound disappointed and failed miserably. She paused. "Is he okay?"

"He's fine," Hunter replied. "Lucy's the one that brought him in."

Lia looked at me, eyes round. "You know Kieran?"

I didn't tell her he was dating my best friend. Well, according to Nicholas he wasn't dating Solange anymore anyway.

"Heads up," Hunter said.

Down below, two Huntsmen emerged, carrying the limp body of a human woman to the infirmary.

"Those are the Huntsmen that came at us in the woods." I recognized the fang necklaces as well as the man I'd pepper-egged.

"Damn it," Hunter muttered. "I can't figure out what they're saying. I knew I should have learned to read lips." It was probably the only thing in the world she didn't know how to do yet.

The Huntsmen rushed the patient under a lamppost. Hunter and I both fumbled for a better angle. The woman had short hair, short enough that I could see the side of her neck.

And the puncture wounds, which could only have come from fangs, dripping blood.

I sucked in a breath. "Shit."

The Huntsmen knew there was a vampire out near the school; Jody and her idiot friends knew Nicholas was with me. And now there was the body of a human woman very clearly suffering from a vampire attack. I knew for a fact Nicholas hadn't done it. And I also knew no one was likely to believe me.

The binoculars dug into my cheekbones but try as I might, I couldn't see anything else. They'd already rushed the woman inside.

"She wasn't a Hunter," Hunter said quietly, thoughtfully.

"How can you be sure?" I asked.

"For one thing they never bother sneaking wounded Hunters onto the campus. They'd just drive right over the lawns if they had to."

"Which means?"

"Which means it was a mundane, a civilian."

I sat back. "Do they do that a lot? Bring them here, I mean?"

She looked at me grimly. "Only if it was a vampire attack and they want to be sure the person wasn't infected. Hospitals would be useless in that case."

"Looks like we do need protection after all," Chloe said quietly.

◆

That seemed to be the consensus in the rest of the dorm as well. When we got back to Hunter's room, there was a small pewter charm hanging on the doorknob. Hunter and Chloe exchanged a grim glance and opened the door. Hunter pocketed the charm and scooped up the folded note on the carpet. It was the number 113.

"Let's go." Hunter turned to leave again.

"Go where?" I asked. "Is that a secret code? Night-vision goggles and secret codes. Okay, this League doesn't entirely suck."

"Hunter runs a secret Black Lodge," Chloe explained quietly.

"Well, sort of secret. It's authorized by Hart but no one else really knows about it."

"Cool."

"Yeah," Chloe agreed, scooping her laptop up off the desk and slipping it under her arm. "It's because of the whole teacher-vampire drug thing. Hunter is Hart's secret eyes and ears at the school."

Hunter shrugged, modestly. "It's no big deal."

Chloe just ignored her. "The Eye of Horus means someone's got info. It calls a secret meeting."

"In Jenna's room, apparently," Hunter said, shoving the note in her pocket. "That's her room number." She glanced at me. "Want to come?"

"Hell, yeah, I do."

"I was going to see if you wanted to join. I think it would be good to have your perspective, just coming into the school and everything. You might see stuff we don't even notice anymore."

"You mean other than the fact that I'm surprised you guys don't run around in black capes and call each other Van Helsing?"

"Yes." She rolled her eyes. "Other than that." She nodded to the door. "Let's move."

Jenna's room was just down the hall, next to a window hung with a hideous lace curtain that was probably meant to be homey. It was just ugly. Hunter knocked once softly and then slipped inside. Jenna was at her desk, her red hair in a braid. There was one other girl and two guys with her, none of whom I recognized. Chloe went straight to the empty bed and stretched out on her stomach, flipping open her computer.

"Where's your roommate?" Hunter asked Jenna.

"At the library, working on a paper," Jenna replied. "She'll be at least another hour."

"This is Lucy," Hunter introduced me. "You know Jenna, and that's Kyla, Griffin, Drew, and Eric."

Eric's dark eyes snapped onto me. "Lucy Hamilton? You know Solange?"

"Yeah," I said. At least he hadn't called me Lucky. I'd probably let him live, despite the tone he was using, as if I'd personally kicked his puppy. "Why? Do you know Solange?"

"I know Kieran."

"Oh."

"She—"

"Stop right there." I cut him off with a narrowed glare. "I might be pissed off at her but she's still my best friend, and I'll kick your ass if you say anything about her."

He leaned back against the edge of the desk. "Yeah? Well, Kieran's my best friend."

"He's my friend too," I replied quietly.

Eric looked at me for a long moment before finally nodding his head once. "Okay."

Hunter sat on the floor. "If you two are done with the macho pissing contest, can we get on with it? Why are you here, Eric? You're not Black Lodge."

"No, but Kieran said you might need this info." He reached over and flipped on Jenna's radio. It was a trick I knew well. It masked conversations in cases of bugging devices or vampires, take your pick.

"Is it about the woman who was just brought in?" Chloe asked. "'Cause we know about that already."

"What woman?" Jenna asked quizzically.

"A wounded civilian," Hunter said. "Bite marks."

Jenna let out a whistle through her teeth. Eric looked at me. I looked back at him.

"What?" I said. "I didn't bite her."

"But you're friends with vampires."

"Oh my God," I exclaimed, disgusted. I flopped back onto Jenna's bed so I wouldn't throw something at his head. Like a chair. "You guys are making me nuts. Kieran's friends with vampires. So's Hunter. So get off my case or I swear I'm going to torch this whole stupid school."

Eric grinned unexpectedly. "That I'd like to see. You're okay, Hamilton."

"Gee," I replied sweetly, sarcastically. "Thanks."

He just laughed. "Anyway, we didn't know there's a civ here, but she's not the first to be bitten this week." He went serious. "She's the third."

I sat up. "The *third?* Why isn't it in the papers? By now at least one of them should be screaming about how this is all because of a government conspiracy or chupacabras or some other weird-ass thing."

"It'll be in the papers tomorrow," he confirmed. "Something about an escaped snake."

"A snake," I said, nonplussed. "What, like an escaped pet cobra? How damned big would the snake have to be to leave marks like that?"

Chloe made a face. "Too damned big." She scrolled down her screen. "Is it in the *Violet Hill Gazette*? Or the *Journal*? Doesn't matter," she added before he could answer. "I can crack either of their servers in my sleep. I could totally delete an article."

"No point," Eric said. "Then they'd really think they were on to a story."

"How did Kieran get the info?" Hunter asked.

"Does it matter?" His teeth flashed white in his dark face.

"I guess not," she grumbled. "But he shouldn't have told you we're Black Lodge. Kinda defeats the whole secrecy thing."

"With an uncle like his, what do you expect?" He shrugged. "Anyway, Huntsmen are all over, vampires are all over, so we need to be out there too. If you're game."

Hunter stood up. "Hell, yeah, we're game. Are you kidding?"

They bumped fists like they were in some action movie. Hunter didn't even glance at me. "Shut it, Lucy."

I grinned at her all the way to the staircase. "You're like Bruce Willis, dude. Or the Rock or something."

"Can I at least be Lara Croft?"

"You don't have the boobs." I was still grinning when I snuck into my room.

Sarita sat up in her bed. "Your dad called like five times." She looked at the clock disapprovingly. "And it's past curfew."

Chapter 11

Solange

When I opened my eyes again the sun was rising, scattering pink and orange light over pine trees and a mountain. But it wasn't my pine trees or my mountains. It wasn't Violet Hill. When I turned around there was nothing but moorland stretching out to a lake in the distance. The heather was purple and interspersed with tiny yellow flowers that looked like birds' feet.

And I wasn't falling into an unconscious sleep. I wasn't even tired.

Dumbfounded, I watched the sun inch higher in the sky. I ran my tongue over my teeth. I still had fangs. I was still a vampire.

But the sun didn't affect me.

I could smell wood smoke so I climbed a hill toward it, dipping down into a valley where a small stone cottage stood on the banks of a wide river. I really had no idea where I was or what was going on. The last thing I remembered was Kala shaking her rattle of dog teeth at me.

And now this.

I kept climbing down to the cottage because I didn't know what else to do. I couldn't just stand there on the moors, however grand and beautiful they were. I heard scratching when I got closer, like an animal digging for roots and grubs. I peeked around the side of the cottage expecting to see a badger or a bear.

Instead, there was an old woman, muttering to herself, up to her knuckles in mud. Her long gray hair was braided and wrapped like a small crown around her head. She wore a long, woolen blue-gray dress with a leather belt hung with bones and pouches and a short dagger with a curved blade. A long chain rattled down to her knees, hooked onto a ring of keys.

She was crouched down, pulling white puffy mushrooms out of the ground and adding them to a pile of herbs in a wooden bowl. When she chortled to herself I noticed she was missing a few teeth. And she smelled like berries and sweat. I wrinkled my nose.

"Excuse me?"

She ignored me.

She got to her feet, creaking and groaning and shuffled toward me.

"Hello?" I tried again, louder, in case she was deaf. Still nothing. Her left eye was milky white. She was blind. Good, she wouldn't see the fangs and freak out. But she seemed to be ignoring me.

Instead, she walked right through me.

I came apart as if I were made out of cold air and smoke, and then melted back together.

It did *not* feel nice.

"Shit!" I burst out, startled and creeped out. "Am I dead? Kala totally drugged me and killed me. Can vampires even become ghosts?"

The old woman shivered and turned her head suddenly, staring at me as if she could see me. Her right eye was clear, black as a jetbead. "On with ye, Fair Folk. I've left milk out and I've cold iron. Your choice, but I've no time to play." She chortled again and bustled off, slamming the door of the cottage behind her. I knew in that dream logic you sometimes had that she'd been speaking Scottish Gaelic, and I'd understood every word even though I'd never learned Gaelic.

I looked at my hands. I seemed solid enough. And I could feel the uneven dirt under my shoes. But I was pale. Not vampire pale; more like I was in a black-and-white movie when the world around me was in full Technicolor.

Clearly, I was hallucinating.

I went to the front door and reached for the handle. My fingers slipped right through it. Frustrated, I tried again. And again. I tried knocking, and my fist vanished through the other side of the wooden door. My arm felt like it was stuck in molasses that was slowly freezing solid. I yanked it back out again, feeling disoriented.

It took me a moment to convince myself that I should step right through, that I should push my body through that weird nonform. That I wouldn't get trapped inside the door. Or inside this dream.

When I'd asked for help, this wasn't exactly what I had in mind.

I took a deep breath even though I didn't need to breathe, and walked through. I ended up inside the one-room cottage, nauseated and exhilarated. The old woman was sitting on a bench in front of a hearth cut into the wall. An iron hook held a cauldron over the flames, but it wasn't filled with toads' eyes or cat tails. It smelled like lamb stew. Dried herbs hung from the ceiling, over a table with two chairs, a shelf with a horn cup and a wooden plate and bowl, and a narrow cot under a window. There was an old-fashioned spinning wheel and washed fleece in a basket. The air was smoky, the floor dirt strewn with flowers.

Just like an old cottage might look in Scotland.

In the 1500s.

Kala had sent me back to witness the prophecy as it was spoken. We'd never known for sure if it was real, if the legendary Scottish madwoman during the reign of Henry the Eighth and Anne Boleyn had even existed.

Now I knew.

A thrill went through me, even as I tried not to panic about finding my way back home. Bats fluttered at the window. The old woman didn't seem to notice. She was too busy drawing a circle on the ground around herself with salt. It seemed to glow brighter than it should for a moment, as if it was made of light.

"Saint Brigid protect me," she intoned. "Bride shield me from harm."

She stirred the mushrooms and herbs into a cup of hot ale.

The smell was cloying and strange. She drew some kind of symbol in the air with her fingertip, over the cup, and then drained it, straining the bits of plant matter through her broken teeth.

Great.

The ancient prophecy everyone was so insane about had been spoken by an old lady drunk on psychedelic mushroom tea.

I crept closer as she closed her eyes and muttered some kind of singsong prayer under her breath. The fire crackled and sparked, belching smoke into the cottage. It hovered in the air and curled around the rafters. She shivered, then her head snapped up and her blind eye stared up at the smoke.

"In the violet hills, the moon's bloodshot eye sees all."

She blinked, her milky eye veined in red.

"When princess becomes queen, the true dragon will be seen. But beware the royal daughter, when the crown tears her asunder; for the dead will return, and the wheel stop its turn. Then only dragon by dragon defeated, and only love by love undefeated."

The fire flared high, scattering embers. The dried lavender stalks on the ground smoldered. She blinked again, blood on her crooked teeth when she spoke.

"A warning: Unseat the dragon before her time, and increase nine-fold her crimes;

And a token: A kiss to wake, a kiss to die, and a kiss to tell the truth from a lie."

She jerked violently, as if she'd been electrocuted, and then slumped wearily. Her hair was coming loose from its braids, and the neckline of her dress was damp with sweat. Her hands trembled. "That's what I see, mistress."

That was when the shadowy corner moved and a woman leaned forward slightly, the warm glow from the fire touching her unnaturally pale face, the gold embroidery on her wimple, the long brown braids wrapped in matching gold cords, and the eyes like frozen water.

Madame Veronique.

I was so surprised to see her there that I jolted, tripped over my own foot, and fell backward.

Through the floor. I fell through dried lavender and dirt and landed on the rocky ground of the cave.

The small fire was turning to ashes in the circle of white stones; Kala and her rattle were gone. I lurched to my feet to squeeze through the narrow tunnels even though I was dizzy and disoriented and felt strange inside my own body. Madame Veronique knew about the prophecy all along, had known the exact words, had watched it being spoken, all while she pretended she had no interest in such things.

I had no idea what that meant.

My head spun, and when I finally stumbled outside, the thirst hit me. My throat felt as if it were full of broken glass, my veins shriveled and on fire. Whatever I'd just experienced—hallucination, drugs, time travel—it left me feeling maddeningly weak. I was so thirsty that the edges of the trees and the rocks and the mountains turned red, like a wash of paint over a photograph. I licked my painfully dry lips and scrambled down the mountainside toward the camp, the prophecy repeating in my head: *only dragon by dragon defeated.*

I was in the meadow on the outskirts when a woman smiled at me from the birch trees, her neck bare and crisscrossed with scars.

"Princess, you look peaked. Do you need to feed?" She tilted her head, baring her throat politely, as if offering me a cup of tea. It was Penelope. I'd fed from her before, when Kieran, Nicholas, and Lucy found me drunk on her blood.

I swallowed. "My family doesn't . . . um . . ."

She stepped closer. "I don't mind. It's why I'm here."

She was offering willingly. And after Kala's magic I felt like a corn-husk doll, papery and lifeless. I needed blood. She was offering. Constantine was right. It was simple. So why complicate it by resisting?

She pushed up the loose sleeve of her sweater and extended her arm, pebbled with goose bumps. I lowered my mouth to the crease of her elbow where her pulse beat, eschewing her neck, silvery with faded scars. It was like sharing a cup that had already been drunk from too many times. My fangs bit down slowly but firmly. I didn't want to hurt her, only wanted the warmth of her blood in my mouth, the flowering of my veins like a cactus taken suddenly out of the desert and planted into a rain forest. It was primal, beautiful. Survival instinct.

I forgot that I should only take a little, just enough to get me back to the tent and the bottled blood, easier to digest. I just wanted more.

Penelope stood still, like a painted marionette whose strings I held. Her eyes were adoring. She barely even winced, only waited patiently.

That more than anything made me stop. There was something faintly creepy about her passive eagerness. I pulled away, wiping my mouth clean. She was still smiling glassily.

"Wouldn't you like more, princess?"

I shook my head mutely. I pushed past her to the camp, my body thrilled, the rest of me utterly conflicted.

"Wait!" She held up her wrists, her veins fierce and vulnerable. "Princess!" She started to beg as I left her behind. "Please. Please, princess."

CHAPTER 12

Nicholas

We waited for Solange in the family tent.

Sebastian sat next to Dad; Marcus and Uncle Geoffrey stood behind Aunt Hyacinth's chair. Quinn and Connor shared a bench, and London lay on one of the sofas, eyes closed. Duncan sprawled in a chair with his arms crossed. Isabeau and Mom stood as severe and beautiful as spears in front of Logan. Even Madame Veronique was here, perched on a bench, pale and still as a bone statue with a handmaiden on either side. She never came to family meetings, preferring to keep her distance and refusing to meet us at all until we'd survived our bloodchange. And we still didn't know what she'd do. She could either take Solange away to indoctrinate her or kill her on the spot. Or buy her a pony, actually. You really just couldn't know for sure.

She'd scared the crap out of me when I was sixteen, demanding I compose a sonnet in iambic pentameter on the spot. In French. *Archaic* French. I didn't even speak modern French.

She still terrified me. And I could admit it freely, because she scared the crap out of everyone. She was just so ... *other*. You couldn't predict what she might do in the name of family honor. And now here she sat, coldly patient.

Just another Drake family reunion.

But at least we were all here and no one seemed to be missing any vital organs.

When Solange came in she smiled at us vaguely, a single drop of blood freshly bloomed on her shirt. "I'm really tired." Then she sighed softly and languidly, as if she was ready to curl up for a nap. But she didn't look tired, she looked painfully energized. "Good night."

Mom moved to stand on top of the trapdoor to the underground bunker. "Solange, we'd like to talk to you."

She paused. "I didn't miss curfew." She saw Madame Veronique and something very close to fear flickered in her face. Madame Veronique tilted her head slightly, like a bird. "Can we do this tomorrow?" Solange whispered.

"No," Mom said sharply.

"I'm afraid not," Dad added, softening his tone. Good cop, bad cop. They did it all the time.

Solange made a complete turn on her heel to eye us suspiciously. "What's going on? What's everyone doing here?"

"We're here for you," Dad answered. "We think you might need help."

Her mouth dropped open slightly. "Is this an *intervention?* That's lame." She shook her head. "I don't do drugs."

"This isn't about drugs."

"We're worried about you, kid," Duncan said quietly.

She made a rude sound. "God, not this again. Honestly, you guys need a hobby." She giggled, then stopped as if the sound startled her, clapping a hand over her mouth. Mom and Dad exchanged a grim glance.

Madame Veronique rose to her feet, like an empress. Solange backed away so quickly she crashed right into me.

I steadied her. "What's the matter with you?"

"I can smell it on her," Madame Veronique murmured. "Blood and something else, something curious. Magic."

Solange backed away again and stepped on my foot. "I thought the Drakes didn't believe in magic."

Madame Veronique arched an eyebrow imperiously. "Due to being exiled, your parents have been . . . isolated in these mountains."

"Did she just call us hillbillies?" Quinn drawled.

"Hey," Duncan broke in mildly. "Some of my friends are hillbillies."

"Are they horror-movie mountain folk like us?"

"I'll be sure to ask Bryn next time I see her." Bryn was Duncan's closest friend. His only friend, actually, and she liked people about as much as he did. She was human and worked as a mechanic, which was how they got to be friends. Her family was even more reclusive than us, living in the mountains and coming down for supplies only a couple of times a year.

"Boys," Dad said repressively. "Stop right there," he added to Solange as she tried to sneak around me. Her cheeks were nearly flushed. That meant only one thing: she'd fed on live blood again. Her eyes glittered. She looked nearly as drunk as the night Lucy and I had found her.

Frowning, Uncle Geoffrey lifted her chin and looked at her eyes carefully, and her triple fangs. "She's taken from the vein," he confirmed flatly.

"Hello?" Solange said. "Vampire. I drink blood. Big shocker."

"Not from the vein, not so young as you are," Dad said. "You know this."

She shrugged one shoulder. "Well, I don't agree. Fresh blood makes me feel strong."

"It feeds the animal, not the soul."

"Oh, Dad, come on. It's not that big a deal."

"Tell that to Kieran," Mom said quietly, almost gently.

Solange recoiled as if she'd been slapped. "What?"

"We know, Solange."

She stared at me accusingly. I held up my hands, palms out. "I didn't tell them," I pointed out grimly. "How could I? *You* didn't tell *me*."

"You could have killed him," Dad said.

"I *know*." She sounded broken, wobbling on the edge of tears. Then she visibly straightened her spine. She licked her lips as if she could still taste the blood. I could smell it, faint and metallic.

"It's addictive," Uncle Geoffrey pointed out. "Not for everyone but for you, certainly. I can see the effects. You don't have the control you need yet."

"You've drunk from the vein."

"I'm considerably older than you."

"In my time," Madame Veronique murmured, "we'd have killed you."

Mom's hand went to her sword hilt. Solange's eyes widened. "For drinking live blood?"

"For being reckless. We didn't have the luxury you have now. Those who were a threat to our secrecy were dispatched."

"But I'm strong," she insisted. "Nicholas, tell them. I fought that Huntsman."

"She's strong," I confirmed flatly.

"It's probably not a big deal," Quinn interjected. "Just lay off the juice until you can handle it. End of drama."

"I can handle it now," she maintained stubbornly.

"By nearly killing your boyfriend?" Sebastian asked, sounding just like Dad. He had the same calm, unruffled tone, the same piercing look.

"He's not my boyfriend anymore," she shot back. "Everyone's always saying how different I am, right? So maybe this is part of it. Maybe it's actually a good thing. Ever think of that?" The roses faded from her cheeks, but her fangs looked just as sharp, and the blue irises of her eyes were ringed in red. "I really don't want to talk about this."

"You can't just ignore it. Not after you compelled two guards." Mom arched an eyebrow. "Did you think we wouldn't find out? The one you compelled tonight never came back."

Solange and I blinked at each other. No one had told me that.

"What?" she asked. "What do you mean?"

"He's ashes now."

She looked horrified. "I didn't do that to him!"

"No one's accusing, honey," Dad said. "But when you use your pheromones like that, there are always consequences. It makes a body slower, befuddled."

"But . . . how do you even know it was the same one? It could be anyone!"

"His clothes were found, and a stake. All human scented."

"A Huntsman?"

"Looks like it."

"It's not your fault," I said softly. "You couldn't have known." It was instinct to comfort her.

"I'm tired of being ganged up on," she said finally. She stalked to the trapdoor.

Mom didn't move. "We're not done."

"Yes," Solange said deliberately. "We are."

Her pheromones were invisible, but I could almost see them coming off her like heat melting pavement in the summer. It was nearly palpable. She leaned closer to Mom, baring her teeth. I could smell a faint combination of lilies and chocolate. "Mom. Move."

Mom just clenched her jaw, her fists, every muscle she could. She fought the compulsion the way she'd fight a *Hel-Blar*. Her eyes narrowed dangerously. "You're very grounded," she said through gritted teeth, as if every word was torn from her unwillingly. Her feet twitched, as did the muscles in her calves.

Dad stepped between them. "Stop it."

"Hey, kid, enough." Duncan put a hand on her shoulder. She grabbed his wrist and flipped him over before any of us could move. He crashed into Connor, then landed on a painted wooden table. He only narrowly avoided staking himself with a jagged splintered leg. Quinn swore, loudly and creatively. Sebastian didn't say a word, only went to stand next to Dad.

"Sol." Logan gaped. "What the hell?" He held Isabeau's hand back when she reached for her sword.

Solange didn't back down. "Just proving my point. I'm stronger than you think. Now get the hell out of my way. All of you."

Mom was still struggling with an invisible enemy, fighting to keep her boots planted on the trapdoor. She lost the battle, which scared us all more than even Madame Veronique striding forward, the air blistering frigidly around her. She spun to confront Solange, wimple fluttering.

"That will do. You will comport yourself with the dignity befitting a Drake."

Solange folded her arms, her expression mutinous and impertinent. "This is none of your business."

Madame Veronique just stood there for a long terrible moment.

They didn't speak again, but it was clear they were testing each other, forcing their wills. Solange exuded pheromones. Madame Veronique was ancient and her direct bloodline matriarch. She had strength we didn't know about. But Solange wouldn't back down. She was filled with fresh blood and had something to prove.

Someone was going to get hurt.

Dad shifted to protect Solange.

"Liam, don't interfere." Madame Veronique flicked her hand and sent him sprawling, never once looking away from Solange. Dad landed hard. Solange looked uncomfortable, then scared. Madame Veronique didn't betray any emotion, as usual.

Mom moved away from the open trapdoor, glancing at me as she eased it open with her foot. I was at an angle behind Madame Veronique. I did the only thing I could have, and barreled into Solange, knocking her into the doorway. She tumbled down the stairs, into the darkness.

I crouched, waiting to see how Madame Veronique would retaliate. It took an age for her gaze to drop, to spear me with those strange and severe eyes. Then she just lifted her foot and kicked me. Hard. I flew into one of the lodge poles, and the tent shivered, threatening to collapse.

A bat shot out of the tunnels and winged desperately in a circle over our heads.

"That little girl is trouble," Madame Veronique said coldly, her voice like an icicle dropping off the roof of a house and impaling you in the head. She grabbed the bat out of the air while we gaped. It squeaked, leather wings frantically beating. Then she released it and stalked away, trailing her silent handmaidens and a disoriented bat smashing its head into the ceiling.

Mom looked bleak but determined.

"Plan B then."

◆

"You threw me down the stairs."

I was in the safe house room I shared with Quinn and Connor, lying back on my bed. There were three cots, each with its own cooler of bottled blood and a chest at the foot for our clothes. Candles burned on a narrow table, flickering gold light over the stone walls. Inside the chest were more candles, flashlights, stakes, and other assorted weapons.

I took out my earbuds, which were blaring music as loud as they could. Sometimes vampire hearing isn't an asset. Connor and Christa were having a Dr. Who marathon above my head. Mom was pacing, furious. When I got tired of sifting through the sounds of mice in the tunnel and dripping water and the rest of my family milling about, I listened to music. Loudly. It worked at home and it worked here. When I first turned, I listened to so much music when Lucy was hanging out with my sister, my ears rang. I was trying to drown out the sound of her heartbeat and her laugh drifting between the walls.

"You threw me down the stairs," Solange repeated, backlit in the doorway.

"Hell yeah, I did."

She smiled slightly. "Thanks."

"Anytime." Music still spilled out of the earbuds on my chest, sounding tinny and thin. "I mean that."

She smiled fully that time; I could hear it in her voice. "I know."

"What's up with you and Madame Veronique?"

Her mouth tightened. "Nothing."

I snorted, propping my head on my folded arms. "You suck at lying."

"She just creeps me out."

"Yeah. Kinda her job."

Solange shifted from one foot to the other. I could smell the blood on her, the lilies and the chocolate of her strange pheromones. "Aren't you ever tempted?"

"To creep you out?"

She rolled her eyes like the old Solange. "Tempted to drink live blood."

I thought of the hundreds of horrible ways I could hurt Lucy.

"No. I'm not tempted."

"It really is different. It's more than a craving. It's what our bodies need, what they were designed for." She sounded earnest and very nearly evangelical.

I shrugged one shoulder. "I'm not sick. I don't need live blood. Not until I have a grip on the hunger."

"But this makes the hunger go away." She shook her head. "I just can't believe you're not tempted."

My jaw clenched around a single word. "Lucy."

Solange's shoulders slumped. "Oh."

I couldn't tell if she was remembering Kieran. "Have you called her? She's freaking out."

"I can't talk to her right now."

"But she's your best friend."

"That's why. And she did Taser me, you know."

I lifted an eyebrow. "Yeah, about that. I can't tell you how great it is that my baby sister and my girlfriend are beating each other up." Truth be told, it was starting to piss me off.

She winced. "Forget I mentioned it. It was a misunderstanding."

"Fifteen hundred volts of electricity was a misunderstanding?" I repeated incredulously.

"Yes."

"At least text her, Sol. You owe her that much."

"She *Tasered* me."

"Lame."

She blinked. "I beg your pardon?"

"That's a lame excuse and you know it."

Her eyes gleamed. "Maybe. But it's not that simple."

"Look, her cousin just got kidnapped and turned, she's at a new school, and her best friend's ignoring her. Think about it from her perspective."

"Yeah, but Lucy can handle it. She can handle anything."

"She can't handle you shutting her out," I said quietly. "Just think about it."

"Okay." She turned to go, then paused. "Nicholas."

"Yes?"

"Do you think I'm . . ." She bit her lip. "Never mind."

"What?"

"Just . . . thanks, Nicholas. I know I can trust you."

She wandered off and I lay there feeling like crap.

I understood a little of what Solange was feeling. Being responsible to such a big family who would gladly sacrifice itself for you was more pressure than it might seem. And finding a quiet moment to think was nearly impossible. And right now, I needed to think.

And plan.

Because it was starting to look as if I was going to have to choose between my little sister and the rest of my family.

CHAPTER 13

Lucy

Monday afternoon

Despite the fact that my best friend, the vampire princess, was going insane, I still had homework to do.

That just didn't seem fair somehow.

Still, my first day of classes went well enough, all things considered. History class, though obviously deeply flawed and biased, was kind of interesting. Training nearly kicked my ass, which made me even more determined to kick it right back. All of the other students were way better than me at kickboxing and martial arts since they'd been training for years. But I'd learned to fight from Helena Drake, so I was confident that off the mat, I could take them.

The other eleventh-grade students were okay, ranging from curious to downright openly nosy, but mostly nice enough. Jody and her bunch weren't the only bullies, but word had already spread that I'd pepper-egged a Huntsman, so most of the comments were whispered with sidelong glances. I could ignore them if I wanted to.

I suddenly had a glimpse of what it must feel like to be Solange right now.

I wasn't exactly a celebrity of her status, but it was still weird to be gawked at or outwardly despised. And Solange needed her solitude more than I did; plus, the vampires who hated her didn't sneer or push her around, they just tried to stake her. Or her family. Or me. So I could feel a little empathy.

Which didn't mean I wasn't still pissed off.

Because I totally was.

I mean, a text message would have been nice, is all I'm saying. I'd only sent her eleven. Granted, the last one was flat-out bitchy, but the first ten were polite if you considered what we'd tried to do to each other.

In the hall, while I was trying to feel empathetic and forgiving, Jody tried to trip me.

I just stepped over her foot, snickering. "Please. I grew up with seven Drake boys. You'll have to do way better than that."

She glared at me.

"That glare could use some work too." I smiled as sweetly and as obnoxiously as I could. I knew better than to display even an ounce of weakness around them.

I walked away, down the locker-lined hall. They were old-fashioned half lockers in army green. A girl in long pigtails nearly closed the door on her thumb as I approached. Her friend nudged her. She nudged back. They whispered furiously to each other. I overheard a lot of "you ask her" and "no, you ask her." And then the second girl shoved her friend right into my path, solving the argument.

"Is it true that you make out with vampires?" She was bright red.

I blinked. "Just the one, actually."

"Does he . . . you know . . . bite you?"

"Dude," I said. "Personal much? And no." I added a mental *Om Namah Shivaya*.

"She's a blood puppet." Jody sneered, coming up behind us. "Don't talk to her, Margaret."

"It's Meg, actually," she shot back. "And I'll talk to whoever I want."

"Then watch your back," Jody advised coldly. "And your neck."

◆

I met my tutor in the library, still planning the nefarious deeds I could do to Jody.

The library would have been soothing if I didn't already feel like screaming. It took up the entire floor, with rooms that opened onto one another, hardwood underfoot, and decorative moldings on the ceilings from the original Victorian house it used to be. There were tall lamps in every corner and green-glassed ones on every table. There was even a fireplace with two overstuffed armchairs. It was the only place on campus that didn't have some sort of weaponry displayed on the walls. A bank of computers shed their blue glow between oak shelves piled with books of every size, style, and description. Christabel would love it. Some of the books even had peeling leather bindings. I was sure there was a basket of rolled-up scrolls behind the librarian's desk. But the librarian himself was kind of scary, so I didn't ask what they were.

I was willing to bet there wasn't a single vampire romance anywhere.

I wondered if I'd get detention for sneaking a few in.

I plopped into a chair next to a lanky guy with a painfully shy smile. "Are you Tyson?" I asked, tossing my knapsack onto the table. The sound echoed, loud enough that the librarian speared me with a look. Tyson winced.

"Are you Lucky?"

"Lucy," I corrected. "So what did you do to get stuck tutoring me?"

He swallowed. "Um . . ."

"No one tutors the freaky new girl without some serious motivation."

"I need extracurriculars," he admitted. "You need activities on your transcript that aren't vampire-hunter related. Not that you're not very nice," he added awkwardly. "But it's you or prom committee."

I paused. "They have prom? Is it formal cargos? Can I decorate the stakes? You should see what I can do with a bit of glitter."

He looked a little bewildered, as if he couldn't quite keep up. I get that a lot. Well, here anyway. My old school friends totally understand me. I had a sudden urge to call Nathan just so he could yell at me some more. I sighed. "Never mind. So what's on the agenda?"

He looked relieved to be back on topic. "Let's start with the basics." He pulled a worn Helios-Ra guidebook off the top of the pile of books next to his laptop. "You got one of these in your orientation packet, right?"

"I already had a copy," I replied. I'd picked Kieran's pocket this summer for it, to be precise. I had my own profile in the cream-colored pages.

Tyson flushed. "Oh. Right. I forgot you're in it."

"I'm famous," I agreed blandly. "Just this morning someone locked me in a bathroom stall."

He flushed ever redder.

"Are you blushing?"

He cleared his throat. "No."

I grinned. "You are adorable."

"Uh . . ."

"Relax, I'm dating the undead, remember."

"Stop teasing poor Tyson," Jenna said from behind me.

I tilted my head to look up at her. "But it's fun."

Jenna hiked her hip on the table and swung her sneaker-clad foot. "You're going to give him a coronary."

We both turned to grin at him, waiting for his retort. He just looked slightly nauseated. Jenna patted his knee. I didn't think she saw the way his ears burned at her touch. Interesting. "Sorry, Tyson. We're just bugging you."

He shrugged a shoulder. She swung her foot wider and nearly kicked him. "So what are you guys doing?"

"Tyson is tutoring me."

Jenna burst out laughing. "Oh, Tyson. You're screwed."

"Hey!" I pinched her.

She just scooted across the table and dropped into an empty chair. "This I have to see."

Tyson wiped his hands on his pants surreptitiously, as if he was sweating. It wasn't just Jenna that made him nervous. It looked like any kind of group interaction might send him into fits. And while I didn't consider three a group exactly, he clearly considered it a huge crowd, and the anxiety it produced might just crush his larynx.

"Sorry, Tyson," I murmured gently. "Go ahead."

Jenna propped her chin on her hands. "I got your back, man."

I eyed her. "You know I hang out with vampires, right? You could be scared of me like the others."

She scoffed. "You and your pretty boys don't scare me."

Jenna's mocking tone was soothing. If it wasn't for her and Hunter and Chloe, this whole transition thing would have been even worse. "Shush," I scolded her primly. "I am learning about the weirdo League of hunters who think they're in a comic book."

"Your family now too."

I drew back, horrified. "Excuse me, but after my parents, the Drakes are family. You lot are riffraff."

"The riffiest."

"That's not a word."

"Is so."

"What's it mean?"

Jenna glanced at Tyson. "Help me out here, Ty. You're the smart one."

He just shook his head. "Are you two always like this?"

Jenna and I exchanged mischievous smiles.

"We're just getting started. But I think we might be," I said.

"Alert the guards," Jenna agreed cheerfully.

My eyes widened. "There are guards?" I'd need to know that the next time I snuck off campus. I thought about the Huntsmen currently lurking on the edges of school property.

"Figure of speech," she said. "But actually, yeah. Sometimes."

"We're not really supposed to be off campus without written permission anyway," Tyson said apologetically.

I wondered if the Drakes could ask Hart to write me a note. Speaking of which, "Does Hart ever come here?" I asked.

"He came to an assembly last year just after he was promoted," Jenna said, sounding disgruntled. "I missed it."

"He's hot," I told her. "Don't skip next time."

"I'll keep that in mind."

A small crowd of students clustered at one of the windows. Jenna and I stood on chairs to peek over their heads.

"What's going on?" I asked.

"Looks like more agents are arriving," Jenna replied. "They're staying here during the Blood Moon."

"That's a lot of cargo pants," I said drily, as I considered making "The Truth about Vampires" flyers to post all over campus.

Tyson cleared his throat. "Uh . . . I should be tutoring you . . ."

"Okay," I agreed, pulling a chocolate bar out of my bag. "Tutor away."

"Well, the Helios-Ra is named after two sun gods, Helios from Greek mythology and Ra from Egyptian mythology. The League was officially formed in 892 C.E. by Alric Skallagrim."

"C.E.?" I asked. "What's that?"

"It means Common Era. It's the archaeologist's version of A.D. And before Alric, hunters had their own tribal traditions, some of which were solidified and spread about by the armies of Rome. But they never all officially worked together until Alric."

"Let me guess, there was a big bad?"

"Several actually. How did you know?"

"There's always a big bad. Didn't you ever watch *Buffy*?"

"Even so, the original tenet of the League was to hunt the undead."

"They're not really undead," I interrupted. "You guys know that, right? I mean, the *Hel-Blar* are, and most of the others, but not the families of the Raktapa Council. Not entirely anyway. I mean, they get sick and die. Sort of. But not really. It's complicated."

"It's never been complicated to the Helios-Ra," Jenna said. "Vampire is as vampire does."

"That's specie-ist," I grumbled, frustrated. "Why doesn't anyone ever listen to me?"

"Vampires drink human blood," Jenna pointed out. "And I kinda need mine."

"They don't have to drink enough to kill you. Just to live. Survive. Whatever." I frowned. "Don't be so greedy."

"Don't be so eager to give my blood away."

"Would you donate blood at a blood drive?"

"I guess so."

"Well, there you go!" I declared triumphantly.

"But that's different."

"Why?"

She frowned at Tyson. He frowned back at her. Then they both frowned at me.

"I don't know," she said finally. "It just is."

"We know times are changing," Tyson added, looking interested enough in the quandary that he forgot to be hand-shakingly shy. Instead he sounded as if he was quoting a professor in his head. "We have treaties with some vampire tribes. And we also have several more departments, at the academy and at the college. And in the League at large as well. Things like Tech and Supernatural Studies."

"What about Vampire Relations?" I asked. Especially with the local newspapers now reporting on the increase in missing persons. Apparently the last time something like this happened was in the eighties. "We need that. I could totally do that."

"Making out with your hot boyfriend doesn't count toward your grade," Jenna teased.

I shook my head. "I knew this place was all wrong."

"Did Bellwood go through the rules with you?" Tyson asked.

"Probably," I admitted. "But she talked a lot. And she's surprisingly intimidating."

Jenna just snorted.

"The basic rules are pretty self-explanatory," I recited. "Don't leave campus after hours, don't tell outsiders about the school or the League, don't get caught or tell secrets, and don't fraternize with vampires. Which is a stupid rule, by the way."

Tyson looked at Jenna helplessly. When she didn't offer any advice, he just handed me a printout. "Here's the homework."

I groaned. "Homework? Really? On top of all my other classwork?"

"Bellwood gave me a list of essays and papers you have to do to prove you're catching up."

I lay my head on the table despondently. "Shouldn't I be learning how to kill things?"

Jenna checked her watch. "Come on, there's a kickboxing match in the gym in ten minutes. Afterward, I'll teach you how to fall down."

"I know how to fall down, thanks."

"Trust me, falling down properly is harder than it looks. Learn the right way and you can get back up faster and keep fighting."

I thought of being in Lady Natasha's dungeons, of my cousin Christabel being kidnapped because they thought she was me, of stakes flying at my boyfriend, and of Hope taking out half the Drake farmhouse. I bared my teeth.

"I'm in."

CHAPTER 14

Solange

Monday, sunset

I woke up missing Kieran.

By the time I'd drunk three bottles of blood and was sated enough to leave my own private corner of the family tunnels, I'd already talked myself out of writing him a letter or checking to see if he'd written me one, about five times. Maybe ten.

The last thing I wanted to do was deal with the aftermath of Sunday night. Mom lost her temper all the time; everyone was used to it. Even Lucy lost her temper enough to give Mom a run for her money. But I never lost my temper. Frankly, until recently you could have been forgiven for assuming I didn't even have one. Now I just felt it there all the time, boiling and searing under my skin.

I knew I should apologize, and I meant to, but the minute I

came up from the safe house and felt everyone staring at me, the anger came back. I actually glanced down to make sure there wasn't steam coming off me. I felt full of embers again, instead of blood.

Duncan was sprawled in a chair, looking wary. I should definitely tell him I was sorry, but I didn't know if he wanted to be reminded that his baby sister had taken him down. Quinn, Connor, and Marcus sat at the table. Only Connor smiled at me. Mom and Dad turned to watch my progress up the last of the metal steps. A candle burned between them. Dad's worry lines were so deeply etched between his eyes they looked painted on.

"How are you feeling?" he asked.

"Fine." I didn't mean to snap the answer; it was just that somewhere between my brain and my tongue everything got jumbled up. "How's London?" I asked before we could get into another painful discussion about my attitude.

"Better," Dad replied. "Not at full strength, but she'll get there. Your uncle's keeping an eye on her."

"Oh. Good." I didn't know what else to say. I took a step toward the door.

"You're restricted to the grounds." It was the first thing Mom had said to me since I'd compelled her. She wouldn't look at me.

"I know." *They want to keep you weak. They always have.*

"That means you stay between the torches."

"I *know*."

"And watch your tone, young lady, or you'll be restricted to this tent."

I slipped outside before I said anything to make it worse. The cold night air helped, and the expanse of the star-thick sky made me feel slightly less itchy and claustrophobic. I didn't know what to do or where to go. I wasn't even sure who to trust anymore. I knew I didn't trust Madame Veronique, but my parents did, so what was the use in warning them? They'd think I was overreacting. They'd think it was pheromones or regular hormones or whatever other thousands of excuses people had when anyone under twenty-one had something important to say. And it was even worse with vampires, whose life spans were so ridiculously long some would barely acknowledge anyone under two hundred.

A sixteen-year-old girl who'd tried to compel her mother and the oldest matriarch of her lineage?

Not likely.

I stepped out from under the tent awning and wandered down the path, aimless. I tried to ignore the vampires who turned to watch me pass and Penelope, who curtsied so deeply and abruptly she nearly tripped an Amrita dignitary from India. I searched for Constantine's black hair and his distinctive violet eyes, while trying not to be too obvious about it. For some reason, he always made me feel better. Or at the very least, he made me forget. Maybe he could take me back to the Bower, where I was a dhampir and it was no big deal, where I was a princess and it was no big deal either. The Bower was technically off-limits for me right now, but the ache to be sitting in the parlor under the trees was palpable. I felt better just thinking about it.

Better enough not to notice the way the crowd was parting in front of me until it was too late.

The Furies.

The sound of white damask silk rubbing over wicker panniers was soft as the wind through the snow. Fangs gleamed, diamond shoe buckles glittered, and black feather tattoos seemed to move on their own. I smelled face powder and blood.

Everyone around us stilled. Morbid curiosity thrummed. My heart would have stuttered in my chest, if it still beat. It gave me a jolt to see them looking so identical to Lady Natasha, even though I'd seen them before. Constantine might consider her to be a colonial backwater wannabe queen, but she was still the vampire who'd eaten a raw deer heart because she thought it was mine. Her Furies didn't intimidate him, not even now, hissing and spitting as one.

Which is why he was the first one to move when the whitethorn stake came at me.

It would have cleaved my heart if he hadn't been there.

"Solange!" he yelled, even as he leaped impossibly fast and high. He kicked the stake, knocking it out of its trajectory just before it sliced through my shirt. It grazed my skin lightly and landed in the snow. At the same time Constantine threw his own stake at the Fury nearest to us. He was as good a fighter as any of my brothers and nearly as good as my mother.

Even so, he was no match for the Chandramaa. No one was.

It all happened so fast, it was as if the snow froze in midair, as if everything else had stopped moving altogether. The Fury who'd attacked me crumbled into ashes, leaving behind an embroidered white dress that drifted to the ground as if it were underwater. Someone shouted but the sound was elongated and strange. Red arrows fell like angry rain, creating a sort of fence between me and the other Furies. Constantine was facing me, about to land on the frozen ground.

He didn't see the crossbow bolt, also red, whistling toward his back.

Chandramaa justice was blind. He'd taught me that.

I had just enough time and presence of mind to kick his knee-cap with my boot. He dropped painfully out of his graceful descent, the look of surprise on his face nearly comical. I threw myself across him, covering him before he'd even landed. The jolt of hitting the ground snapped my jaws together. I lay there with my eyes scrunched tight, wondering if I was about to feel the bite of a crossbow bolt in the back.

Nothing happened.

I opened one eye, then the other. Constantine lay very still under me.

"I'm not dead?" I asked.

His mouth curved in a half smile but his eyes were fierce. "Too many bats."

I blinked, turned my head slowly. He was right. There were just enough bats dipping and somersaulting over us to block any arrows or stakes from the trees. The Moon Guard couldn't see us to kill us. The Furies were still hissing, but they were too frightened to cross the line of red-tipped arrows.

I told you I'd protect you. We are stronger together.

I stayed where I was, sprawled on top of a very handsome vampire. "Now what?"

"I have no idea, princess."

For someone who'd just saved my life and had nearly gotten staked for his trouble, he sounded pretty calm.

But that was only because he'd never met my mother.

"Solange Drake!" Mom's black braid snaked behind her like a whip as she and the rest of my family shoved through the crowd. She paused, seething when an arrow nearly stabbed into her toe. Sebastian put his back to her, guarding her and glaring calmly at the trees. "I can't even begin to express how much trouble you're in," Mom said between her teeth.

"It's not my fault!" I tried to glare at her, but I couldn't quite contort my neck that way. "They tried to stake me."

"What?" Mom's voice dropped until it was such a cold, dark whisper several of the bystanders backed away. Dad's fangs gleamed. The crowd chattered so loudly among themselves that when they stopped abruptly it made me flinch.

A woman marched toward us. She was young, with short black hair. "I represent the Chandramaa," she announced, as if the red moon stitched on her black leather jacket didn't give away her or her vaguely menacing stance. She was too young to be full Chandramaa and she'd let us see her face, so she was clearly not a full initiate. "Release him to us," she said to me.

I knew what that meant. Constantine would be executed for saving me.

I was *not* going to let that happen.

"No."

The guard blinked, nonplussed. "Perhaps you didn't understand me. I was sent by the Chandramaa."

"Solange," Dad said tightly. "What are you doing?"

"Constantine saved my life," I answered as the bats grew agitated overhead. "Don't let them kill him." *They don't understand. They never will.*

"He interfered with Chandramaa justice," the girl said sharply. "There are no exceptions."

"Kill her!" the Furies chanted, softly, viciously. "Kill her now! Blood traitor!"

Constantine moved so that his hands were on my hips. His eyes were like amethysts. "What do you want to do, princess?" he asked quietly, so only I could hear him. His lips tickled my cheek.

What did I want to do?

The fact that he'd asked me, the fact that he was waiting for me to decide my own fate made me all the more determined to save him from his.

"We run," I whispered back.

"Kill her!"

I wasn't sure yet how I seemed to control bats, but I thought about them now, as hard as I could. I imagined them swarming through the trees toward us, floating like a fanged black cloud, swallowing the stars and the arrows of the Moon Guard. I was visualizing them so intently that it took a moment for me to realize the sounds of hundreds of leathery wings weren't in my imagination. Bats darted and dive-bombed around us, cutting off anyone who tried to get too close, even my parents.

"Solange, wait!" Dad shouted, ducking as a bat flew past his head. "You don't know what you're doing!"

Let go. Let me protect you.

"If you cross the Chandramaa, you're exiled from this place," the guard added, looking angry and confused. A bat went for her eyes and she shrieked. "An instant death to you and yours should you return to this place."

"Solange, don't!" Mom pleaded. I'd never seen her sound so scared or look so torn.

But I couldn't just stay here and let Constantine be killed. That wasn't justice; it was murder.

"Are you sure?" he asked as I tensed to jump to my feet. "There's no turning back."

I met his violet eyes. "I'm sure."

He launched off the ground in one fluid movement, one arm pinning me to his chest. Bats crowded around us. Everyone was shouting. Chandramaa bolts snaked between the bats, but they just landed in the frostbitten dirt. Only snow hung in the cold air, not ashes.

Constantine and I broke into a run, dodging helpful hands and harmful ones. We plunged into the dark forest, still trailing bats. Someone gave a strangled yelp from the top of a pine tree. A crossbow fell to the ground. Bats winged between the trees, as if they'd been released by an invisible slingshot. I ran as fast as I could, convinced I was going to be impaled on an arrow or a stake flung from above. Constantine held my hand tightly, dragging me over roots and under moss-draped branches. Ferns flattened at our passing.

We left the torchlight of the Blood Moon camp behind us, along with my family and everything I'd ever known.

CHAPTER 15

Nicholas

Monday, early evening

We were patrolling on the very edges of the forest when Karim, the guard walking next to me, fell apart into ashes.

The bolt pierced his heart and thunked into a pine tree. Splinters ricocheted as I reached for a stake and launched into a run at the same time. There was no smell of mushrooms or rot, no clacking of teeth. Not *Hel-Blar*, but definitely vampires. They moved too fast to be hunters.

I could hear them in the trees, up in the branches, down in the ferns, everywhere. There were a lot of them; that much I could tell. I ran faster, until everything blurred. It wasn't enough. Another crossbow bolt whistled by my head. A stake landed in the dirt by my left foot.

I was seriously outnumbered.

I hit the alarm on the GPS tag Connor had just recently programmed for everyone in the family. If we activated it, a message was sent immediately with our location. Assuming I was in range of any signal and assuming anyone else had a signal to even receive it.

Assumptions that could get me killed a whole lot faster.

I darted around a hemlock and slid into the yellowing grass of a narrow valley on the edge of the forest. I was far from the encampment, far from the farmhouse, even far from the royal caves. I'd never even seen this part of the mountains. I thought I heard screaming, faintly, but it faded and I was running too hard to be sure. If I'd still been human, my heartbeat would have drowned out every tiny sound; as it was, the rush of my blood through my veins was like needles of rain and wind. The part of me my mother had trained remained calm and removed, as if I were watching a movie. Clods of mud and dead flowers broke up under my boots as I pushed on. If I lost my cool now, I'd be dead for sure.

I had a moment to feel grateful that none of my brothers were with me. Losing Karim was bad enough. He was dead because of me. He could have been back at the encampment with his own family, or at home, wherever that might be. I'd only just met him before setting out. I didn't even know his last name.

But dying now wouldn't help him.

I could try to shake them in the labyrinthine caves of the mountains, but I was as likely to trap myself in a dead end as not. I might be able to outrun them, but there were no guarantees. There was also no decent place to make a stand, nothing solid to put at my back besides the mountain. A quick glance showed rock and stunted wind-bent pine trees, and another vampire sliding down toward me from up high. A flash of pale skin on my right, a gleam of fangs behind me.

"Enough play," someone barked, violent laughter in his voice.

The first grab caught my jacket and yanked me to a stop. I had just enough room to maneuver out of the sleeves and leave it behind. The cold air slapped my bare arms, but I wore the coat mostly out of habit anyway. I didn't need it. And I certainly didn't need it to fight. I managed to get just out of reach, but the way was blocked by a pile of boulders from some long-ago avalanche. Moonlight fell on moss and frost and the leaf-bare silhouette of twisted trees. I leaped forward, intending to scale the uneven pile. I'd take my chances with gravity over the lot behind me.

Not that I had a choice.

A length of rope snaked over my shoulders and yanked me backward. I landed hard, my back teeth snapping together. I rolled into the fall and twisted back on my feet, shrugging out of the rope. I threw my stake as I rose out of a crouch. It caught one of my pursuers in the chest, right over his heart. I grabbed for one of the rocks I'd landed on, tearing up my pants and my knee underneath the thick fabric. Blood dripped into the mud. The vampire clutched at the stake stuck between his ribs. I threw the rock as hard as I could, and it hit the wooden stake with an audible thud. The point slid past muscles and bone, straight into his heart. He collapsed into dust, leaving behind a pile of dark clothes.

There was an angry yell from one of his companions. The rope slid away, was tossed back at me. I managed to dodge out of the way, barely. It nearly took out my left eye. I had weapons, but I had no room, no escape route. My only chance was to wear them down before I tired myself out. I wasn't hopeful. I might have eliminated one, but there were still four others.

They circled me and I couldn't stop them. I was too busy ducking rope and stakes. They didn't seem to be aiming for my heart, but a pointy stick in the throat or the arm wasn't any more fun.

"Who are you?" I snapped. I was surrounded now. There was nowhere else to go. "What the hell do you want?" Because with every moment they were proving if they'd wanted me dead, I'd be ashes already. This was about something else. Solange, my mother, my last name. It was all the same in a dark crevice in the mountains. And I wouldn't give any of them up.

They grinned at me, showing fangs and bloodstained collars. They held thick branches, a combination of pointed-stake and short staff. They didn't use the odd staves to run me through or bash me in the head. Instead, they held them end to end and closed in until they were close enough to punch. I raised my fists. I had every intention of going down fighting.

Instead, the one closest to me whipped a handful of Hypnos at me before I could duck. It wouldn't have mattered; the others threw their own Hypnos and the white powder dusted over me, stinging my eyes, catching in the back of my throat. It tasted sickly sweet, like wilted lilies, chocolate, and copper.

"Stop fighting," the vampire who seemed to be the leader ordered.

Colors changed, as if I were in an overexposed photograph; too much light here, too much dark there, and a strange acidic green to the pine trees. My fists unclenched, arms lowering. I was trapped inside a cloud of passive panic, aware of my surroundings, aware of my desperate need to put up a fight and utterly unable to do anything about it. I bared my fangs but it was all I could manage. I couldn't even hiss.

I had a very uncomfortable moment of empathy for the guards Solange compelled. At least when she'd compelled me I was reasonably certain she wasn't going to hurt me.

The leader nodded to the vampire on his right. "Leash him."

The strange colors turned red as sour rage smoldered inside me. I tasted smoke over the lilies. They used the rope to knot my wrists together behind my back and a strip of cloth over my eyes to blindfold me. It was like looking through heavy fog. I could see faint shadows and the shifting of light, but not enough to be sure of my footing or my direction.

"Walk." The order was accompanied by a shove to get me moving. Pain shot through my knee, blood dripping from a gash that would take some time to heal. I was still so young and and close enough to the bloodchange that only shallow scratches healed almost instantly. After a day's sleep, I'd be fine. Assuming I made it through the day, of course.

They pushed me into a forced shuffle-walk, my muscles only barely cooperating. Try as hard as I could, I couldn't fight the movement of my wounded knee, the forward momentum of my legs, the push of the Hypnos as it slid through me, finding every tiny secret place, like water. I slid down a steep incline, scattering pebbles. A hard hand on my shoulder shoved me back onto a trail.

"Come on, princeling," he sneered. "We've got a gilded cage just for you."

"Where are we going?" Useless to ask, impossible not to. I didn't get a reply, of course.

We walked until the terrain changed underfoot to smooth rock. I stumbled again, was wrenched back into place. I'd hoped that enough falling and being pushed around would loosen the rope, but it held tight. I could tell by the smell of mildew and cold that we were nearing a cave of some kind. The darkness felt thicker, damp. There was another combination of scents underneath, rust and blood maybe. There were no dogs howling, and no drumming, so the Hounds weren't nearby. They managed to find distant private caves no one had ever entered before; but clearly these weren't them. I could smell humans and vampires both. I was jerked to a stop. I hunched my shoulders as the Hypnos began to wear off, expecting a stake in the back. Someone ripped off the blindfold.

I could never have imagined anything like this was even possible.

We were in a huge cavern, with fissures in every wall, blocked off with metal grates like homemade dungeons. Pale, wretched faces showed briefly at the bars. Someone wept in a dark crevice. Someone else grunted in pain. There were chains everywhere and the clank of iron. Torches burned in brackets drilled into the stone. The light flickered over the murky milk-gray water of a sinkhole, like a small pond. An arm bobbed to the surface. I couldn't tell if it was attached to a body.

I was pushed toward long metal tables set against one corner, under a string of battery-operated lights. Camping lanterns glowed with a clear unnatural light, glinting mercilessly off glass beakers, jars of strange liquids, test tubes, iron-tipped stakes, jagged daggers, and implements of torture I couldn't look at without sweat breaking out on the back of my neck. We liked to tease Marcus that he was the mad scientist in the family, following in Uncle Geoffrey's footsteps. But his laboratory was for the pursuit of knowledge, not pain.

Even at a glance, this place had no other purpose.

A half-dead vampire slumped unconscious, hanging on chains attached to her wrists. Blood ran in rivulets down her side, dripping off her elbows, her fingertips, her feet. It gathered in a narrow trench dug into the ground, clogged with water and bodily fluids. I gagged on the stench of old blood and festering wounds.

This wasn't politics. This was something else entirely.

But I had no idea what.

I made an instinctive move toward her, though how I thought I'd free her with my hands tied behind my back, I had no idea. A boot kicked me in the back of my wounded knee and I toppled, my cheek hitting stone. I saw stars, jerked away from the trench.

Human guards stood at the edges. They looked like Huntsmen, though I thought I saw the glint of at least one Helios-Ra sun pendant. They didn't even flinch when I sprawled at their feet. The four that captured me stood in a clump, grinning at a man wearing a leather apron smeared with blood and bits of flesh, like Dr. Frankenstein. Beside him, standing quietly alert, was a vampire wearing a familiar brown tunic I'd seen before.

On Montmartre and his Host. Right before he tried to abduct my sister.

I pushed to my feet, hissing, fangs extending so completely my gums bled. The Host flung a rusted iron spike, like a giant horseshoe nail. It slammed into my shoulder, knocking me back and pinning me against a wooden support beam hung with more chains. Pain bit down with jagged teeth. At least pinned to a post with convenient chains and splinters, I could work my hands free. The rope snagged on a sharp spike, and I bore down, fraying it into strings I snapped easily.

Frankenstein glanced at me. "I guess the Hypnos wore off."

"Am I a hostage?" I forced myself to ask, choking as I yanked myself forward, pulling the spike out.

"You could say that," my captor answered. "Hostage, test subject, prey. You're whatever the hell we tell you to be."

Frankenstein waved his hand. There was blood under his nails. "Do something with him."

"Don't you want a closer look?" The tone was smug and self-satisfied.

Frankenstein narrowed his eyes, circling me slowly. "And?"

"He's a Drake."

The Host vampire moved so fast it was no wonder humans thought we could fly. All I saw were fangs and fingers digging viciously into the wound in my shoulder. I jabbed out with my thumb and first two fingers in a claw shape, the way Duncan taught me. He fought dirty, even dirtier than Mom. I aimed for the windpipe. The Host gagged, taken by surprise. I went for the eyes next, but he'd recovered and had a stake pressing into my chest.

"Wait!" Frankenstein shouted. "Stop!"

The Host pressed the stake deeper, until it bit through my shirt and several layers of skin. His amber eyes flared, his fangs gleamed.

Frankenstein pushed the stake away from me, with effort. "Patience, or you'll spoil the fun."

Then he smiled slowly, as someone in the dungeon behind me started to whimper.

Chapter 16

Lucy

Monday night

"Are you sure you're up for this?" I asked Kieran again, leaning forward between the seats. We were in his friend Eric's car, driving to town. Jenna, Chloe, and a handful of the rest of the Black Lodge were following in one of the unmarked school vans. Kieran was in the passenger seat, a bandage taped on the side of his neck to cover Solange's bite marks. "You did just have a blood transfusion, what, two days ago? Three? Shouldn't you be on the couch watching bad TV or something?"

"It wasn't a full transfusion," he answered, staring stonily ahead. "I'm fine." There was something hard about him now, something final and sad in his voice. I frowned. Beside me, Hunter nudged me and shook her head.

The fields narrowed and turned to lawns and parks until finally we were in the downtown quarter of Violet Hill. All three blocks of it. Cafés, health-food stores, and used bookshops were sprinkled between New Age stores selling everything from crystals to Tibetan prayer flags. We passed the shop my mom worked at, but it was closed. The only places open were restaurants and pubs and a bookstore behind the movie theaters.

Eric parked behind an abandoned glass factory. He grinned at me, white teeth gleaming in his dark face. He tossed me a messenger bag full of stakes and Hypnos-stuffed putty eggs. Apparently, he liked being snapped at, because after I got mad at him at the Black Lodge meeting, he was now treating me like an old friend.

Kieran just methodically checked the weapons strapped to his shirt under his jacket. The school van pulled up and the others spilled out of the doors. They were vibrating with contained excitement. Chloe shot us a thumbs-up, her curly hair exploding out of her ponytail.

"Follow the plan this time," Hunter told her sternly. "I mean it. I'll kick your ass."

"Yeah, yeah."

"What was that about?" I asked Hunter, when Chloe vanished back into the van for her knapsack.

"The last time we were here, she totally blew the plan, got stabbed, and Quinn had to bail us out."

"Let it go, Wild," Chloe called out.

Hunter made a face but didn't say anything else. Instead she nudged me and stepped back out of earshot. "Keep an eye on

Kieran," she said quietly. "He won't pair me with him for the sweep."

"How do you know?"

"Because I'm worried about him, and he thinks if he pretends he doesn't know that, I'll leave him alone."

"He's met you, right?"

She smiled but there was no humor in it. "Exactly. Like I'll let him backslide."

I blinked. "Backslide? Backslide to what?"

She took a deep breath, looking as uncertain as I'd ever seen her look. Usually she was quietly confident. "This is strictly confidential," she murmured. "Okay?"

I nodded. "Okay."

"After his dad died, Kieran went through a bad patch."

"Understandable."

"A really bad patch. I barely recognized him."

I thought of Solange. "I'm beginning to know how that feels."

"It sucks. He was bitter and hard and so focused on vengeance and finding his father's killer that he dropped out of college."

"The one in Scotland." There was more to Kieran than met the eye, clearly. I wasn't even sure if Solange knew this much about him. They hadn't been going out for long, and with her pheromones, they weren't exactly heavy on the philosophical debates lately.

"He basically didn't show for orientation, and the Blacks have been going to that college for nearly as long as the Wilds. His mom fell apart and was no help whatsoever. Believe me when I tell you that Solange saved him as much as he saved her. He needed his whole world put right side up again."

"And now they've broken up."

"Exactly."

"Solange isn't talking to me," I admitted. I couldn't save Solange from herself right now. So I'd damned well better save Kieran. "But he will."

We exchanged grim conspiratorial nods just as a motorcycle pulled up and everyone tensed, except for Eric and Kieran.

"Easy," Eric said. "It's only Connoly."

"Kieran's friend," Hunter explained before I could ask. "The three of them went through the academy together. They're the reason one of the Common Room windows is nailed shut."

"I definitely want to know *that* story."

"If you girls are done with the whispering," Kieran said blandly, "we can start."

"I can both help and kick him in the ass, right?" I muttered to Hunter.

"In fact, I insist."

Connoly took off his helmet and locked it in the seat of his bike. He had long hair and more tattoos than Bruno, and that was saying something. Bruno had been getting tattooed twenty years longer.

"Now that we're all here, are we clear on the objective?" Kieran asked. "We're looking for hot spots mostly, the ones vampires might be using to prey on the civs. They don't necessarily know the town, so don't assume it's the usual areas. If you see a Huntsman, don't engage unless you have to." We all nodded. He looked unyielding enough that I didn't even tease him about sounding like James Bond. "No one goes alone. Chloe and Kyla—you're with Eric, Connoly's got Drew, Hunter's got Noah, and I'll take Lucy. Blend as much as you can. The townsfolk are getting nervous about all of these disappearances; they might be watching out their windows more carefully. Meet back here in two hours and keep the lines open."

The groups went in different directions.

Kieran glanced at me. "Got your weapons?"

"Dude, who are you talking to? Of *course* I do."

He nearly smiled. "I know this is a foreign concept to you, Hamilton, but you follow orders in the field. Period."

"Yeah, yeah."

He just stared at me.

"What? I said yes."

"Mm-hmm." He didn't sound remotely convinced. He crossed the parking lot toward the sidewalk, his boots crunching through broken glass.

"So where are we headed?" I asked.

"We'll go down Main Street and then check the alleys behind the movie theaters. I got intel that there've been some disturbances there in the last couple of days."

"Yeah, because there's a bar next door. A gross one where all the drunks hang out. Half the knife fights in town happen there." I slid him a glance out of the corner of my eye. He looked calm, dressed in black cargo pants and a jean jacket. His short hair made him look older. He suddenly reminded me of the Kieran who'd once dosed me with Hypnos powder in the Drake living room. I couldn't help but poke at him a little for that. "And intel? What's with all the lingo?"

He shrugged. "This is who I am."

"Mm-hmm." Now I was the one who didn't sound convinced.

"Just come on."

The streetlights cast a watery yellow glow on the pavement. There was frost on some of the store windows. The tip of my nose was already cold. "Solange hasn't talked to me since I Tasered her," I said, jumping right in when I couldn't think of a subtle way to broach the topic.

"You'll work it out."

I waited. Waited some more. "Will you?" I pressed when he didn't say anything else. "I know you broke up," I added gently.

"It's not a secret."

"Are you *trying* to be infuriating?"

He sighed. "I don't want to share my feelings and do each other's hair, Lucy."

"Too bad. It's what friends do." I rolled my eyes when he shot me a look. "The sharing part, 007."

"I'm fine."

I ground my teeth. "I swear if I hear that from you or Solange one more time I'm duct-taping your mouths shut."

"Can I duct-tape yours shut?"

I grinned. "Like that would stop me."

He grinned back. It was so brief I nearly missed it. "Can we just do this recon thing?"

"I can multitask," I assured him, peering into the shadows of the first alley we passed. "Cat, raccoon in Dumpster, smell of pee," I catalogued for him. "See? Now talk."

"About what? We broke up. It happens."

"Did you break up because you don't like each other anymore?" He paused. I jumped on that like it was made of chocolate. "Ha! See? That means you broke up for some other stupid reason."

"How do you know it was stupid?"

"Because any reason other than I-don't-love-you or You-make-me-miserable is stupid."

"Real life isn't that simple."

I stopped walking, fished a pack of gum out of my pocket because it was all I had, and threw it at his head. He jerked his back. "What was that for?"

"You don't get to condescend to me. My best friend is all crazy and mad at me, my cousin just died and turned into a vampire, and people are constantly trying to kill my friends. I *know* things aren't simple."

He rubbed his temple. "Sorry."

"Good," I said crankily. "You can't shut people out. Not now. Solange is shutting us out and you see how well that's working for her. Things are going to get worse, Kieran. We all know it."

He hunched his shoulders but he didn't argue with me, which I counted as a victory.

We patrolled the alleys, stepping over a drunk guy snoring while propped up against the back door of the bar. He still had his car keys in his hand. I plucked them carefully out of his grasp and tossed them into the nearby garbage can. Then I knocked on the door. When one of the busboys opened it, the drunk fell back over his feet. The busboy just sighed. "Thanks."

The back of the movie theater was deserted and smelled like popcorn. We saw three cats, two squirrels, and a fox, but no vampires. We crossed Main Street to check out the other alleys, passing the little park where I used to hang out with Solange on Saturday afternoons, drinking coffee and complaining about how there was never anything to do in Violet Hill. It seemed like forever ago.

"That alley connects to a back street behind the high school," I told Kieran as it began to snow very lightly. It wasn't cold enough to stick to the road, it just sort of floated in the air around us. The stars were still visible between thin wispy clouds. We skirted the debris of a tipped-over garbage can between a shop selling crystals and one selling ski equipment.

"It's pretty quiet," I said. I stopped, winced. "I just said that out loud, didn't I?"

Kieran nodded, checking over his shoulder. He aimed his flashlight down the mouth of the dark alley. The light glinted off soda cans and a metal fence.

"I just totally jinxed us," I groaned. I pulled my miniature crossbow out of my bag and loaded an arrow into it, just in case. I still carried stakes but I was more skilled with the crossbow. I had better aim than arm strength. It wasn't easy pushing a sharp wooden stake through a rib cage. Not to mention distressingly gross.

Kieran and I both paused at the sound of a scuffle. He eased forward slowly, switching off his flashlight. A broken moan trailed toward us, went high-pitched and kept ululating. The hairs on my arms rose. We crept closer as the sounds got louder.

And then a shadow knocked a can across the alley, clattering suddenly. It leaped toward me, yowling. I scrambled back, slipped on a puddle of liquid, and landed hard, knocking the breath out of my lungs. Kieran fumbled with his flashlight. Cat eyes gleamed at us, then vanished with a hiss.

"Cat," Kieran said shortly.

"I fell on my ass over two cats fighting?" I pushed myself up. "That's just embarrassing." Kieran's light swung over me. His eyebrows lowered. I looked down.

I was covered in blood.

"Are you hurt?" He rushed toward me.

I shook my head. "Not my blood."

The puddle I'd slipped on wasn't rainwater or spilled garbage runoff. It was blood.

A lot of it.

I grimaced at the state of my pant cuffs and tried not to gag. Kieran crouched down to get a better look. The puddle was quite deep and thick, not yet dried.

"I don't think anyone could lose this much blood and survive," he said darkly.

I frowned. "Vampires wouldn't waste that much though."

He glanced at me, straightening. "Not the ones you know." The beam of faintly blue light followed a trail of droplets so red they were nearly black to the brick wall of the nearest building. He pointed the flashlight to the metal fire escape, wet with melting snowflakes and something else entirely. "More blood on the bottom step."

"But no body," I confirmed after checking behind the Dumpster and a pile of crates full of empty bottles. "And no blood leading anywhere else."

Kieran tucked the flashlight in his belt. "Will you be okay if I go up?" he asked.

"I've got this thing." I adjusted my grip on the miniature crossbow. "I'm good. I'll cover you." God. The lingo was contagious.

"If there's incoming, don't wait for me," he said, climbing the steps. "Just run."

I rolled my eyes at his back. Then I turned my shoulder blades to the wall and kept an eye on the mouth of the alley leading to the road and the fence to the school on the other side. Litter pushed around my feet when the wind picked up. Wind chimes from someone's back door shivered through the frigid air. A car drove slowly down the street, tires crunching through a very thin layer of ice, headlights spearing the drifting snow. A dog barked farther down the road, probably because of one of the cats. I heard the slight scrape of Kieran's boots as he hauled himself up onto the last balcony. It was only a three-story building so it didn't take him long. I risked a glance up and saw him pulling himself up to the roof as if he were doing chin-ups.

There was something unnerving about standing in a dark cold alley, the ground stained with mysterious blood. I went back to cataloging sounds, jumping when Kieran spoke, even though it was softly enough that I nearly didn't hear him.

"I found a body," he said tightly. "Female."

I stared up at him. "Should I call 911?" I fumbled for my phone with cold fingers.

"Too late for that."

I shuddered. Kieran was standing on the roof with a dead body. "What do we do?"

"She's been exsanguinated," he said. "Puncture marks on the neck. We'll have to call it in to the League. They have a cleanup crew for this kind of thing." He dialed and spoke into his phone in low tones.

"Remind me not to sign up for that department," I muttered, hunching my shoulders against cold and trepidation. I was very aware that the cuffs of my pants were stiffening with a dead woman's blood. I swallowed against the bile burning in my throat.

And then I realized there was something worse than being covered in blood.

Being covered in blood in a town overrun with vampires.

A shadow moved to fill the mouth of the alley. I couldn't smell mushrooms over the rotting garbage in the Dumpster and the snow, but I knew it was a vampire regardless. Pale, too fast and too agile; just not *Hel-Blar*. It was a man, fangs gleaming. A woman stepped up behind him, smiling. She wore fur and pearls. Definitely not from Violet Hill.

"Oh, good," she murmured, sniffing the air. "I'm starving."

"I'm not food." I lifted my crossbow. "And I'm under Drake protection." I angled slightly so they could see the Drake family insignia cameo I wore around my neck.

"We just want a little bite." The man shrugged. "And I don't see any Drakes here. Do you?"

"There are still treaties," I argued, suddenly nervous. I glanced at the other end of the alley. I shifted from one foot to the other.

"Treaties, bah. All I see is one little girl, all alone."

"Then you're not looking close enough," Kieran said from the rooftop, just as he aimed his flashlight at them. It only blinded them momentarily, but it was just long enough that I could launch into a run. Kieran kept pace with me, jumping from roof to roof. A shingle slid and crashed to the ground behind me. I ran as fast as I could, trying not to slide in the snow and ice. My leg muscles twitched, my lungs burned, and still I ran. I could hear them behind me. They were faster than I was and could have caught up easily enough. They were playing with me.

Aunt Hyacinth told me a story once about organized hunts in the nineteenth century when she was turned. Vampires would use terrified humans instead of a fox. The fear and the adrenaline made blood sweeter.

The hell I was going to be their fox.

Which was a great theory I had no idea how to put into practice.

My throat was dry from gasping, and sweat gathered under my jacket. I forced my legs to keep moving. Dirt rained down from Kieran's boots. A gutter broke and he stumbled, nearly falling. He swung above me like a human pendulum. I glanced up, and the tiny break in focus made me slip on a patch of frost and snow. I crashed into a metal gate. It was locked. I couldn't get through, and I couldn't reach Kieran to help him. His flashlight was on the ground, the beam slicing across the toe of my boots when I spun around. The fence dug into my shoulder blades. Miniature dust devils of snow and discarded chocolate bar wrappers skittered into the corner. I lifted my crossbow, hand trembling slightly in the cold.

There was just enough light to see the vampires strolling around the corner, blocking the only exit. Kieran cursed and dropped from the edge of the roof, where he'd been clutching a broken gutter. He landed hard and limped to my side, a stake in each scratched and bleeding hand.

He was a good fighter. And I had good aim. But these vampires were old, I could tell that right away. And that meant we were no match for them, training or not. And I was covered in blood, maddening them. And I'd run away, which I knew I wasn't supposed to do. It only made vampires more eager to chase you. But sometimes, standing still was simply not an option.

Speaking of options.

We had none.

I could tell Kieran agreed. His face was grim, his shoulder cutting across mine in an effort to shield me. So I did the only thing I could think of.

I opened my mouth and screamed.

I didn't just scream, I shrieked and screeched and caterwauled. This wasn't a damsel-in-distress scream for help. This was every decibel of noise my lungs and vocal cords could possibly muster.

Vampires needed a certain amount of secrecy, even these who clearly weren't following the rules. The Blood Moon attendees were strictly forbidden from feeding in town. There was a blood supply available in the encampment and some of the older tribes traveled with their own human donors. So the ones who decided to troll through Violet Hill thought they could get away with it.

"Shut her up," the woman snapped. She flinched when I made my voice even higher-pitched.

And I still had my crossbow. I fired a bolt, still yelling. It caught her right under her collarbone. She hissed in pain and surprise. Next to her, the man jerked in surprise, then his eyes narrowed furiously.

Oops.

One day I might learn not to seriously piss off vampires.

Today was clearly not that day.

Kieran flung his stake. It grazed the man's throat, drawing enough blood to splatter the air. I coughed, drew a deep breath and kept on screaming.

A light switched on at the other end of the alley.

"What the hell's going on out here?" an old man bellowed grumpily. "It's the middle of the damn night. I'm calling the cops. Damn kids." He slammed his window shut.

The screaming, combined with the GPS in Kieran's phone, had some of our team charging up the alley behind us. Hunter used a Dumpster on the other side of the gate to climb up, aiming her own crossbow. Eric and Chloe came up behind the vampires.

Crossbow bolts and arrows flew through the alley. One of them nearly got Hunter in the thigh. She leaped off the Dumpster, landing in the shadows. The vampires, wounded and annoyed, scaled the brick wall and vanished over the rooftops. I stopped shrieking. The silence thrummed around us. My throat was raw.

Kieran rubbed his ears. "Is there blood? Am I blind?"

"Don't you mean deaf?" I croaked.

"No." He half smiled. "You scream louder than mere ear damage." He nudged me, like two comrades-at-arms in a war movie. "Nice moves, Hamilton."

"You two scared the crap out of me," Hunter muttered from the other side of the fence.

"And what the hell's that smell?" Chloe added. "Gross."

"We better get out of here," Kieran said. "League's on the way. You know how they get when there are students around."

"And we saw a Huntsman not far from here," Connoly added.

"Crap. Let's go."

CHAPTER 17

Nicholas

"Is it true?"

The voice was so soft I barely heard it. It was coming from behind a hole in the cave wall, fitted with iron bars. It must open up into another crevice like the one I was lodged in. I sat with my back to the rock where I could keep an eye on a portion of the main lab.

"Are you really one of the Drakes?"

I slid closer to the gap. A female vampire with long brown curls matted with blood and cracked lips bent into view. They weren't giving her enough blood, if any. I tried not to think about what would happen when the sun went down tomorrow and I woke up with a newborn's thirst. It was nearly two years since my change, and that wasn't nearly long enough to get by on a mouthful of blood.

"Yes," I whispered. "It's true."

"You're young, boy." Her accent sounded Greek. "Is the other dhampir your sister?"

"Do you mean Solange?" I asked. She nodded. "Then yes."

She was trembling all over, lightly, like an aspen leaf. Pain had made marks in her face, which was dark with dirt and streaks of burned skin, as if she'd been doused in bleach. No, not bleach. Holy water. I cursed, softly.

"You might survive, then," she said. "If they need you." She huddled into herself.

"Better pray they don't need you and let you die," another voice said. There was someone else in the cell with her, a man with cuts on his face, crusted with blood and accented with bruises. He was human. He was human, he was locked up, and the vampire hadn't eaten him, even though she was clearly in dire need of blood.

"You're . . . human."

"Figured that out, did you?" he said, disgusted.

A clatter of iron chains and a thin wailing scream cut us off. We froze.

"Keep your head down," the man snapped. "Get out of the light."

I slid closer to the gap, deeper into the dank shadows.

"What the hell is this place?" I asked when no one came to the gates for us.

"Hell," he shot back. His jaw bristled with gray whiskers. I could smell the sweat on him. "They've brought half a dozen vampires here. Some are still chained up, others are dust."

"But why? What do they want?"

"Who knows? They like pain. They don't like vampires."

"But half of them *are* vampires."

"Better to serve the devil than burn in hell," he said, sounding exhausted. "Whatever they're looking for with all their tests and torturing, they haven't told me."

"Why are you here? You're human."

"They take our bodies and dump them in town. Took a woman just tonight. I don't know why. At first I assumed I was just food, though Ianthe here has very politely held back."

"I wouldn't eat you, Lee," the vampire said with weary amusement. "You know that. You smell terrible."

Lee's smile was brief. When he looked at me, it died. "I hope you're stronger than you look."

"I hope so too."

There were too many sounds: iron chains, Hunters talking, victims sobbing or trying to claw their way out, rats scurrying, water dripping. I leaned my head back, covering my head with my arms, but the screaming pierced through, was so broken, it was jagged and hot in my ears. I stood up and went to the bars. The woman hanging from the bars was weeping soundlessly through seizures of pain. Frankenstein stood near her with an expression of detached curiosity, a metal device full of spikes in his hand, dripping blood.

"If you pierce around the heart but not quite through it, you get the most interesting reaction," he was saying to one of the guards.

"Stop it!" I yelled when he lifted the device again and the vampire shivered and begged. "Leave her alone!"

Frankenstein turned slowly toward me. "I'll stop," he said pleasantly. "Provided you're willing to take her place."

The vampire woman hung like meat. Her eyes were nearly dead. Even if the rest of her survived, she'd go mad. Fear was metallic and bitter in my mouth, like pennies in vinegar.

"Deal."

CHAPTER 18

Solange

Late Monday night

Constantine took me to the Bower. The bats followed us the entire way though their numbers thinned a bit. I stumbled along, Constantine's hand gripping mine tightly as I tripped over roots and was generally the exact opposite of a graceful vampire with excellent night vision.

I was a little busy freaking out.

One of Lady Natasha's handmaidens tried to stake me. I'd just been exiled from the Blood Moon where my mother's right to the throne would be ritualized later this week under the full moon. I was persona non grata, to be staked on sight. I was hearing voices.

And it wasn't even midnight yet.

I wanted to call Lucy, but this was too dangerous for her. I wanted to call Kieran, but I didn't know what to say. I wanted to turn the clock back and stay inside the family tent so the Furies never saw me and none of this even happened.

Instead, I sat on a dusty brocade sofa under a wreath of bats. We were alone, snow falling lightly between the branches. I smelled pine and cedar and ice and the burning wicks of candles in tin lanterns. Ice glimmered here and there, dripping off evergreen boughs and iron candelabras. It was haunting and beautiful, but I barely noticed.

"What am I going to do?"

"Whatever you want, love," Constantine answered, smiling gently as he sprawled in a chair with the carved feet of a lion. He looked utterly comfortable and unconcerned that he'd been marked for Chandramaa execution.

"They just tried to kill you," I felt compelled to remind him.

He shrugged one shoulder. "We're safe here."

"You can't know that." I rubbed my palms on my knees. Vampires rarely sweat. Our body temperature didn't even approach lukewarm unless we'd just drunk a lot of blood and it was running at full tilt through our systems. Still, I was anxious enough that my hands felt damp. A hundred thousand thoughts crowded in the black space of my mind, like stars on a clear night. And they were just as difficult to catch. "I didn't even know we *could* be exiled," I said. Even though the Drakes had been exiled from royal court for centuries, this was different.

"Moon Guard don't concern themselves with renegades outside

the encampment borders. They won't come after us here. They won't even bother with us unless we try to go back. It's as if we don't exist to them anymore."

I swallowed. "What about my family?"

"What about them?"

"Will they be punished? For what I did?"

He shook his head. "Doubt it."

"But you don't know for sure?"

"No one's been exiled in my lifetime, love. We're breaking new ground." He reached for a bottle of blood from one of the lace-covered coolers. He lifted one in a toast. "To us."

I didn't drink when he offered the bottle. My throat felt too tight. "I don't know what to do," I said again. *Drink.*

"Enjoy," he suggested. The bottle swung negligently from his fingers, like a hypnotist's watch. When he offered again, I drank deeply. "What else can you do?"

I could go back to the farmhouse. Bruno or one of my parents was probably already there waiting for me. But I didn't want to go home. And maybe that was okay. Certainly, my family would be safer for it. As they proved nightly.

Unsurprisingly, my mother was the first one to find us.

She marched into the Bower wearing swords instead of the pearls I imagined normal mothers wore. She looked so angry, if she'd had Isabeau's magic, I'd have worried her braid would turn into a hangman's noose with Constantine's name on it. Her furious glare snapped onto him as soon as she saw I was unharmed.

I stepped in front of him to shield him. "Mom."

I could tell it was a struggle for her to shift her gaze. It softened to sparks instead of outright nuclear war. She hugged me so tightly the hilt of the dagger strapped across her chest left an imprint on my neck. "Solange, are you all right?" I nodded and tried to disentangle myself. She tightened her grip. "Come back to the farmhouse. We'll figure out what to do."

Don't let them take us. They'll lock us away. They think you're a monster.

"She can figure it out for herself," Constantine said.

Mom actually hissed. "You stay away from my daughter."

"Mom, he saved my life!"

"Which is why he isn't a pile of ashes as we speak," she said between her teeth. "I'm grateful." She glanced pointedly at Constantine. "Which is why you're not dead."

"He didn't do anything wrong," I insisted.

"Solange, you don't understand."

Right there.

Without even meaning to, Mom set me off again. I could feel the blood I'd ingested smolder inside me. Guilt and worry sizzled into irritation.

"I understand *fine*," I snapped. "I'm sixteen, not stupid!"

She frowned. "I never said you were." Her frown turned to a scowl when she looked at Constantine. "He smells wrong."

I tugged my hand out of hers and folded my arms across my chest. "I trust him."

"That's what scares me."

I turned slightly toward Constantine. "I'm sorry. We're kind of an insular family. And Mom's chronically suspicious."

"I'm also your queen," Mom cut in. "So leave my daughter alone."

"That's for her to decide, surely," Constantine replied smoothly, as if he wasn't inches from a pointy death. He'd never met my mother.

You should be queen, Solange. Then you'll never be at anyone's mercy ever again.

I was suddenly embarrassed by my mom, which was marginally better than being terrified by the growing strength of the girl's voice inside my head. I knew Lucy was mortified by her hippie first name, by protests and group hugs in front of city hall and the way her dad insisted on stopping the car to leave a tobacco offering every time he saw a turtle. I'd yet to feel that squirming humiliation. Mom was fierce and kick-ass. But she was also bossy and demanding.

Stifling.

"Mom, stop it," I said sharply. "You can't control everything that happens to me."

"I can damn well try. I'm your *mother.*" The moonlight reflected on the pommel of the sword on her back. "Remember when we thought Logan was dead to a Hound spell? I can't go through that again. I won't. Come back home with me. We can talk about it there."

"I'd rather stay here."

"Solange. This isn't a game. I'm worried about you. And so's your father."

"Very worried actually," Dad said tightly.

I stared at him over Mom's shoulder as she whirled to face him.

A vampire I'd never seen before had a knife to Dad's throat and a stake dimpling his shirt, right over his heart. Dad's head was tilted back, his neck muscles straining, his fangs gleaming. Beside him, Logan, Quinn, Duncan, and Sebastian were in the same danger, forced on their knees in the snow with weapons aimed at their hearts.

Mom's sword flashed. Logan made a strange "*urp*" sound when the stake pierced through his shirt, drawing blood. Mom froze.

"Stop it!" I shouted. The bats hissed and screeched above us. Logan's eyes were wild. Dad was tensed to fight, but blood bloomed on each of my brother's shirts, in the same place.

"You heard the princess," Constantine said, stepping forward. "Release them." The guards stepped back as one so suddenly Logan and Quinn pitched forward. Sebastian was on his feet, a stake in each hand before they'd even landed in the dirt.

"Behind me!" Dad shouted, keeping his body between the guards and his sons. But the guards didn't move; they only glanced at Constantine for order.

I looked at him too. "What the hell is going on?"

"Forgive me." He bowed slightly to me, as if we were in a ballroom instead of the woods. "I have men loyal to me. They must have come as soon as they heard I'd been exiled."

Adrenaline and blood, fear and anger, made my hands shake. My gums ached around my fangs. "Oh." *He understands us. He'll protect us.*

"Not good enough," Mom said. I was vaguely surprised, in some distant part of my brain, that her head hadn't actually exploded yet. Fury had her cheeks looking flushed. Her cheekbones looked too pronounced, her eyes haunted.

She didn't know Constantine like I did. "Mom, it's okay. Really." I winced at my brothers. "Sorry."

"Hell of a welcome, kid," Duncan grunted.

I narrowed my eyes at the guards. "You're never to harm my family. Ever."

"That's an order," Constantine agreed.

I stalked forward and marched down the line of them, as if I were a general and they were at military school. I looked each of them in the eye. I exuded pheromones, as best I could, imagining heat waves and electricity arcing off me.

"You will never harm my family," I repeated, making sure they were thoroughly compelled. They nodded mechanically, dead-eyed. I turned to Mom. "There." I expected her to be proud of my initiative and my unique tactic if nothing else. I didn't expect her to look even more scared. I couldn't do anything right.

"Solange, please come with us. Don't make me order you." It was the same tone she used when Lucy and I used to sneak out.

Blood curdled in my belly. "No. I need some time to think."

"You can think at home."

"We can't force her," Dad said.

"The hell we can't!"

"Helena."

"Liam, don't use that rational tone with me. I am *this* close to pulling that man's kneecaps through his nostrils."

"She won't thank you for it," Dad whispered just as I stepped closer to Constantine.

"It was an accident," I said. "Constantine would never hurt me. Or you."

"Again, I apologize. I didn't know they were out there. But I hope, if nothing else, that I've proved that your daughter is perfectly safe here."

"I'm not feeling particularly comforted," Mom said viciously.

"Retreat to fight again," Dad murmured. Then he handed me a small walkie-talkie that would work inside the Blood Moon camp since we weren't that far away. He looked older and sad. It made me feel awful. "Use this at any time," he said, "and we'll come." His face, when he looked at Constantine, was stone and ice. "We'll be posting our own guards," he added before he had to physically drag my mother away.

I was alone in a way I'd never been before.

And despite the fear inside me, there was a kind of nervous excitement as well, as if anything could happen. If I went back home, everything would stay the same. I'd feel guilty and everyone else would feel worried. I'd have to hold back.

I was tired of holding back.

Constantine motioned to the guards and they melted back into the shadows. "I am sorry about that," he said again. "But you did the right thing. It's not safe for the Drakes outside the encampment."

I snatched the bottle off the table and drained it before I could even manage to speak. "I'm a Drake."

"Yes, but you're so much more."

I wiped my mouth, feeling wired. "You saved my life."

"I'd say we're even." He smiled when I reached for another wine bottle of blood. "It's all ours for the taking, love." He had an angel's face, the kind that cracked open worlds with fiery swords. It was mesmerizing, especially when he looked at me like that. As if I might be able to crack open worlds too.

I looked away, not sure what to say. "Where are the others?" I finally asked.

"They'll be along any moment, I'm sure," he replied, still lounging in his chair without a care. There were little lines at the corners of his violet eyes though, if you looked closely enough. "Word travels fast, as we've discovered."

He was right. They came streaming between the red pine and in less than half an hour every seat was taken, including a few low branches of the nearest trees. There was Marigold in her distinctive tulle skirt and bare toes, Spencer, Elijah, Jude, Eliane, Fay, Toby, and a few others I didn't recognize.

Marigold grinned at me around a red lollipop. "So you're a rebel now, are you?"

I nodded, feeling glad to have stood my ground and miserable to have hurt my family.

"Cheer up," she said, perching on the arm of the sofa. "That's what the Bower is for."

I smiled back tentatively. "Thanks."

She crunched down on the candy. "Don't thank me. That's the beauty of this place, in'it? It doesn't belong to anyone."

I looked around. "Where's Ianthe?" I asked. She was soothing. She thought I was ordinary and not worth all this fuss and bother.

"She's gone," Jude said. "We haven't been able to find her." He tossed a scarf onto one of the chairs. "Only this." He looked frustrated. "It reeks of her fear."

Constantine's jaw clenched. "We're being picked off. And the Chandramaa and the council care only for their own politics." He touched the nape of my neck. "We have to be more vigilant."

Marigold tilted her head. "They're saying you killed three Furies and kicked a Moon Guard in the teeth and then gave everyone rabies, Solange."

"I gave people rabies?" I asked, insulted. She nodded to the bats still circling. "Oh," I said sheepishly. "Right. I'm sure they're not rabid."

"So what really happened?" Elijah asked. "I heard you staked a baby bunny."

I gaped at him as Constantine chuckled. "Vampire gossip sucks," I said. "To be clear: I never wanted Lady Natasha's stupid crown and I don't kill bunnies. God."

"Bigger picture," Constantine said. "Do you want the crown now?"

Yes. I blinked as everyone turned to stare at me. "No!"

"And why not?"

"Because anyone who touches it gets a big fat bull's-eye on their back," I pointed out. "No thanks."

"Sometimes the only way to change the system is to work within it."

I stood up even though I had nowhere else to go. "My *mother's* the queen. I think I've traumatized her enough for one night, don't you?"

"She's made it abundantly clear that she's holding the crown in trust for you. She's more of a regent, really."

I shook my head mutely. *You could protect them all if you were queen. Let me help you.*

"Think about it," he suggested. "The Moon Guard would have killed us both tonight, if you hadn't broken the rules."

He was right. If I complained about a system that had exiled me, put my family in constant danger of assassins and bounty hunters, and then tried to stake a man for trying to protect me, then it was time for me to do something about it. Maybe this was the reason I was so different. If I found a way to use my power, it might not burn so uncomfortably inside me. I might not hurt people so much.

That voice might go away.

"Are you really tired of the old structures?" Constantine asked the others. "Because you've heard about the prophecies."

Dragon fighting dragon. Although it also said, "Unseat the dragon before her time and increase ninefold her crimes." Was the dragon Mom? Or me? He didn't realize just what he was asking for.

"Are you ready to follow a new queen into a new way? A better way?"

"This is all going too fast." I grabbed his arm. "I'm not ready for this, Constantine."

"Of course you are," he said, standing close to me, his arm around my waist. I wasn't sure if he was supporting me or keeping me from running away. "Look at them."

The vampires gathered around us were kneeling, one by one. They stayed on one knee in the snow, waiting for me to do something queenly. I was utterly at a loss.

They'd chosen the Bower over the monarchy and the Chandramaa.

And now they were choosing me.

I felt exhilarated and sick at the same time. The bats drifted lower, as if they were watching the proceedings too.

"Sorry, mate," Marigold said, her fangs dimpling her lower lip. She looked like a particularly savage little doll in her candy-colored skirt and the flowers woven through her hair. "I'm with you but I don't kneel. Not to anyone."

I just nodded. Constantine must have sensed my agitation because he bent his head toward mine, lips tickling my cheek. "It's just a symbol," he assured me. "It buys you some protection, some followers to guard your back."

"I'm not sure I like it." I shifted uncomfortably.

"You will," he promised.

CHAPTER 19

Nicholas

Tuesday, just after midnight

I waited until I was out of the cell before I fought back.

I dropped so suddenly I was able to slip free, the sleeve of my shirt ripping off, where it was already torn from the rusty nail. I rolled, knocking two vampires down like undead bowling pins, then I kicked up, booting a Huntsman in the thigh. He flew back and landed on a metal table, shattering half the jars and bottles. The clatter was loud enough to bring all of the other prisoners to the grates but not loud enough to wake the woman still swinging on her chains. She was now as close to dead as a vampire could be without being ashes. Even if I managed to cut her down, I couldn't drag her with me and I couldn't heal her. If I got away and brought the others back, Uncle Geoffrey might know what to do.

The silhouette of a Host blocked the main exit just as another charged out of a tunnel on the other side of the murky pond. I threw an entire table at him.

"Behind you!" Lee shouted, propping Ianthe up at the bars. Between us stood a Helios-Ra agent with a loaded crossbow aimed at my back. She looked young enough to have been in the same year as Kieran. As soon as I had the time, I'd worry more about Lucy being in that school.

Right now, ducking was a priority.

The arrow missed me but caught the Host behind me in the side. He doubled over, hissing in pain. I grabbed the crossbow before the Hunter had time to shoot again and slid it to Lee and Ianthe. Lee grabbed it, contorting so he could stick his arm through enough to shoot it. One of the vampires who'd captured me exploded into dust. Frankenstein shouted. Ianthe knocked the Helios-Ra girl off her feet.

It was enough of a distraction to help get me to the exit, but not enough to get me through it. Someone tackled me and I went down, cracking my head on the wall as I fell. I saw double. I blinked furiously, holding my bruised head in my hand as I struggled to get back up. I stumbled, dizzy, and tried to push through.

No such luck.

I was pinned between a Huntsman and a Host. Lee managed to fire one arrow but the shot went wide. The Hunter smashed it out of his grip with his boot, breaking his fingers. Lee grunted but didn't yell. Ianthe slumped, hissing as she tried to find the strength to pull Lee back into the relative safety of the cell.

I was dragged back toward Frankenstein. He didn't speak for a long moment, just surveyed the damage that had been done. He had a kind of clinical displeasure that made me cold.

"Now that wasn't the deal," he said. "And you've made a terrible mess. I suppose we'll have to renegotiate, won't we?" He pointed to Lee and Ianthe. "Bring them."

"What are you doing?" I struggled violently until my shoulder started bleeding again.

Lee tried to pull the guards off Ianthe, but they were stronger. In the light of the torches I saw he was older than I'd thought, the white of his whiskers like salt in his dark face. Ianthe was thin, the bones poking out at her collar and hips. There were cuts in the crease of her elbows and her wrists. She hadn't just been starved, she'd been leeched. They'd cut her veins and let her bleed until she was too weak to heal.

"No!" I kept fighting even though it was useless. Lee tried to use his body to shield Ianthe, but they dragged the three of us inexorably toward the pond and Frankenstein. Ianthe used the last of her strength to buck and jerk when she saw the water. She keened and spat curse words in what I thought was Greek.

"A valuable lesson." Frankenstein raised his voice so the other prisoners could hear him. They were still at the bars, but they were silent now. I saw at least seven vampires and three humans, and I had no way of knowing how many others were chained in the dark. There were fangs and hisses but little other objection. There was nothing anyone could do to help us.

And nothing we could do to help Ianthe.

"A little reminder," Frankenstein said. "There's no escape."

At his nod, Ianthe was tossed into the water. No, not just water. Holy water.

She went under and resurfaced, shrieking. Lee didn't make a sound, tears running into his beard as her skin blistered and oozed, her hair falling away with chunks of her scalp. She tried to claw her way out, but there was too much holy water in the pond. It wasn't really blessed water, it was just infused with UV rays and vitamin D in such concentrations as to be toxic to vampires, like pure sunlight.

Lee slid his eyes away from her for the barest moment, looking at me, then at the ground. I followed his gaze to the spike near his foot. He flexed his fingers, glanced back at Ianthe, choking on her own cries. The smell of burned flesh was making me nauseated.

Lee leaned back, using the guard's grip to hold his weight as he kicked the spike in my direction. I caught it, jerking my head back at the same time and breaking the nose of the Helios-Ra agent on my left. Where the hell had he come from? I didn't bother trying to free my other arm. This wasn't about escape. We knew we couldn't get out, not this way.

Instead, I threw it as hard as I could at Ianthe. It cleaved her heart and she smiled briefly before turning to ash that coated the surface of the pond.

"Interesting." Frankenstein studied Ianthe's remains. He flicked his fingers at us, not even bothering to turn his head our way. "Take them back to their cells," he told our guards before wading into the water to his ankles to further his inspection of the muddy ashes. "But I haven't forgotten our deal, prince."

CHAPTER 20

Lucy

Tuesday, 1:00 a.m.

Hunter, Chloe, and I went to Kieran's house. Kieran said he was busy, but Hunter was worried about him, so we snuck right back off campus again. Kieran wasn't home, so we waited on a bench near the garden, under a maple tree. We hid out of the glow of the porch light so his mother wouldn't see us. Hunter didn't want to bother her.

Chloe was eating a chocolate bar and Hunter was texting Kieran again. It was a cold night, and we were bundled in scarves and extra-thick sweaters. Hunter wore some kind of special-issue long underwear, prepared as always. She looked sleek and comfortable. I looked like a top-heavy penguin in great danger of toppling over.

"He's on his way," she said, just as we heard the rumble of motorcycles a few streets over. The Drakes tended to use bikes because they could go places cars couldn't, especially in the woods. I assumed vampire hunters used them for the same reasons, plus they had a better chance of outrunning vampires that way. On foot, humans had no hope. We just weren't fast enough, no matter how hard we trained around a racetrack.

It wasn't long before Kieran and his friends Eric and Connoly came around the corner, the spears of their headlights touching cars, windows, garbage cans, and one startled raccoon. Kieran broke off from the others and turned onto the driveway. Eric and Connoly continued on with a wave. Chloe made yummy noises.

Kieran pulled off his helmet. "What's wrong? Another vic?"

"No," Hunter assured him.

He turned off his bike, pocketing his keys. "I don't need a babysitter, Hunter."

"No, you're special. You need three," I broke in. "There are three girls waiting for you on your doorstep, Black. Aw. Poor you."

He shook his head. "You're a pain in my ass, Hamilton."

I grinned. "I practiced on seven vampire brothers, remember? I could give classes."

"And I brought chocolate," Chloe added, tossing him an extra bar from her bag.

I eyed her. "Hey, you said you were out."

"I lied."

Hunter snorted. "She also stole that chocolate from my stash."

Chloe was cheerfully unrepentant. "You're running low by the way."

Hunter smirked. "I have another stash you don't know about."

It was the same kind of banter Logan and I used to fall into to distract Solange from being all stressed out over her bloodchange. Both Hunter's and my phones beeped at the same time. I felt a small clutch of anxiety as we looked at each other.

"Quinn," Hunter said.

I frowned at my phone's display before answering. "Logan? What's up? Where's Nicholas?"

"He's patrolling," Logan answered. "He's fine."

Relief made my voice squeak. "Then what is it?"

"Solange."

Relief fled like smoke in a high wind. I glanced at Kieran, eyes wide. He frowned questioningly.

"What?" he mouthed.

I was already jumping to my feet. "We'll be right there." I disconnected as Hunter slipped her own phone back into her pocket.

"Solange was just exiled from the Blood Moon," I explained for Chloe and Kieran's benefit.

Kieran was the first to respond. "*What?*"

"Apparently she fled with Constantine and they've set up camp. She nearly got half her brothers killed for good measure." I checked my inside pocket for stakes and then adjusted the Hypnos-filled cartridge under my sleeve. "Connor will send me the coordinates as soon as he finds a signal. But it's in the woods, and we can get at least that far on our own. So let's go."

"Um, Kieran?" Chloe interrupted, staring up at the house. "Is there supposed to be a guy in your room?"

Kieran's head whipped around. The silhouette of a man showed briefly at his window, then was gone.

And he moved too fast to be human.

"My mom's in there," Kieran said, already running for the front door with a stake in his hand. "We need to move the fight outside. She can't know."

There was no question that there was even going to be a fight.

"Chloe, with me. We'll take the back door," Hunter said in her best commando voice. "Lucy, go with Kieran."

Kieran pushed the door open in one quick shove so the hinges wouldn't squeak. We stepped onto the thick rug in the foyer and paused. Vampire hearing was preternaturally sharp. They'd hear our heartbeats if they were listening for them, but with any luck they'd attribute any other sound to Kieran's mom. Ice clinked in a glass as the refrigerator ice maker grumbled.

Kieran nodded to the kitchen, then waved me to the other side of the stairs leading to the second floor. He pointed to himself, upstairs, then the door.

Great, charades.

I slipped into the shadows where he'd told me to wait and hoped to hell I'd deciphered what he'd said properly: Wait until Kieran had lured the vampire out before following. Keep his mother safe.

"Hey, Mom," Kieran called out. "I'll be out in the garage working on the bike. Don't worry if you hear some clatter."

"Okay, sweetie."

Kieran went back outside. I held my breath, raising a stake.

The vampire was down the stairs and out the door before it had clicked fully closed. I barely saw him move, just the blur of his white shirt and a shift of cold air. He didn't even glance my way. I waited to make sure there wasn't a rear guard. At the first sound of fighting on the driveway, I rushed out.

Kieran's motorcycle was on its side, and a garbage can rolled noisily into the street, shedding banana peels and yogurt containers. Kieran's sleeve was shredded and his cheek scraped. He had a stake in one hand and a long, thin dagger in the other. Kieran stabbed at the vampire with the dagger, but he was out of reach, grinning, fangs fully extended.

I edged closer, trying to figure out a way to throw my stake without accidentally impaling Kieran. My aim was good, but logistics were logistics. They weren't exactly standing still. I picked Kieran's helmet off the driveway as the fight moved onto the grass, in the shadows of the garden. I swung it from its strap. If I threw it right, I could hit the vampire in the back of the legs and knock him off-balance. Even if it was only for a moment, it would help. Right now he had all the advantages; not only was he faster, but he was a better fighter. I crept closer and closer, swinging the helmet to get better momentum. By the time it left my fingers, the vampire had already turned toward me.

"I don't think so, little girl." He kicked the helmet with his heel before it collided with him, sending it back toward me.

I didn't have time to dodge. It hit me full in the chest, knocking me back into the cold grass. I landed hard, the breath knocked right out of me. My lungs seized up, then cramped around a violent cough. Tears burned my eyes as I struggled to gasp air back into my chest. I thumped a fist on my rib cage, scrambling to get back up. Apparently, Jenna needed to keep training me on how to fall properly. Everything hurt and if the vampire had been focused on me, I'd be dead now.

At least my spectacular failure had given Kieran a brief distraction to work with. His dagger sliced through the vampire's shoulder, deep enough to lodge into bone and stay there. There was a hiss of pain. Kieran jabbed up with the stake, aiming for the throat. It wouldn't kill him but it sure would stop him. I remembered what Hunter had once told me about aiming for the eyeballs.

A tip I could use right about now.

"Lucy, on your left!" It was Hunter, blood in her hair, chasing after another vampire darting around the side of the house, from the backyard. He was pale and wispy, and looked surprisingly fragile.

Big fat faker.

Vampires were never fragile.

I darted past Kieran and jumped, grabbing hold of one of the maple tree branches. I threw myself forward, as if I were a gymnast. My old gym teacher would have wept with pride. And shock. I swung, ankles tight together to make a battering ram out of my legs. I hit the vampire with the bottom of my boots, the force sending shocks of pain up to my knees. He fell back and Hunter was on him, stake at the ready. He kicked up, hitting her in the arm. The stake in her hand dropped. She grunted in pain, suddenly the one on the ground. He reared back, fangs out.

I let go of the branch and clamped onto him like a barnacle on a ship. He grunted. I held on tighter. He reached back, seizing me by the throat. I choked, using one hand to claw at him. Hunter squirmed to the side, slid out from under him while he was busy trying to strangle me, and then jabbed him with a stake. He went to ash, and I sprawled in the dusty grass, coughing painfully. If Hunter was any less skilled, she'd have hit me with the stake as well. But her grip was perfect, the arm tensed to rock, stopping the forward momentum and pulling back at just the right second.

"Thanks," I croaked.

She helped me up. "No problem."

We rushed to Kieran's side just as he managed to twist his arm at the proper angle. Hypnos powder burst out of the cylinder strapped under his sleeve. "Drop!" he yelled to the vampire as he tilted his head back sharply, holding his breath. Hunter and I yanked the collars of our sweaters up to cover our nose and mouth. The vampire went down like a rock, lying paralyzed at the feet of three hunters.

Kieran frowned at Hunter. "You're hurt."

She pushed her hair off her back, grimacing at the blood. "It's my nose, no big deal."

"He broke your nose?" I asked.

She shrugged. "I'm fine. I put it back."

"Where's Chloe?" Kieran asked.

"Inside doing a full sweep," Hunter answered. "I caught the other one climbing out your dining room window. Your mom's still in the kitchen."

He jerked a hand through his hair. "That's something, at least."

He pulled out his cell phone. "I'm calling for a bodyguard detail for her. You guys might get busted for sneaking off campus."

"Bound to happen sooner or later," I said.

After he'd hung up, he crouched over the vampire. "What the hell are you doing here anyway?"

"Kill Kieran." He sounded drunk, fighting the sticky web of Hypnos and his own rage.

"Yeah." Kieran wiped blood off his face. "I got that part."

"Who sent you?" Hunter demanded.

"Don't know."

I scowled down at him. "You're making vampires look bad, you undead asshat." I glanced up at the others, as Chloe joined us. "Can I kick him? Just once?"

"House is clear," Chloe confirmed.

"Are you sure?" Kieran asked.

She nodded. "Full sweep. I'm sure."

"Thanks."

Hunter crouched next to Kieran and blew another dose of Hypnos into the vampire's face. She flung herself backward, holding her breath until the powder had settled. "Who sent you?" She asked again.

"Kill Kieran."

She pressed the tip of a stake over his heart just hard enough that his eyes rolled, the whites practically glowing around pale blue irises. "*Who* sent you?"

"Don't know," he ground out. "Kill Kieran."

She sat back on her heels, scowling. "No use. They must have figured he might get dosed and didn't give him any info we could use."

"Now what?" Chloe wondered. "Do we stake him?"

Hunter shook her head firmly. "You know how I feel about killing unarmed, defenseless prisoners. I'm not an executioner."

"You killed that other vampire."

"Yeah, because he was killing Lucy."

"Well, we have to do something," Chloe insisted.

The vampire just lay there glaring at us. He might not be able to move, but he could see and hear just fine. I pulled my MP3 player out of my pocket, cranked the volume as loud as it would go, then shoved the pink skull earbuds into his ears.

The others just blinked at me.

"Um," Chloe said. "What are you doing?"

"He has vampire hearing. This is the only way we can plan without him knowing what we're saying," I told them. "So? Next step?"

"We need to let him go," Hunter insisted, wiping blood from her face and hair with a bandanna she fished out of her pocket.

"He tried to kill me," Kieran reminded her grimly. "He might have killed my mother."

She met his eyes unflinchingly. "We can fight about that later. Right now, we let him go, and we track him back to his hole."

He nodded once, grumbling. "Yeah, okay."

"Chloe and I will follow him and email you GPS coordinates as we go. You two get to Solange as soon as you can, after the League guards get here. But we have to move fast. If they get here first, they'll take him into custody and there goes our chance."

Kieran hauled the vampire to his feet, gripping his shirt with his fist.

I yanked the earbuds out, saving my MP3 player before it got trampled. "Go home, asshat," I snapped. "To whoever put you up to this."

He hissed ineffectually and then shambled off, a slave to the Hypnos. Hunter and Chloe trailed him. They were barely out of sight when a car pulled up from the opposite direction. Kieran hurried to right his motorcycle.

"League," he told me shortly. "Keep your mouth shut, Lucy."

I was, frankly, mutinous.

"I mean it," he said. "These are hunters, not students. Different rules. And not everyone's pro–vampire treaty."

"Fine," I muttered, crossing my arms.

A woman approached us first. She was wearing jeans and combat boots and looked perfectly normal. "Black," she greeted him. "Got the call."

Another hunter followed her, young enough to be a new agent. He had that kind of swagger. Kieran had it too when we first met him, but I made it my mission to kill the swagger. I eyed the newcomer consideringly. Kieran stepped back, nudging me. Spoilsport.

"Thanks for coming, Janelle," Kieran said to the woman. "Mom doesn't know."

Janelle looked relieved. "Good." She nodded to the other hunter. "Diego, take the back."

"Yes, ma'am."

Janelle glanced at me. "Student?"

I nodded. "Yes."

"I'm taking her back to campus," Kieran lied smoothly. "I need to know my mom'll be safe when I'm not here."

"Detail's here for the foreseeable future," Janelle assured him. "So go on, before this one gets bathroom duty." She cracked a smile my way. "Trust me, it's not worth it."

Kieran popped his head into the house to tell his mom he was going and then came back, holding a second helmet for me. We drove away, the scratched-up bike grumbling and muttering to itself.

Chapter 21

Nicholas

Lee and I came up with another escape plan.

I'd take the screws out of the grate that blocked his cell from mine, but slowly so no one would notice me hunkered down in the same spot for too long. There were enough shadows that one of us could hide. The next time the guards came to take one of us away, the other one would launch out of the opening and take them by surprise. After that, the plan involved a lot of staking and breaking of various bones.

It might have worked.

But we didn't get the chance to find out.

One of the Hosts came for me before I'd managed to loosen all of the screws. Lee was trapped in his own cell, patiently seething. The Host grinned at me, showing one nicked fang.

"Time to go, pretty boy."

I got to my feet before he could reach in and drag me out. It just felt better to walk on out on my own two feet, even if my knees felt full of electricity. I wanted to dash for the exit with every bit of my being, but there was another Host guard and two more human hunters in my way. I shifted toward them anyway but the guard at my back kicked me at Frankenstein and one of his metal tables. Ominous instruments clanged together.

Frankenstein looked up from a notepad in front of him. "Excellent. Thank you. Secure him to that post and then give us space, if you would."

I struggled, determined to make everything as difficult for them as possible. I managed to dislocate the shoulder of the hunter assisting him but the Host guard was too fast. I was chained to the post, the blue-tinted light from the camping lanterns winging over us. It barely took any time at all.

So much for my great revolt.

"Now where shall we start?"

Frankenstein's ruthlessly pleasant chitchat was grating, building the itch of foreboding. I thought I caught a glimpse of Lee's grizzled beard out of the corner of my eye, pressed at the bars of his cell. I yanked on the chains once. They were heavy, cold iron, and locked tightly.

"What's the point of this?" I asked, cringing back away from the sharpened railroad spike he held in his hand. "You won't get a ransom if you kill me." Keep them talking, Dad would have said. Keep calm and negotiate.

Mom would say kick him in the balls.

But there were chains looped around my ankles.

Frankenstein used the tip of the spike to pull the frayed edge of my shirt away from the dirt-and-blood-encrusted arrow wound. The rusty point of the spike sliced through the ragged flesh that hadn't had a chance to knit together. Blood seeped. I gritted my teeth and refused to react. A shrill scream echoed from one of the cells.

Frankenstein smiled, almost gently. "This is noble work Dawn has charged me with."

"Dawn? Is she the one behind this?" I asked. "What does she want?"

"She's very clever. She knows it's not enough to kill the vampire, but one must find out how he works so we might eradicate the plague from humanity." There was an unholy glint of mad joy in his eyes. Blood and viscous fluid were dried to his leather apron.

"Are you Helios-Ra?" I asked, hoping to keep him talking, desperately searching for a way out of the chains. "Or a Huntsman?"

"I was Helios-Ra," Frankenstein said, whipping his head back to stare at me. The point of the spike pressed deeper. I clenched my jaw against any sound of pain. It might be the only currency I had left, and I wouldn't hand it over until I absolutely had to. "Before they kicked me out. Said I was unstable, said I needed help." He spat. "Bah. They didn't know genius when they saw it, no one did, not even my own parents. Not until Dawn. Not until the worm in the heart of the Helios-Ra ate at the rose." He laughed. "Treaties." He jabbed deep with the spike and I jerked back, grunting.

Muscles split, blood oozed. "They make us weak, vulnerable to the plague."

"Then why the humans?" I forced out, cursing. "Why do this to your own kind?"

"It's science. Sacrifice. They are casualties serving a grander purpose." He wrenched the spike back out, and the yank of iron scraping against my shoulder bone, the tear of flesh, the vicious bite of pain, made me thrash in the chains for a moment. My fangs extended as far as they would go; sweat gathered on the back of my neck.

I tried to remind myself what Mom would do in a tough situation like this, how she'd fight her way free, how she'd survive—but I couldn't think at all. There was just pain, like fire nibbling at every part of me, consuming, burning, eating away as if I were made of paper.

When the rattle of the links quieted again, the Host guard was grinning at me over Frankenstein's shoulder. He handed his dagger to the scientist. "Here, use mine."

Frankenstein circled me once slowly. The dagger darted in and out, stabbing under my other shoulder blade, over my kidney, under my ear. He circled back to the front, slashing shallow cuts on my chest, my neck, my arms, even my palms. I hissed, jerking violently at each slice. I tried to picture Lucy's face, tried to imagine the exact way she smiled at me.

It helped a little.

I'd used Lucy as a talisman to pull me through the worst of my bloodchange, and I'd do the same now. And all I had back then were mostly memories of her punching me in the nose.

The dagger jabbed into me, and Frankenstein turned it as if it were a key and I the lock.

The way Lucy smelled like cherry bubble gum and pepper.

Blood dripped into the foul trench in the ground. It seeped from leaching strength and healing. I struggled, feeling every drop as it trickled down my body.

The way Lucy giggled when she thought no one could hear her.

Even my pupils dilated painfully when he swung a UV bulb liberated from a tanning bed into my eyes. It seared into my brain, left me feeling weak as if it were noon.

Lucy playing her guitar.

Frankenstein reached for a beaker of clear liquid and dipped the spike in. "Holy water," he said, almost conversationally.

Lucy and I stretched out on the grass watching the northern lights.

He flicked drops into my cuts, inspecting them curiously as they blistered and peeled. I choked on a yell, gagged, fought.

The way Lucy's mouth moved under mine, the way her body fit against mine, the way she whispered my name.

He dipped the spike in the holy water and dragged it lightly over the wound, enough to make my eyes roll back in my head, but not enough to cause the kind of lasting damage that might take me out of the game.

Lucy and I sitting in the secret tree fort, listening to music.

Shallow cuts over my heart. More blood, more pain.

Lucy...

CHAPTER 22

Solange

Tuesday, 3:00 a.m.

I didn't know what to do with myself.

The walkie-talkie Dad gave me was wedged in my pocket. I itched to use it. I could call Mom to apologize, or Lucy to help me figure out why I kept insisting on ripping my life apart like I was looking for the caramel in the middle of a chocolate candy. I could call Kieran.

I fisted my fingers together before I could give in. This was no time to crawl back home. There was too much that needed figuring out. Too many questions, too many secrets.

Constantine passed me a wine glass of blood-doctored wine. The others were talking quietly, shooting me curious glances.

Candle flames flickered inside the lanterns, casting patterns of light on the rugs and the tree trunks, like fireflies. It was getting colder, snow sticking to the grass and branches.

"What just happened?" I asked, drinking the wine.

"Destiny." Constantine sat back comfortably, his leg pressed against mine. "No one said it would be comfortable."

He's right. It's our time now. My time.

Everyone else probably thought I was throwing a tantrum, but he understood there was something else burning under my skin. I just had to figure it out. Sometimes, I didn't even feel like myself anymore. And I wasn't sure how to figure out who I was if I wasn't Solange, rare vampire daughter, Drake princess, baby sister.

"My brothers were nearly staked." I still felt a little shell-shocked about that.

"An accident," Constantine said, his hand tickling my lower back, as if I were a wild cat that needed soothing. I did feel a little bit like purring. It was like there were two of me: the Solange who knew better and the Solange who didn't care. "It won't happen again," he assured me. "You have my word."

I wasn't worried about it happening again, not with my phero-mone compulsion. I was just worried that it had happened at all. It dulled the shine of being on my own.

On my own.

I could make decisions for myself now. Like the one to save Constantine from an unjust execution. I felt good about that. I just had to hold onto that for the moment. It had to be enough.

But I couldn't help but wonder what Madame Veronique was doing right now.

I shivered. "What do we do when the sun rises?"

"I have a spot, love. Not to worry."

"So what are we going to do about these disappearances?" Elijah asked. "How do we find Ianthe?"

"We've tried tracking her," Jude said, frustrated. "But aside from her scarf, we found nothing."

"How many are missing?" I asked.

"At least seven that we know of."

"Even with the Chandramaa?"

Marigold snorted, stretching her legs out onto the table. There was glitter on her toes. "Chandramaa care about the encampment and the queen, nothing else."

I frowned. "Wait, so my mom could order them to search?"

"Yes," Constantine replied.

"*Technically*, yes," Elijah corrected. "Chandramaa might protect the queen, but they take orders from someone else. Whoever that might be. And they're not likely to split their focus with the ceremonies and councils starting so soon."

"That doesn't seem fair."

Marigold shrugged. "Doesn't have to be. But realistically speaking, there's no need for any of us to leave the camp. It's secure and they have enough blood for everyone. If we leave and we get nabbed, it's our own fault, really. They were clear on that when we set up the Bower."

"But who's doing it?" I asked. "Hunters? Other vampires?"

"Does it matter?" Marigold yawned, rooting through her beaded bag. "I need more sugar."

And then my mother, Madame Veronique, and missing vampires were suddenly not the worst thing that could happen to me.

Lucy.

"Solange! Let me go!" I heard her yell from the woods. "She's my best friend!"

I leaped to my feet, dashing to the guards. "Lucy?"

"Yes, me. Ow!"

"Let her go," I said quickly.

Lucy stumbled out of the tree, pushing her hair off her face. Her sweater was crooked and she looked furious. "What the hell, Solange?"

"Constantine posted a guard," I said sheepishly.

"No shit." She straightened her clothes. "Bruno says hi."

"Bruno's out there too?"

"Yeah." She turned to peer into the shadows. "So's Kieran. He's waiting for the all-clear. Bruno seemed to think your guys would jump him for being a hunter."

"Kieran's here?" I sounded as freaked out as I felt. I wasn't ready to see him, or for him to see me like this. I didn't have sunglasses to cover my eyes. My fangs still wouldn't retract. "You couldn't have warned me?"

"I've been calling you for the past hour!" Lucy grumbled. "Not to mention the six thousand texts this week."

"My phone's back at the camp."

"What the hell's going on? Logan said you took off and nearly got them all killed."

I scowled. "That's not what happened. The Furies tried to kill me and Constantine saved me. And then I saved him back. Sorry, I didn't stop to text you," I added sarcastically.

"Oh, you are not pulling that crap on me, Solange Drake."

"Back at you, Hamilton." I wasn't even sure why we were fighting. Lucy knew me better than I knew myself sometimes. I should have been asking for her help. Especially with Kieran lurking in the woods.

"Are you going to let him in, or what?" Lucy asked. "He came all this way with me to make sure you're okay. You know, after you broke up and forgot to tell me about it."

"Let him through," I called out loudly, knowing they'd hear me.

Lucy stepped closer to me. "He misses you," she said quietly as Kieran came out of the tree line. She glanced at me. "And I know you miss him too."

"It's better this way," I said. She had no idea the thirst that screamed inside me, even just seeing his silhouette. Even when I looked at her, she was faintly edged with red, as if everything were soaked in blood. My gums hurt around my fangs. And there was that little thing about my going crazy. "You guys shouldn't have come."

"Too late now," she said cheerfully.

Kieran looked good. He wore his usual cargos, his dark hair tousled from the wind, his shoulders hunched against the press of the cold circle of vampires in the shadows. I knew he'd have already catalogued the glint of eyes in the dark, the pale skin, the movement of guards on the other side of the Bower.

He stopped in front of me. I couldn't quite meet his eyes. "Hey."

"Hey."

There was a long awkward pause during which I contemplated staking myself just to end it.

"Pathetic," Lucy finally huffed to herself. "Whoa!" she added when she caught sight of the Bower. The lanterns swung gently. From here you couldn't see the moth-eaten edges of the lace or the worn patches on the velvet sofas. "Okay, that's cool."

"It's the Bower," I said, smiling slightly. "Isn't it great?" Kieran barely glanced at it. My smile died. "What are you guys doing here?"

"Oh, I don't know," Lucy said with dry nonchalance. "Kinda heard my best friend was going dark side."

I scowled. "I was saving a life, actually."

"And I'm grateful," Constantine said, joining us. He was on my right, just behind me, and Kieran was in front. It was like a sandwich from hell. I shifted uncomfortably.

"Constantine," I said. "This is Lucy and Kieran."

"Ah," he drawled. "The best friend who electrocuted you—"

"Hey!" Lucy interrupted.

"And the hunter ex-boyfriend," Constantine continued smoothly.

"Constantine," Lucy seethed, her hands curling into fists.

"Lucy," I said. "Stop it. God, you're as bad as my mom." I shook my head. "Look, it's not safe in the forest for humans, especially hunter humans. You should go."

Lucy flinched as if I'd punched her. "Did you just call me a hunter?"

"Aren't you?"

She muttered one of her mantras under her breath. Constantine looked amused. Kieran looked grim.

Lucy exhaled slowly before speaking again. "I can't believe you just said that."

"Look, I'm sorry, but this is no place for you guys right now. Vampires are missing. Everyone's high-strung."

"So are humans," Kieran said grimly.

"Then you get it. I'm trying to keep you safe." I didn't know why they couldn't just leave it at that.

"Mm-hmm." Lucy sounded just as annoyed as the time Nicholas had hidden her homework back when they picked on each other incessantly.

"Lucy, I'm fine."

"Okay, well you know what? It's not just about *you* anymore, princess." I knew she was only calling me that to get back at me for calling her a hunter. "It's also about the two vampires who tried to kill Kieran."

Now that I didn't know. Dread soured my stomach. "What? When?"

"Just now, at my mom's house," Kieran replied quietly.

"Is she okay?" I asked, wanting to hug him or touch him in some way just to be sure. "Are you okay?"

Constantine arched an eyebrow at him. "You look all right, lad."

Lucy pinned him with her patented glare. She wasn't the least bit intimidated. I missed her. "Did you have anything to do with it?"

He just smiled, amused. "Why would I? I'm not the big bad wolf, little girl."

Lucy shifted her glare to me. "Solange, can we talk alone?"

I couldn't afford to let her back in.

"I trust Constantine," I said.

"Good for you. I don't." She tugged on my elbow, pulling me into the relative privacy of a spruce canopy. "Sol, you can't be serious."

"He saved my life tonight. What's *wrong* with everybody?"

"Well, you ran away from home. It's not like you."

She doesn't understand us. Forget about her. She's weak. Human.

"You've been running away from home since you were six." Usually to our house. "And now you're at the Helios-Ra high school. And you never even mentioned it to me before you went!"

Her eyes narrowed to slits. If she'd been a vampire they would have gone clear and cold as ice. "I tried to tell you."

"When?"

"When you compelled my boyfriend to kick me out of your house for talking about Constantine," she pointed out. "Remember that?"

I bit my lip. "Sort of."

She blinked, nonplussed. "What do you mean sort of?"

I sighed, wishing Kieran wasn't standing right there listening.

"Look, sometimes things get a little fuzzy when the hunger's on, okay?"

"Are you blacking out?" Kieran asked sharply.

"No. It's not like that. It's just . . ." I shrugged, unable to find the right words. "I don't know." I didn't mention the female voice, or the things she whispered to me. It was probably stupid not to, but I didn't want them to think I was insane on top of everything else. Then they'd *really* insist I couldn't take care of myself. *I'm only here to protect you. You don't have to be afraid.*

"What does your family say?" Lucy asked.

"Uncle Geoffrey wants to run more tests." I grimaced. "I'm his undead pincushion."

Lucy half laughed. "I can just imagine. Still. Something big's going on, Sol. Shouldn't you stick with your family?"

"And sacrifice someone who saved me?"

"I guess not." She sounded disgruntled.

"Why's everyone so determined to think the worst of Constantine? He saved my life. When Kieran saved my life, everyone practically gave him a key to the house. And he's a *hunter*. And after *Isabeau* saved my life, Logan went and fell in love with her. No one even blinked."

"Are you in love with him?" Kieran asked quietly.

Lucy took a step back and pretended she wasn't avidly eavesdropping. I honestly didn't know whose side she was on, and I couldn't blame her. I squirmed.

"Are you?" Kieran repeated.

"No," I answered. "Of course not." I wasn't in *love* with him, just . . . intrigued. And I missed Kieran. I missed that he didn't play games, that he stood up for what he believed in, even when others tried to knock him down. He was like one of those knights in the medieval stories. And I was the dragon. "We just broke up," I reminded him. "Are *you* in love with someone already?"

When the wind shifted, the query became less about retaliation and more of an actual question that needed an answer. Right now.

Because I could smell girls all over him.

And for some reason it made my gums ache around my fangs.

"Sol," Lucy said. "Your eyes are . . . weird. Are they usually that red?"

My nose twitched. "I can smell them on you."

Kieran looked confused. "Who? The vampires?"

"No, girls."

"Girls? What are you talking about?" *He's lying to us. He can't be trusted.*

A part of me recognized that he was truly mystified by the change of topic and that I was overreacting. But the rage inside me, always looking for a place to land, just didn't care.

"At least three different girls on you," I said, lips lifting off my teeth while I sorted through the scents. Kieran's hand hovered over the stake in his belt. I grabbed the lapel of his jacket, keeping him still. "Didn't waste any time, did you?"

I was close enough now that the perfume of my enraged pheromones made his jaw clench. His fingertips grazed the top of his stake, but he didn't pull it loose. His other hand shot to my hip, fighting the pull of my grip on his coat. We were frozen in a feral dance, with only the music of the blood pumping viciously in my veins. His breath was warm on my cheek.

"Who are they?" I demanded.

Lucy rolled her eyes. "Me, Hunter, and Chloe. We were fighting off vampires sent to kill him, remember? Get a grip already."

We both ignored her.

He eased closer, the lines of his face harsh. "What about Constantine?"

"This isn't about him."

"Then what's it about?"

We were so close and he felt so right, as if it were just the two of us in the safe house under the ground where we'd first really talked as a girl and a boy, not a vampire and a hunter, that I nearly kissed him. Or he nearly kissed me. I couldn't be sure. I was all fire and sharp edges. I was still angry, and the bloodlust snaked through me like a drop of fiery poison in a glass of water.

He's not worthy of us.

I leaned closer. For what, I wasn't sure.

"Uh, guys?"

We were still locked together. The intensity of Kieran's eyes went soft. I was leaning in toward his neck, which was still healing from our last encounter in the woods, when Lucy made a strange "*eep*" sound.

"Solange!" she added, trying to shove between us. "Don't!"

I saw through a red veil, as if it were raining blood. I could already feel the give of Kieran's skin under my bite, taste his blood in my mouth. Lucy's elbow dug into my sternum, but it didn't stop me. She was like a tiny firefly trying to move a boulder. Her feet dragged on the ground as she tried to find purchase. "Stop, stop, stop!"

"Yes, do." Constantine was suddenly there as well, his voice gentle and dark in my ear.

I didn't let go, but I didn't press forward either. He slipped a goblet of blood between us, waited until the scent had distracted me enough to break eye contact. Without the full force of my pheromones, Kieran pulled free so abruptly that Lucy stumbled back a step.

Kieran shook his head like a wet dog. Lucy had no idea what to do, and that never happened. I drained the cup with trembling hands.

And then the walkie-talkie in my pocket warbled, changing everything. Mom's voice was sharp as nails in the soft bower.

"Nicholas is missing."

CHAPTER 23

Lucy

Tuesday morning, before dawn

For a long frozen, broken moment, everything stopped.

The blood in my veins, my heart in my chest, my breath in my lungs. There was no space for anything inside me but shock and fear. I was watching myself from far away, standing in the woods by candlelight in torn jeans and a sweater my mom crocheted for me out of hand-dyed, multicolored wool. The smallest details stuck: the glint of tin lanterns, the frayed edge of the rug under a single chair under the tree, gilt paint peeling. The arms were carved to look like dragons. I was cold, too cold to move.

Solange was the first to break the tableau of shock. She grabbed for the walkie-talkie so fast it whipped out of her hand and crashed into the trunk of a black maple and broke. Bats formed a cloud over our heads. Kieran stepped closer to her, and she looked up at him, eyes wide and impossibly blue.

I shook my head violently. "Let's go," I said finally, my voice grim as a rusted lock clicking shut.

"Where?"

I bared my teeth like a wounded badger. "To find Nicholas. To talk to your parents."

"I could—"

"*Now*, Solange."

She flinched at my tone, but I was already stalking away, systematically checking my weapons, Kieran at my heels. He bent to pick up a fallen branch as we walked. It was long enough to be used as a staff. He was sharpening one end of it with a hunting knife when I shoved past Constantine's guard. I nearly burst into tears when I saw Bruno's familiar face waiting on the other side of them.

"Come on, lass," he said gruffly, his Scottish accent suddenly thick as mist on the heath. The lines at his eyes were pronounced. Even his tattoos looked stark. "Where's herself?"

"I'm here," Solange answered quietly, suddenly standing beside me. Even Bruno hadn't seen her move, and he was as used to vampires as he was to his morning coffee. Constantine was there too, but I ignored him. I didn't have time for anyone but Nicholas.

Bruno patted her shoulder gingerly, as if he wanted to offer comfort to the little girl he'd been protecting her entire life but wasn't sure if his hand might get broken for his trouble. Solange smiled at him wobbly.

We followed him quickly. Constantine was on Solange's right, his hand on the back of her neck. Kieran was on her left, and she was holding his hand in the shadows, gripping so tightly I saw the muscles in his forearms twitch. But he didn't let go. And he didn't say a word to me, just passed the staff over with his free hand. It was whittled to a killing point, like the staves I was learning to use with Hunter. I felt better with the weight of it in my hand.

The Drakes waited in a concerned huddle over a map laid out on a tree stump. A thin creek meandered beside them, glittering like a broken mirror. I couldn't help but think of Lady Natasha's mirrors in the royal courts. Nicholas had survived her; he could survive this too. Whatever this was.

There was instant comfort in the calm, authoritative way Liam ordered the guards to patrol, even with the haggard tension around his eyes. Connor and Quinn were identical lean swords of anger under the pine trees. Marcus frowned and Duncan's jaw was stone. A scatter of guards stood around them. Sebastian was listening patiently as always, noticing everything. He was the first to see us approach and he nudged Liam. Liam turned, smiling a little when he saw us. Solange's brothers eyed her warily. There was blood on their shirts.

Helena marched toward us, sword glinting. "Lucy." She caught me up in such a tight hug I felt my shoulders grind together, but I didn't care. I hugged her back and tried not to cry. She finally let me go, touching my cheek, before the battle fire flared in her eyes again. I knew she'd do whatever was necessary to get her son back, and she knew I'd do whatever necessary to get my boyfriend back. It was an unspoken pact, and it helped push down the frantic panic boiling in my belly.

"Mom, what happened?" Solange asked. She was closest to Nicholas and always had been. Kieran was still holding her hand.

"We don't know yet," Helena replied. She looked at Constantine and nodded once. "Any help is appreciated," she said bluntly. He nodded back courteously. I could guess their last conversation hadn't been this polite.

"Nicholas activated his GPS tag," Connor told us. The friendly computer geek was hidden under a layer of pure Drake wrath. "I only found out just now when I went out looking for a signal."

"And?" Solange pressed.

"And they found his guard's clothes, ashes, and nothing else," Duncan answered tightly.

"Ransom?" I asked. "Like with Christabel?" Ransom meant he was still alive. You couldn't collect if your victim was . . . no. I couldn't go there.

"No way of knowing yet," Liam said. Bruno joined him at the map, already barking orders into his phone.

"Logan and Isabeau have already left," Duncan added. "They're hoping Charlemagne catches Nicholas's scent before any more snow falls, or worse, rain." He looked up at the white winter sky without much hope. There was already very light snow hanging between us. But Isabeau's dogs were legendary. They'd once tracked Montmartre through this same forest.

"Aunt Hyacinth is out already too," Quinn added. "Uncle G. is staying back at the camp to make sure this isn't a decoy of some sort. And to keep an eye on Christabel and London."

I nodded, because I couldn't seem to find my voice. My fists clenched around the staff, splinters digging into my palm. The family had marked the spot where Nicholas had called for help. It was a red circle, like blood. There was nothing but mountain and forest around it for miles.

"You should go back to school," Liam told me gently.

I found my voice real fast. "What? No way!"

"He's right, Luce," Sebastian added quietly in his serious way, which was so like Nicholas my throat cramped around tears.

"Are you high?" I asked, blinking furiously. "I'm not going home until we find him."

"It's not safe here," he said. "The forest is all vampires and Huntsmen right now."

"I don't care!"

"We could give you a guard duty, but that would be at least three guards not out searching for Nicholas," Sebastian pointed out gently.

It was like he'd punched me. He was usually so quiet and kind that you could forget how ruthless and blunt he could be.

But he was right.

The thought of going back to sit in my dorm room and wait helplessly made me want to throw up, but he was right.

"I'll keep you in the loop," Connor promised.

I nodded. I knew if I said anything now, it would be squeaky and unintelligible.

"I'll take her back to school," Kieran said. "My bike's not too far from here."

"I'll go with you, at least that far," Duncan said, pushing away from where he'd been leaning against a tree. "I'll double-check your bike to be safe, before you take off. The trails are a bitch on the battery cables." Bats dipped and somersaulted around him. Duncan's jeans were frayed at the cuffs and stained with engine oil. He looked tough, like he belonged in an old James Dean movie. But when he glanced at Solange, he was all hurt puppy. I just didn't know who to be mad at anymore. Now that the Drakes were fighting among one another, defending them was becoming a full-time job.

"Try not to worry," Liam said, kissing my forehead. My lower lip wobbled embarrassingly.

Solange stopped me. Bats lowered around us like a leathery curtain. "We'll find him," she whispered. "Lucy, I promise." Her eyes were pale blue as moonlight on snow, veined with red like winter lightning. The veins at her wrists and collarbone practically burned like a gasoline trail to dynamite. "No matter what."

We hugged briefly, and hard. The bats drifted away. Duncan and Kieran were waiting for me.

"If they don't find him tonight, I'm going out searching tomorrow anyway," I said as we left the grove, ducking under branches and scrambling over fallen logs bristling with snow-encrusted mushrooms.

"I know," Kieran said. "I've already texted Hunter."

I tried to smile at him. "Solange was stupid to break up with you."

He just snorted.

◆

I didn't go to my room after Kieran dropped me back off at the campus. I couldn't stand the idea of sitting there with Sarita staring at me as I struggled not to fall apart. And I didn't want Hunter or Chloe or Jenna to come find me. Pity was poison right now. I needed to be alone.

I doubled back and darted into the edge of the woods, stopping just inside the shadows. I couldn't hold back the tears for one more second. They made my vision waver and stung my cold cheeks. I sobbed until I was coughing on salt and tears and fear.

Nicholas had to be all right.

He just had to be.

The bark of the tree pulled my hair, keeping me anchored. I wanted to scream and kick and give myself over to the panic, but I had to be strong. Didn't I have to be strong? I couldn't remember exactly why right now, but I tried to catch my breath anyway. I scrubbed my face.

I still had the makeshift weapon Kieran had given me. And even if Sebastian was right that they couldn't spare any guards, there was no reason I couldn't go right now, by myself. No one had to know. And it was better than sitting around. Anything was better than sitting around.

I fished a tissue out of my pocket, blew my nose, and skirted the lawns back to the parking lot to get my car. I'd be busted for driving out in the middle of the night for sure. I couldn't sneak out the Lemon Drop, which is what my Dad called my car. I could walk to the mountain, but it would take most of the night and most of tomorrow too, and the trails weren't exactly reliable. And I really only had a vague idea of where I was going. A red dot on a map. Which would already have been picked clean by vampires with a better sense of smell and excellent night vision.

My steps slowed as I realized how futile my big gesture really was. It was enough to make me want to cry again.

"Busted," Hunter said quietly. I looked up, blinking back more tears. All this crying was annoying. And it froze to my eyelashes.

"What are you doing here?" I asked.

She was leaning against the front door of my car in her plaid flannel pajama bottoms and three layers of thick sweaters. The tip of her nose was already red. "Are you kidding?" she asked. "You might have fooled the parentals by giving in, but you just put the rest of us on high alert. Kieran called me right after he dropped you off."

"I was pretty much talking myself out of it," I conceded. "I don't even know where to start looking."

She slung an arm around my shoulder, hugging me. "I'm so sorry, Lucy. But we'll go out with you tomorrow. And Kieran's pretty sure Eric and Connoly will help. Connoly thinks you're cute, so he's definitely in."

"We barely know where to start," I said, shivering when the wind snaked between the rows of cars.

"We'll know more tomorrow," Hunter said comfortingly, steering me back to the dorms. "I called Quinn. He sounds about as good as you look. But between the Drakes and Bruno's guys, there'll be people searching twenty-four seven."

"That's true." I felt infinitesimally better.

◆

I woke up at dawn, confused and nauseated. I lifted my head groggily. The pretty pink light filtering through my window was a personal insult.

As the light grew stronger, Nicholas grew weaker.

Wherever he was now, he was in even more trouble.

I checked my phone again, but there were no updates. My eyes felt hollow with fatigue, but I was itching inside my skin. I pulled on another sweater and a scarf and went up the back stairs to the dormitory roof. It was ringed with an old-fashioned and ornate wrought-iron fence, snow gathering in the corners. The wind was vicious. I could see where the forest gave way to the mountains in the distance, under the wispy glow of the moon, fading into the pink sky.

Mom always told me that when you don't know what else to do, you go outside. She said the sky and the sun and the trees were healing. That the stars and the rocks could shelter you, the moon could protect you. And that chanting and burning incense and praying could help you when nothing else could.

I wasn't in a chanting sort of mood.

I did tilt my head back for a moment to let the light touch my face. The clouds seemed tattered and moth-eaten, trailing snow and fitful moonlight. I begged that moon to keep Nicholas safe.

But moonlight wasn't enough.

The cold wind wasn't enough, the ice on the fence and the snow weren't enough, and the rising sun especially was not enough.

Because when the snow turned to rain, I wanted to scream. Rain would wash away his scent and his tracks. I suddenly felt so sharp and dangerous, you could have used me as a rapier. I was filled with so much rage I practically glowed. The rage helped to smother the sickening fear and the cold iron weight of sorrow that might drag me under and keep me there. I couldn't give up. I *wouldn't* give up.

Nicholas was strong. The Drakes were great hunters and even better fighters. Helena would burn the forest down if she had to. I had to believe he was okay and that he would come home, even if I had to force my will on the entire cosmic order. Mom said that people created their own reality. If you believed in something deeply enough and sent it enough energy, you could make it happen. She was full of stories of miraculous cancer cures and dreams that warned people off planes that fell from the sky. Isabeau might have said the same thing, calling it magic.

I just knew I couldn't contain this pain inside me.

So I'd use it as a weapon.

I screamed so long and loud, the pigeons on the roof flapped away hysterically.

I screamed until my voice was hoarse, my throat was raw, and my face felt red enough to explode. I screamed until two teachers I didn't know burst onto the roof, armed with stakes. One of them tried to hold me up, but I collapsed to my knees. I was still sobbing and crying and screaming when Theo pushed his way through. He crouched down in front of me, his voice sharp and practical.

"Lucy. Lucy, stop it." He shook me once. "I'll sedate you if you don't stop and breathe."

I gagged on a sob and dragged my sleeve across my face. My lips felt cracked and I tasted blood. Salt crusted my eyelids, making them feel sticky and unwieldy. Theo took my pulse while I tried to swallow. "I'm thirsty," I added.

"You think?" he shot back, but not unkindly. He checked my pupils. "You okay now?"

I nodded. "Sorry."

"You need water and rest." He helped me to my feet. I felt weak, as if I'd just had a bad flu. "And a visit to the school counselor tomorrow."

A few students hovered near the doorway. Mr. York ushered them back inside.

"Oh, great," I muttered. "Cue the rumors that the new girl is a headcase . . . now."

Theo half smiled, then glanced at the other teachers. "She's fine."

I pushed my hair off my face. I'd never freaked out like that before. It was *not* fun. And it didn't help. Nicholas wasn't any less lost.

I shivered, suddenly freezing.

"Come on," Theo said. "Let's get you to your room."

CHAPTER 24

Solange

Tuesday night, after sunset

I woke up confused.

I knew the sun had set, knew I was so thirsty I was seeing red, but I couldn't remember where I was. I wasn't in the family safe house. I couldn't hear my brothers rummaging around the adjoining rooms, or my mom avoiding the guards until she'd had her morning blood. The room I was in was smaller, cramped, with water running down the cement ceiling and down a drain in the floor. There was a shelf with lit candles set in one corner and a narrow army cot under me. That was it.

And then I smelled her.

Human, warm, willing.

The hunger actually growled inside me. I wasn't sure how the rest of my family felt it, but sometimes I felt it like thirst in the throat, sometimes like hunger in the belly. And when it was this pronounced, it was always painful; as if I were desiccated and crumbling, as if blue sparks arced from my every movement. Only one thing made it better: blood. And live blood, despite my family's objections, worked faster and better. And it was impossible to resist when presented so agreeably just after sunset.

"Please, princess."

It was Penelope again, kneeling by the side of my bed, extending her bare arms. Constantine stood in the shadows behind her. I wanted to ask him what was going on, but her wrist was right there, blue veins pulsing, and the hunger took over. I bit down, warm blood filling my mouth, flooding me with vitality. I drank greedily, pinning Penelope's wrist to my mouth. The more I drank, the less my gums ached, the less I itched under my skin like it fit wrong, the less weak and confused I felt. Penelope's head fell back, her long curly hair trailing the dirty ground. I drank until she started to sag and I started to come back into myself enough to know to stop.

Constantine stepped forward at the exact moment when I wondered how to make myself push her away. He eased Penelope's wrist out of my grip and helped her to her feet, pressing a scrap of clean cloth to the little puncture wounds. "Go on, Penelope," he said gently, nudging her out. "Someone's waiting upstairs with food for you, and iron pills."

"Thank you, princess." She wandered away, smiling as if she were drunk. I felt the same way, only I wasn't smiling.

I scrambled to my feet. "Why did you bring her here?"

"You need blood," Constantine replied calmly. "She's willing to provide it. What's the problem here, love?" He pushed a lock of hair off my cheek.

"Live blood just makes me . . ." I shuddered, trying to sort through all the feelings ripping through me. Satisfaction, strength, lust. I took a step back, struggling to control myself. Constantine closed the distance between us. His violet eyes gleamed.

"You don't have to be scared," he said softly. "It's natural."

I swallowed the coppery taste of blood on my tongue. "I . . ."

"Don't make yourself smaller for other people," he added. "Be brave, Solange. Give in."

And then he was kissing me.

It happened so quickly. He just pulled me into his chest, his hand digging into my hair and tilting my head back. His lips were clever, teasing and slow as a hot, humid summer day. His tongue stroked mine, retreated. I fell into him. The combination of a newborn's hunger, fresh blood, and his mouth on mine made my head spin. I had to clutch his arms to stay upright. He crowded me back against the damp wall, pinning me in place.

The kiss was languid and dark. He coaxed and took and smiled against my mouth when I made a small sound I didn't understand. I kissed him back, hungrily. His lips were cool, like ice cream, but I'd never wanted ice cream this much, even when I was human. I could have gorged myself on him, cavities and ice-cream headaches be damned. And he knew it. That smug confidence should have been off-putting, but it just added to the dangerous appeal of him.

But as the last of the blood coursed through me, everything came flooding back.

Nicholas.

I pushed away from Constantine, my lips still tingling. His hair was tousled from my fingertips.

"My brother," I said hoarsely.

He passed a hand over his face, as if he also needed to compose himself. The seductive smile—the crooked tilt to his grin that made me feel as if I were on fire—was gone. "I checked. No word yet."

I pushed past him, darting up the metal steps and through the open gate. The forest glittered and gleamed as if carved from diamonds and obsidian. The snow had melted and more rain had fallen during the day. As night fell and the temperature dropped, ice formed on every surface. It dripped from branches, shone between flat cedar needles like lace, and crunched underfoot. Even the tiny veins on fallen oak leaves were traced with frost. I picked my way delicately through it, afraid to make a single sound and crack the frozen world into pieces.

The Bower was even more beautiful. It was strung with crystal beads of ice and draped with shawls of frost. Candles burned, melting little pools of water under the lanterns which reflected the flickering light. Someone had built a fire in an iron cauldron, and it snapped cheerfully. I wanted to sit in a velvet chair and soak it all in.

I turned my back on the winter fairy-tale beauty. "I need to hunt for Nicholas."

"Of course you do," Constantine agreed. "I'll come with you."

"You will?"

He half smiled. "I know the Drakes are ferocious and all, love, but I've been doing this longer than you have."

I nodded, feeling grateful and slightly embarrassed for kissing him. And a little guilty. Kieran and I had broken up, but I still loved him, and he'd been there for me when I needed him. I hadn't cheated on him, but I still felt awkward, as if he could see me. I pushed it out of my head. No time for that.

Time only to find Nicholas.

There were search outposts set up between the encampment and the Bower, as well as where Nicholas had activated his GPS tag. I checked in with them and kept the family channel open on the new walkie-talkie I'd been given after I accidentally broke the last one by whipping it at that tree. There were maps with color-coded pushpins to keep track of the search pattern.

I had so many guards trailing me, both from my parents and the Bower, that when Constantine ignored me to concentrate on hunting, it felt just as good as his kisses. I stayed away from my family. It just seemed easier.

They'd narrowed down Nicholas's whereabouts to the mountain, the only other possibility being that he'd been taken up through the trees and the scent had dispersed already. I couldn't bear to think about that. Anyway, I couldn't search outside of the woods, not with my triple fangs and flared eyes, like red ink in water. Bruno and his detail would take the roads and the town, and so would Lucy and her friends. I'd concentrate on the caves with some of the others.

It seemed simple on paper: find the cave where Nicholas had

been taken. But there were hundreds of caves and hundreds of dead ends. Not only did we need to search each one, we needed to map and chronicle our search so we didn't double back and waste precious time.

But even with our large family and allies, time was running out.

We didn't even know if he'd survived the last day. He could be trapped out in full sunlight for all we knew. I couldn't stand it. He wasn't just my brother, he was my friend.

That voice whispered inside me again, like water closing over my head. *I can help you. Let me out.*

I pushed it aside.

We hunted for hours, following half trails and suggestions of scent. Half the time it led to another one of my brothers, not Nicholas.

And then we heard it.

A hoarse scream echoing from somewhere inside the mountain.

CHAPTER 25

Lucy

Friday, late afternoon

We still hadn't seen or heard from Nicholas.

Helena refused to sit at any council table until her son was found. Once the ceremonies began, Liam, being a better negotiator than tracker, would sit in for her. They needed to maintain the illusion of control over the tribes, or the ensuing feuds and fights would make finding Nicholas even more difficult. Vampire wars could decimate the countryside and would definitely obliterate any clues. All the brothers hunted too. Solange went out on her own and though we hadn't spoken since we'd fought in the Bower, we sent texts. One from me at night and one from her at sunrise: *nothing yet.* Christabel tried to help too, even though she was still a city girl and didn't know a dogwood from a poison sumac, let alone how to read footprints and broken twigs. The rain had washed away most of the vital evidence.

Kieran was helping, and so were Hunter and I when we managed to sneak off campus. It wasn't easy for me right now; all the teachers were keeping an extra concerned eye on me, and my parents alternated days for visits. Mom used one of the pendulums she sold at the shop, but it only pointed to the mountains, and they were huge. Even Tyson was worried and kept trying to lend me schoolbooks. Sarita didn't say much, but she still ratted me out when I tried to sneak out at night. And after my screaming episode, there were rumors circulating about a werewolf on the roof. Also, that I was crazy. I went to see the school counselor in the morning, who assured me I wasn't crazy, that countless hunters before me had struggled through loss and anger over senseless tragedies.

But I could see crazy from where I was standing. I barely ate, mostly surviving on protein shakes Hunter shoved at me every time she saw me. I spent all the daylight hours not in class driving around Violet Hill and the countryside around it, listening to a mixed CD Nicholas had given me. When I couldn't see through the tears, I switched it off and kept driving.

I was determined to find him, or at the very least, clues to where he was. I found a rusted-out school bus, seven abandoned shoes, a full sixteenth-century embroidered dress with a hole in the corset over the heart, and a homeless man who threw a can at my head when I tried to give him spare change. I spent every penny of my allowance on gas for the car, and then I begged my parents for more money.

All for nothing.

I shoved the map I'd been poring over off my lap and got to my feet, too restless to sit still. The sun was setting on the other side of the window, glistening on the last of the ice. I could see Jenna running the track again, her breath puffing white over her head. A class in the backfield practiced with their crossbows. Only the older students were allowed to practice with them at night. I was safe in my warm room, sitting on my Jack Sparrow blanket. I was safe and warm and Nicholas wasn't.

Abruptly I couldn't stand it anymore and stalked to the door.

"Where are you going?" Sarita asked, glancing up from her homework.

"Out."

"Where?"

I sighed, turning back. "Why?"

"Because it's dark now and you're not allowed off campus. Headmistress Bellwood was very clear on that when she talked to me."

I gritted my teeth. "I'm not going off campus."

"Oh." She bit her lip, looking unconvinced. "Are you sure?"

I just left, slamming the door behind me. It wasn't her fault she was stuck with a crazy roommate, but if I had to explain myself to one more person I'd punch someone. I went back up to the roof where I could be alone to watch the last of the sunset. It was my new ritual, to stand and witness the lavender and indigo light sink between the trees, to see the stars brighten, the mountains darken. And hope and pray with all my might that Nicholas was safe out there. Somehow, if I was there watching over the light fading, I could protect him.

And freeze my ass off.

I tucked my chin into my scarf just as the door to the rooftop squeaked open. I refused to look away from the woods. Sarita or Hunter or whoever it was would just have to wait.

"Hi, sweetie." Mom's arm came around my shoulder. She leaned down to kiss my temple.

"You're on duty today?" I asked. Dad had come yesterday, sneaking me real ice cream and a bag of candy.

"You're never a duty, Lucky Moon." It was finally dark enough that the lights flicked on and I let her turn me around. She scrutinized me. "How are you today?"

"I'm okay," I assured her, smiling wanly. "Really."

"We miss him too, honey."

"I know."

She hugged me, smelling like Nag Champa. It was comforting, making me think of simple things like drinking tea in the kitchen and family movie nights. "I know he's okay," she said. "You'd feel it, if he wasn't." She sounded so sure of it that I nodded, wanting to believe that too. "Why don't you come home?" she asked again.

I shook my head. "It's better to be busy. And I'm busy here."

We stood there, just watching the stars and the moon, Mom singing one of her favorite chants softly. She pressed another bag of art supplies into my hand before leaving. Between her and the counselor, I was going to have to take up art therapy as my new major.

I stayed up on the roof for a little longer, letting the cold air clear my head and sparkle through me. A strange flash of light from the woods on the edge of the field had me squinting. Just when I wondered if I'd imagined it (great, hallucinations now), it flashed again. It bobbed erratically, like the reflection off a mirror. My cell phone vibrated in my pocket.

"Hello?"

It was Logan. "Meet me in the woods."

"Is that weird light you?"

"Yeah, it's a mirror. I don't want some student screaming 'vampire,' so get down here quick and don't get seen. We'll be past the willows."

I would have scaled down the outside of the building if I'd thought it would get me there any faster. I rushed down the stairs and burst outside, my heart in my mouth. I had to force myself to slow down so no one would notice me. I skirted around the far edge of the crossbow field and ducked down into the undergrowth, not straightening until I was well hidden in the trees.

I took the path Hunter and I usually used, crossed a narrow half-frozen creek with the help of my staff and turned left at the willow trees. Logan waited there in his favorite velvet frock coat, next to Isabeau and her wolfhound Charlemagne.

"Any news?" I asked, hugging him as hard as I could.

He hugged me back, shaking his head. "Not yet. But we have an idea."

I eased back, smiling at Isabeau and scratching Charlemagne's head when he shoved it under my hand. "Okay. What is it?"

Logan looked exhausted, but over the layer of grief there was a spark of something else. "Isabeau found a spell."

I blinked at them both. "I'm in."

"Do you not want to know what the spell is?" Isabeau asked.

"Don't care. I'm in."

She smiled briefly. "Logan said you would say this. Come with me."

We crossed between more willows and into a grove of spruce trees so thick and twisted you couldn't see into the center. Isabeau pushed through, holding back the branches for Charlemagne and me. Logan was behind us, casting a last probing glance before letting the evergreen snap together like a locked door. It smelled like Christmas and winter.

A single candle burned in a bowl of water in the center of a very cramped, uneven circle. Around the candle there was a pouch made of red flannel stitched with runes, a rattle made from a painted dog bone, and a scatter of crystals. It looked like the tables my mother set up around the house for holidays where she burned incense and left offerings of milk. It might have freaked some people out, but I was instantly comfortable. The ground was bumpy with tree roots when I sat down, crossing my legs.

"So what's the deal?" I asked as Charlemagne wedged himself between me and peeling trunk and rested his head on my knee.

"There is a spell that might help us to locate Nicholas," Isabeau explained, the candle light glinting off the chain mail on her dress and the pendants around her tattooed and scarred throat. With her long dark hair and green eyes, she was pretty as a doll. You know, the kind of doll that came to life at night to kill monsters. "Kala is stronger, you understand, but she will not leave the caves, and humans are not welcome."

"And Isabeau thinks we need you for this," Logan added quietly. "Your connection to Nicholas could make the difference." He pulled a shirt out of a bag and handed it to me. "You need to wear this."

I shrugged out of my coat and pulled the black T-shirt over my head. It smelled like Nicholas, like black licorice and sandalwood. I hugged myself, forcing the lump in my throat to dissolve. "What else?"

"Isabeau is going to dreamwalk," Logan answered. "Kind of like astral traveling."

"Right."

"You know what this is?" She sounded surprised.

"You've never met my mother." Logan and I smirked at each other. My mother made power bundles of sacred objects for each of the Drake brothers on their sixteenth birthdays, to help them through the bloodchange. And she danced naked under the full moon in our backyard all the time. A little astral travel was nothing.

Isabeau nodded once, impressed. "*Bien*. This will make it easier." She jabbed more painted bones in the ground in a circle around us. One of them was wrapped in copper wire. She passed me an amulet made of garnet beads and tarnished silver. I slipped it over my head.

"Ready?"

I wiped my palms on my jeans, feeling a nervous giggle well into my throat. I was finally *doing* something. Something useful. I felt the jaws of panic which had been clamped around my throat for days release, just a little. I could breathe again.

"I'm ready."

"I will take you," Isabeau said. "All you have to do is relax and follow me."

"It's a little disconcerting," Logan warned me. "Hell, when it happened to me the first time, I thought someone had slipped me drugs."

I nodded. "I can do this." I took a deep breath and muttered Mom's mantra. Logan sat where he was, a sword balanced across his knees. He stayed focused, guarding us.

At first nothing happened. I took deep breaths, as my butt got numb from the cold ground. I breathed some more. And then it was like the pendant Isabeau gave me started to heat up, slowly, then like an ember cradled over my belly button.

"Open your eyes," Isabeau murmured. "Lucy."

"I don't feel any different. I don't think it worked." I opened my eyes, disappointed. "Whoa."

Isabeau was standing in front of me, and yet I could see right through her to where her body was still sitting among the tree roots. Charlemagne sniffed me, then put his chin on his paws. The edges of the branches and the dog bones glittered. Logan's sword was so bright it was hard to look at. The world had been bleached to bone and then certain areas painted with carnival colors. Even I was glowing faintly.

"Why am I pink?" I held up my hand, looked right through it. It made me feel really weird. "I look like bubble gum."

"It's your aura," Isabeau replied.

"My aura's cotton-candy pink? Dude. That's embarrassing."

"Come, we haven't much time."

I stood up, feeling all floaty and lightheaded. My boots hovered just above the ground. I could feel the wind, but not the cold bite of it through my clothes. And the hot pulse of the amulet burned, shooting sparks.

"Um, is it supposed to do that?"

"Think of Nicholas. Think of him as hard as you can."

I hadn't done much else in days so that part was easy. I imagined his tousled dark hair, his serious smile, and the way he looked at me just before he was going to kiss me. I saw his favorite black tie, the photo of us on his desk, the winter-storm gray of his eyes. I visualized him so intensely, so completely, that the sparks whirling off the amulet like a Catherine Wheel stuck together. They clung to each other until they'd formed an outline, his outline. His shoulders, his tall lean body, the gleam of his fangs.

I reached out a trembling hand to touch him because I couldn't help myself. My fingertips dragged through the sparks, and they came apart like fireflies. I snatched my fingers back, but he was already gone. The tiny floating lights shot away from us, between the boughs.

"*Viens.*"

Isabeau grabbed my hand and dragged me out of the tiny grove. We half ran, half flew through the forest, following the trajectory of the streaking lights. They took us over a swamp, around massive red oaks, through a herd of sleeping deer. A buck lifted his head, antlers pale as butter.

The sparks turned red, like embers. They swirled in a whirlwind, hovering over a flock of bats. Beneath them, Solange and Constantine sniffed the air and searched the undergrowth for prints. Isabeau shot me a curious look.

"Nicholas!" I ordered the sparks, hearing the deep velvet of his voice, his dry laugh, the sweet way he had of saying my name when we said good night. A few of the sparks stayed where they were, the rest continued to fly between the trees. They led us to the mountains, which wasn't surprising. They fell apart drifting through the stone. Caves glowed briefly, as if candles had been lit inside.

"What does it mean?" I asked Isabeau frantically. "Where is he?"

"In a cave."

"Which one?"

She looked sad, annoyed. "I don't know."

A few trailing sparks found one another, like static. They flared brightly once, burning Nicholas's face into my eyes. I blinked, the afterimage of him blinking back at me. When they faded, the light had a blue tint, smearing everything with indigo and turquoise and lavender. I blinked. She swore in French. "We must go. Your body is pulling you back."

"No! Not yet!"

She grabbed my hand again. "Now, Lucy."

"No!" I struggled. She just spun me around and yanked on the chain of the amulet. It came away in her hand, and I felt myself being sucked back, the trees blurring in the wrong direction, colors smearing into a hundred shades of blue.

I landed in my body, as if I were cliff diving. I gasped loudly, then pushed up, groaning. "Ouch." The tip of my nose and my cheeks were numb. My left foot was asleep.

Isabeau sat up, smiling triumphantly. I scowled. "Why are you smiling? We didn't find him!"

"No, but did you see the way sparks flashed briefly into his silhouette? At the end, by the caves?"

"Yeah. So?"

"So," she explained. "Now we know he's alive."

Logan and I both stared at her for a long moment, afraid to believe her.

"He's alive?" I asked in a small voice. "You're sure?"

She nodded, touched Logan's hand. "I'm sure."

Relief made me giggle through the tears, and if it had a slightly hysteric tinge, no one commented on it. Logan was too busy grinning just as idiotically.

Isabeau just looked at us, calmly, as if we were nuts.

CHAPTER 26

Solange

Saturday night, 8:00 p.m.

I paced the Bower, wanting to hiss at everyone and everything. We still hadn't found Nicholas. I was still fighting with my family. I was still fighting with myself, conscious of red-soaked needs I couldn't articulate.

The others lounged about, drinking from glass bottles and arguing over politics. I didn't care about politics. But I was beginning to wonder if it was the only way to get things done.

Constantine motioned Penelope and two guys out of the shadows around the outdoor salon. They came willingly, as always. My fangs poked into my lips.

Spencer, who'd been sprawled on a couch, sat up frowning. "Bloodslaves?" he asked.

I just shrugged and looked away.

"Not cool," he added. He shook his head before he left the clearing.

Marigold reached for a lollipop then followed, tossing me a careless smile. "Sorry, princess, but he's cuter."

I just sighed. I felt too big for my body, like it was too crowded inside my head. I wanted blood. I wanted to be left alone. I wanted to march into the Blood Moon camp and demand they all go out and search for my brother.

I can help you do that. I can help you find your brother. But you have to help me first.

I paused, bats dipping out of the treetops.

Nicholas had risked his life again and again for me. I'd damned well do the same for him. Even if I had to take down the entire Chandramaa and Blood Moon encampment to do it.

But there was only one way to do that.

Despite our differences, I felt sure my mother would agree. That made it a little easier.

A little, but not much.

Constantine must have seen something in my expression because he stepped closer. "What is it?"

"Vampires have been going missing. My brother's missing. Only another vampire could do that, in this place, under our noses, right?"

"Probably. Or at least someone working with one."

"So, in all likelihood, that same vampire, or vampires, are at the Blood Moon camp right now. They know what's happened to Nicholas. And they're getting away with it."

Constantine smiled slowly and bent to drag his mouth along my neck. I shivered. "What do you propose, princess?"

"A coup." Something in me stirred, like embers busting into flames. I felt hot all over, burning from the inside. The soft female voice purred like a cat. *Yes. When we are queen everything will be better. I promise this.*

Constantine laughed, softly, darkly. "Finally."

"No one gets hurt."

"I can't promise that." He said it gently, but his violet eyes gleamed fiercely.

Your family is weak. They only bring you down, want to make you submit and kneel. We're better than that.

"*My family* doesn't get hurt," I amended.

"That seems perfectly reasonable," he agreed. "When?"

"Now." Before I talked myself out of it. Before word got out. Before Nicholas ran out of time entirely. "It's the first night of the ceremonies. We go in fast."

"Then you'll need blood," Constantine said.

Yes, more blood.

Who are you? I asked.

Viola.

What are you?

Your friend.

Constantine snapped his fingers and Penelope tripped over herself to get to us. She was looking a little pale. I should drink from somebody else. But I couldn't worry about that right now. She pushed her sleeves up. I drank as Constantine went to talk to his

men, still lurking protectively around the Bower. Nerves and antici-
pation danced in my belly. Once the live blood hit my system, I felt
like I could take on the world.

Let me out.

Constantine waited with the others. Elijah elected to stay
behind. Everyone else was with us. It was a little daunting. Or would
have been, if I weren't intoxicated on blood. Right now it felt like
a game, and, at the same time, as if I were fulfilling some higher
purpose. It was heady, invigorating. Terrifying.

Constantine's guards had a lot of weapons.

And a map of the encampment.

"You knew this would happen," I said, strapping on extra stakes
and daggers.

"I prepared for the possibility," he said. "The prophecy says you
will be queen. And so you shall."

"When dragon fights dragon," I quoted softly to myself
again.

"What's that?"

"Nothing. Never mind."

Constantine pointed to an area of the map. "This is the only
field large enough for the crowning ceremony. Your mother gets
officially recognized as queen tonight." He looked up at the moon
and the length of the shadows it cast on the newly snow-dusted
ground. "Within the hour. We have to hurry."

"Bruno will be with them. The rest of his crew will be out
searching for Nicholas. There'll only be a couple left to guard the
Bower." I let my pheromones waft like perfume, imagined the heat

waves of lily-scented compulsion reaching everyone. "No one gets staked. Drakes are off-limits. Understand?"

They nodded mechanically. Constantine just tilted his head. "That's not necessary, love."

"It is to me. The bats should keep us covered from Chandramaa fire." Penelope's blood danced inside me. I felt feverish, strong, confident. "Let's go."

Let me out.

We marched out, trailing bats like Aunt Hyacinth's mourning veils. Bruno's men dropped the minute I got close enough to compel them. They didn't stir, even as we filed past them. I didn't even glance at them, just focused on what had to be done next.

The bats thickened around us as we crossed into Blood Moon territory. Arrows bit into the ground around us. A bat squeaked, pinned to an oak tree. A dagger hit one of the motorcycles outside Duncan's garage tent, clanging. A warning whistle ululated over the treetops. It was too late for that. I was prepared for this sort of plan and attack. Ironically, prepared by my own family on the best way to take them out.

I could hear drums and smell smoke and blood. Someone cheered. The tents were mostly deserted, except for the odd blood-slave who watched us with wide, fearful eyes. A dog barked. A vampire went flying into a pole when she tried to stop the first of the Bower guards. Her gold-embroidered sari caught the light. Three muscular Joiik men with long blond hair cut us off and were taken down. A vampire wearing the Chandramaa crest got through three of our numbers, reaching me. He wasn't real Chandramaa, since he let us see his face. And his eyes.

Big mistake.

I stopped, smiled. Pheromones flung from me like daggers. He paused, confused. I kicked him between the legs and he collapsed, wheezing. I stepped over him, Constantine offering me his hand like an old-fashioned gentleman helping a lady across a muddy street.

The field was ringed with torches and various tribes. Isabeau stood with Kala and the other Hounds. Their dogs growled and snarled at us. Lucy's cousin Christabel stood with Saga and Aidan, looking nervous. Saga held a *Hel-Blar* on a chain, wearing a copper collar and clacking his jaws.

In the center there was a small mound, where my family stood. My brothers looked impatient. Even London was there, bandaged and wan. Madame Veronique looked haughty and cold, as always. She was the first of the Drakes to see me. She was part of this some-how and I didn't trust her. Not anymore. Neither did Viola; I could tell by the frigid dip in her voice.

Let me out.

Murmurs preceded us, like wind on water. I could barely hear it over the rush of blood in my ears, the sound of self-satisfied laugh-ter in my head. I shook my head, willing it away. The bats lifted, leaving us vulnerable for a moment, then lowered again.

The drums stopped.

"Solange?" My mother stepped forward; the pearls-and garnet-encrusted crown dangled from her fingers. My brothers reached for their weapons. It made me sick to see it, but I couldn't turn back now. Vampires moved out of our way as we approached. Bats and sword points made them step even farther back.

"Oh, crap," Connor muttered. "She's going Darth Vader on us."

I climbed up onto the mound. Madame Veronique came at me, but with a flick of my wrist, bats attacked her, tangling in her hair, going for her eyes. Aunt Hyacinth twitched her veils closer to her face.

"Someone here knows where Nicholas is," I said coldly. "It's the only explanation."

"You don't think we know that?" Duncan snapped. Blood Moon ceremony or not, he was still wearing jeans. "That we don't have a plan?"

He thinks you're a useless little girl. He has no idea what you can do. What we can do.

I pressed one hand to my ear. The voice was stronger now, nearly corporeal. My arm dropped. I wasn't even sure if I was in control of my movements. Or my voice. "It's time I used all this power inside me. Time I stopped fighting this prophecy and finally used it to my advantage."

Mom didn't look away from me. She lifted the crown. "I would never fight you for something like this," she said. "You're my daughter."

"Mom," I said, voice strangled. Why couldn't they see that this wasn't me? That I was trying to stop myself, trying to save them.

Sebastian reached for his sword.

He would betray you, cut you down even though you are his sister. Traitor!

She wanted him dead, wanted his ashes in the dirt under my boots. Our boots. It was too confusing. The bats descended on Sebastian. His hands bled in rivulets when he covered his face, until Quinn threw one of the decorative shields at me to stop me. I wished he'd hit me with it. But I ducked, or Viola did.

"Don't," I begged, but to whom, I wasn't sure. "Beware the royal daughter . . ."

They have to pay. Let me out, Solange. Let me out!

I exuded pheromones as hard as I could. "Kneel." I gagged on the word, tried to clamp my lips shut together. *No, Viola, please no.*

My family members all knelt, struggling fruitlessly. Bats dipped and whipped over the heads of the other vampires, forcing them down on their knees as well. Constantine was the only one who remained standing, at my side, the air currents from so many bat wings whipping his hair about. My own lifted like silky black snakes, hovered.

"I'm sorry," I said.

I snatched the crown out of Mom's hands.

The moment it touched my head, my hair lifted higher, the bats screamed, and a wall of power exploded out of me, knocking everyone flat.

CHAPTER 27

Lucy

Saturday night, 9:30 p.m.

"Don't be a wuss, Lucy."

"Hello to you too," I said as I picked my way through the prickly remains of a cornfield at the edge of Megan's family farm because I'd promised Nathan I'd show my face at Megan's party. I was wearing one of Logan's old frock coats that he'd outgrown, over a white slip dress with lace at the hem and jeans. Cows mooed grumpily from the comfort of the barn. A light dusting of snow covered everything from the iron weathervane to the dead chrysanthemum on the border of a pumpkin patch. Jenna and Tyson were with me, moving with the stealth and grace you'd expect from a couple of young vampire hunters. Only they were here as fellow "art students" today. And Tyson was here under duress. I'd bribed him with an essay. I wasn't really in the mood for a party but it was the only way to get out from under adult scrutiny for a few hours. And it appeased my school counselor.

And it might give me a chance to do some scouting in the area.

My boots crunched loudly as I left the lawn for the scraggly woods. I hadn't been here in three years, but I knew there was a field on the other side. All I had to do was follow the flickering light of bonfires and the noise.

"Where are you?" Nathan asked. "You said you'd be here. I don't care if there's snow."

"I'm here, you lunatic."

"I don't believe you." He was pouting. Nathan didn't pout unless he meant it.

"I can hear MJ DJing again," I said to placate him. "She always plays the worst music no one can dance to."

"You *are* here!" Nathan exclaimed before he hung up on me.

Climbing over a sagging wire fence bristling with ice and rust, I could smell the wood smoke when the wind shifted. The bonfires crackled and snapped invitingly as my old classmates milled around them wearing thick scarves and mittens. It was way too cold for a backfield party, but since it was the last one of the year, no one complained. Until spring the parties would have to be in basements and living rooms, too close to adult supervision for any real fun.

Megan's parents had a profitable working farm; they weren't selling crystals and homemade pickles and plowing snow in the winter to make ends meet the way mine did. Mom talked about this farm all the time. Apparently Megan's grandmother grew the best squash. I hated squash. Regardless, Megan's parents let her have parties out here when they were out of town. Possibly, they didn't know about them.

"Try not to look like a cop," I told Jenna. She shook her shoulders and tried again. "Or a bodyguard."

She winced sheepishly. "I can't help it."

"Try looking scared to death like Tyson instead," I suggested. Tyson just swallowed, his Adam's apple bobbing frantically. I patted his shoulder. "You'd rather come face to fang with a *Hel-Blar*, wouldn't you?"

"Hell, yeah. Way less scary than girls," he muttered.

Jenna was trying not to look too curious. "And you want to take notes, don't you?" I shook my head. "You guys are in serious need of socialization."

"H-R is a small school," Jenna agreed. "And a small world."

I knew everyone, and it was easy to slip into the old rhythm. The only difference was that one of the school bullies, Peter, now went out of his way to avoid me. Christabel had kicked him in the balls for threatening Nathan. I was glad to see Peter avoided him too. Nathan, being far nicer than me, wouldn't take advantage of the situation.

"Hey, Lucy." Megan waved, tottering on a pair of boots with ridiculous heels. She wanted to be a big-city girl so badly she gave herself frostbite the year Crocs were in fashion. "Are you back?"

"Just visiting," I said, accepting the paper cup of apple cider she passed me. There was an iron cauldron full of the stuff boiling over one of the fires. There was beer and cheap wine too, but I pre-ferred something warm. Jenna and Tyson did the same. I knew they weren't comfortable enough to let their guards down, not this close to the forest at night. And especially not with a Blood Moon going on. "Great turnout. Have you seen Nathan?"

"The fire on the left there," she said, turning back to her gig-gling friends. I said hi to a few more people as I found my way to one of the smaller fires. The embers shimmered. Nathan sat on a bench, his feet practically inside the fire.

"You dyed your hair!" I exclaimed, plopping down next to him. The rickety bench wobbled. Usually his hair was bleached white, but now it was black enough to shine nearly blue in the firelight.

"You got contacts," he accused.

I scrunched up my nose. "Had to. Long story."

"Do you eat hamburgers now too?" he grumbled.

"Aw. You missed me," I grinned, tugging on the end of his red-and-white-striped scarf. It was way too long, brushing the ground when he sat down. I'd made it for him three years ago when my Mom taught me to crochet.

"Did not, traitor," he grumbled, but he slung his arm around my shoulder. "Where's your gorgeous boyfriend? He's the one I really wanted to see."

"He has a family thing," I told him, trying not to let my smile slip. Knowing Nicholas was alive wasn't the same thing as know-ing he was okay. "But these are my friends Jenna and Tyson."

"Hey." He gave Tyson a considering look then glanced at me. I gave a near imperceptible shake of my head. Nathan sighed.

"Bummer," he said under his breath. He nudged me. "You are useless to me, Hamilton."

"I know, sorry. There's this guy Jason, but I don't know him well enough to know if he's your type." Nathan liked to play at being casual, but he was actually a romantic at heart. I had no intention of setting him up with anyone who didn't deserve him, no matter how cute they were. When Nathan fell, he fell hard.

"This music really is awful," I said cheerfully. "We should fire her."

"Too dangerous," Nathan said. "MJ's a biter."

"And how exactly do you know that?"

"She bit me in grade six. I still have the scar."

"Do I even want to know why she bit you?"

"She claimed I stole her X-Men comic book." He sniffed. "When clearly, she stole it from me. She didn't even know who Gambit was."

"Oh well, I'm surprised you don't shun her even now." I was used to Connor geeking out over comics and sci-fi movies. "Let's run her out of town, Nathan."

"If she plays Celine Dion again, no one would blame us."

Jenna was chatting with the girl next to her, and Tyson looked as if he wanted to flee into the woods. The music was bad, the fires were cozy.

It was nice. Normal.

You know, until the screaming.

And that kind of scream in Violet Hill could mean only one thing.

Vampire.

The rest of the party assumed it was someone fooling around, an ordinary scream of a girl being scared by some drunk idiot jumping out of the shadows at a field party. But I knew better. I followed Jenna and Tyson, pulling my embroidered purse in front of me in case I needed easy access to a stake or a pepper-Hypnos egg. I pushed through the branches of a stand of slender birch trees, barely noticing when they slapped me in the face. I skidded to a halt in the frozen dirt and decomposing leaves. I didn't know the girls well because they were a year ahead of me, but I knew their names. Rachel was hyperventilating and weeping, her fist stuffed into her mouth.

Libby was sprawled in the undergrowth, blood on her neck.

Tyson knelt beside her, checking her pulse and lifting her eyelids to see if her pupils responded. Jenna was already sweeping the grove for vampires. I turned to Rachel, my hand still hovering near my purse, just in case.

"Did you see who did this?" I asked.

Rachel just continued to fall apart. "Rachel!" I grabbed her shoulders and tried to make my tone firm and strict, like an angry teacher. "Pay attention!" She just hiccuped pitifully and made me feel like a monster. But we couldn't help Libby without certain answers. "Rachel! Answer me!" I shook her.

She gagged on a sob but tried to answer. "I just saw a shadow running away." She choked. "Pale and . . ." She dissolved into tears again. "Libby's bleeding. Why is she bleeding?"

I sniffed the cold air, smelling snow and fire and old pine

needles but not mushrooms or rot. I didn't think it was *Hel-Blar* but best to be sure. "Did you smell anything . . . weird?"

She blinked, momentarily distracted by the strange question. "What, like pot?" She shrugged.

"No, I mean something . . . kind of rotten."

"No, nothing like that. Why?"

"Not *Hel-Blar*," I told Jenna quietly when she circled back to us.

"Thank God for that," she muttered as Tyson rose from his crouch with Libby in his arms.

He looked calm and utterly capable. There was no bumbling shyness about him when he looked down at two guys in his path. "Move." They scrambled to get out of his way.

"Where is he taking her?" Rachel shrieked, trying to grab at Tyson. "Wait!"

"He knows first aid," Jenna explained. "And he has a car. It'll be faster than waiting for an ambulance." Translation: she'd been bitten by a vampire and was unresponsive and we had no idea if she'd been infected or not. No hospital could help her now, not even in Violet Hill. She needed the Helios-Ra doctors.

I was about to follow Tyson and Jenna when I saw it.

It was a faint glint in the flattened grass and old leaves. I knelt down and grabbed it, easing back behind a tree. No one saw me. Well, no one but Jenna. She frowned at me, using her body to shield us from prying eyes.

"What did you find?"

I held up the medallion. It had the royal vampire crest on one side—a sword and bleeding crown—and the Drake insignia of a dragon with ivy in its mouth on the other side. "This is Solange's," I said bleakly.

"How do you know? Hunter's got one too. I heard everyone who was at the coronation got one."

"Yeah, me included. But this one has her name on it," I explained grimly, flicking it so it twirled. "The brothers got personalized ones too."

Jenna's eyes went so round she had to blink when they dried out.

I didn't for one second believe that Solange had snuck into a party for a snack. For one thing, if she had, she wouldn't have been stupid enough to leave behind such a damning piece of evidence. Even if she was going through a dark patch, she was still a Drake. She instinctively knew better than that, thanks to years of training.

But no one else would believe that. Not a Huntsman out for a kill or a Helios-Ra hunter claiming justice for the drained humans in town. They might just act first and look for proof later. We didn't know who was killing humans, who had attacked Libby or who was behind the vampire disappearances I'd heard about.

But I knew one thing, and I knew it for a fact.

Solange was being framed.

You'd think I'd have learned by now that field parties never end well.

I went crashing through the trees, across the fields and into the wide dark mouth of the forest that clamped its jaw around the mountain.

"Lucy!" Jenna called out. "What the hell?" She caught up to me, running easily. She spent enough time at the track that I wasn't surprised when she was just there at my side, keeping pace. Her red ponytail swung judgmentally. "Just what the hell are you doing?"

"I have to get to Solange," I answered, looping the silver chain of the medallion around my wrist. "She's being framed. She didn't attack that girl."

"And going off alone into a forest full of vampires will prove that?" she asked. "Did you take stupid pills this morning?"

"Just go with Tyson," I panted. "I'll meet you back at the dorms."

"You really did take stupid pills if you think I'm going to let you do this suicidal idiotic thing alone." She flipped her phone open and told Tyson to get Libby to the infirmary and we'd meet him there. "He was already on his way," she added to me after she'd hung up.

"Jenna, seriously, you don't have to do this. Kinda goes against training to help a vampire, right?"

"It goes against training even more to let a fellow hunter go off into a trap all by herself."

A fellow hunter. So not a compliment to me, even if she meant it as one. "It might not be safe. And you'll probably get suspended."

"Just run. You sound like a lame goose," she added conversationally.

"We're not all born with the workout disease like you and Hunter."

She just shrugged. "Do we even know where we're going?" she asked as we split paths around a huge tree and met up again on the other side.

"I have to find Solange. Or at least one of the Drakes, but they're all out of range. Worse comes to worst I can text Connor. He's the one most likely to sneak off to find a signal."

"We're not going to help anyone by getting lost and being eaten by a vampire. Or a bear."

"I'm not lost," I assured her, ducking under a low branch before I ran right into it. "I grew up in these woods. We'll be on Drake property in about fifteen minutes, if my heart doesn't explode, and after that someone's bound to find us even if we can't find them."

"Not terribly comforting actually."

After another ten minutes, my running turned into more of a jog. A stitch seared my side every time I tried to take a deep breath. I was wearing fuzzy boots with purple pom-poms. I made fun of Megan's footwear but mine were giving me blisters.

And then blisters and burning lungs were the least of my worries.

The first vampire dropped in front of me so abruptly I ran right into him. I didn't recognize him beyond knowing he wasn't a Blood Moon Guard. He wasn't wearing insignia of any kind. I knew this intimately since my nose had bounced off his jacket. I tripped on a root and fell back into the dirt, hard enough that it felt as if electrical shocks were shooting from my tailbone. My palms scraped down a boulder half-hidden under the mulch, breaking open the skin. Scrapes flared on my elbows.

The second vampire grabbed Jenna's ponytail. She yelped, jerking backward. I fumbled for a stake with my bloody hands. I threw it, but it went wide when the first vampire kicked my arm. The second backhanded Jenna hard enough that she flew into a tree and slumped to the ground, blood on her temple. She didn't move.

I opened my mouth to scream, but the vampire yanked me to my feet, fingers digging into the painful bruise already throbbing from his boot.

"Humans, not Moon Guard," he said to his companion.

"Constantine will still want to know. Bring them."

"Constantine?" I said. "I'm looking for Solange Drake."

"Sure you are, duckie. That's the problem."

"What? What's wrong? What do you mean?"

He shook me hard enough that my teeth rattled. "Shut it."

I stopped talking and went for another stake instead. Since I was dangling a few inches off the ground, there wasn't quite enough power behind my swing. The stake only went into the flesh deep enough to make him angry. Blood stained his jacket. His fangs flashed, lips lifting. I aimed for them with my elbows. There was a crack and he let go of me.

I didn't get far.

Jenna stirred briefly. I didn't think the others noticed. I ran to the right, knowing vampire instincts would have them following. I waited until Jenna's dazed eyes met mine, until I saw her hand reach inside her coat.

I dropped, sudden and hard as ship's anchor with a loose chain.

Jenna's stake flung past the spot where I'd been and embedded itself between the ribs of the vampire who'd hit her. The point pierced flesh and muscle and finally, heart. He crumbled to ash with a stunned cry. Horrified, his friend paused just long enough for me to scissor kick the back of his knee. He stumbled.

But it wasn't enough.

He was going to kill Jenna. I could see it in his face.

She'd lapsed back into unconsciousness and was defenseless. I scraped my scratched palm along the nearest tree, pressing hard enough that blood dripped down my wrist when I pulled my hand away. I flicked it at him and then shot to my feet, running as fast and as far from Jenna as I could.

He caught me in less than a minute. I kicked and punched but I couldn't get loose.

And then he cuffed me on the back of the head and everything went black.

CHAPTER 28

Solange

Saturday night, 10:00 p.m.

When I sat up again, I felt distant, small.

Powerless.

I tried to rip the crown off my head, but instead my fingertips caressed it greedily, lovingly. The pearls were soft and cool, the garnets bumpy.

What just happened? I felt my lips moving, felt the words come out, but when they left my mouth they changed. "I am now your queen."

It was my voice but not my words. Viola was somehow in control of my body. This couldn't be happening. I struggled, but it was like fighting spider webs and air. There was nothing to hold on to. I was floating, helpless.

Mom sat up first, eyeing me warily. Dad was next, glancing at the rest of his children, assessing damage. Sebastian wiped blood from his face. Blood seeped through London's bandages. Aunt Hyacinth's veils were knocked askew, showing the burn on her cheek. Uncle Geoffrey just blinked at me.

Help me!

But they didn't hear me. They just heard *her*.

They didn't see me. They saw *her*.

Even the bats drifted away.

I panicked, thrashing about inside my own head. I felt her annoyance. *Hush, little girl. You'll spoil it for me.*

Stop it! Leave them alone!

She sighed, as if I was bothering her. I wanted to stake her so badly my hand twitched. I felt her inner glare.

"We shall retire," she said. "You may see my family out. They are banned from the camp until I say otherwise." She smiled sweetly. "I don't want anyone to get hurt."

Constantine! Can you hear me?

But he was talking to the guards and didn't even glance my way. Their numbers had tripled now that I wore the crown. When Viola walked to the Drake tent, hundreds of eyes tracked our every movement, some impressed, some vengeful. Isabeau struggled to stop her dogs from attacking us. They snapped their teeth at me, spittle flying.

Inside the tent, Viola reclined my body into a chair. "I need blood." We were alone in the tent. Viola felt the tip of my fangs with her tongue. "Lovely. You never did use these properly."

Why are you doing this to me?

"Quiet. I have to think."

I don't know what she did, but it was like a heavy iron-studded oak door shutting in my face, separating us even farther. I could see what she did, hear her thoughts, but I couldn't voice my own. I was trapped in a stone tower. Panic was like rat's feet, soft and insidious.

Marigold and Spencer burst into the tent. "So it's true?" Marigold asked, dropping into a chair and swinging her feet. "Crossed over to the dark side, did you?"

"What?" Viola asked coldly.

Marigold grinned. "You became the man, Sol. You're a bleeding queen." She shook her head with mock pity. "And I had such high hopes for you."

"Yes," Viola replied mildly. "Didn't we all?"

"Camp's all abuzz," Marigold informed her cheerfully. "Your mam must be right pissed."

She had no idea.

I could only imagine what my family must be thinking. I was living it and I didn't know what to think. I guess I should be grateful I'd compelled so many guards not to hurt them, while I still could. I just wanted them to know I hadn't betrayed them. Wanted them to know I'd meant what I'd said about finding Nicholas. Where was Isabeau? Did she realize there was magic involved?

Marigold frowned. "Are you crying?"

Viola wiped her eye roughly. "*Stop it,*" she hissed at me quietly.

The tent door wavered, interrupting us by letting in more

torchlight and sounds of conversations. A guard I didn't recognize stalked in, dragging someone behind him.

Lucy.

There was blood on her clothes and bruises darkening her skin. The guard shook her roughly when she tried to bite him. He cuffed her and she stumbled, landing on the rug. She looked up, holding her split lip. She blinked at Viola.

"Are you wearing a *crown?*" she blurted out.

Viola glanced at her. "I'm queen, haven't you heard?"

"You're mental," Lucy said. "Solange! Seriously?"

Viola felt a flare of fury at being called names. She hated it even more that Lucy didn't cower. She didn't realize that Lucy never cowered, ever, and especially not to me, her best friend.

Her best friend. God, Viola could do anything to her. She could get right under Lucy's defenses.

I wondered briefly if I could stake myself on the sword lying across the arms of an empty chair.

I'll kill her before you reach the chair, Viola warned me.

I retreated, terrified at what might happen to Lucy. Lucy noticed Marigold and Spencer. She frowned at Spencer. "I know you."

"I don't think so," Spencer said.

"No, I know I recognize you from somewhere. A photo, maybe?"

While they talked, I tried to find a way around the door, tried to pick the metaphorical lock or use myself as a psychic battering ram.

Viola looked between the two of them, frowning. She arched an eyebrow at Marigold and Spencer. "Leave us."

"Well, listen to herself," Marigold muttered.

"Wait!" Lucy turned toward them but the guard knocked her back down before she could get up. "My friend *Jenna from school* is in the woods south of here, wounded."

Spencer paused, paled. And then he was out of the tent before Viola could even remark.

Lucy!

Lucy looked up, peering at me closely, as if something didn't make sense, as if she saw more than the others. Viola didn't like it. Rage bubbled inside her, but she smiled prettily at the guard. "Could you get rid of her?"

"Certainly."

Lucy pulled a long silver chain and medallion out of her pocket. "Solange, damn it, at least hear me out. Someone's trying to frame you for murder."

"On second thought." Viola rose with all the deadly grace of a predator. "Let me."

CHAPTER 29

Lucy

Saturday night, 10:30 p.m.

I didn't believe Solange attacked Libby, even when I found her medallion, but I also couldn't have imagined that she'd break from her family and set herself up as some kind of rebel queen. She hadn't been human for a few months, but I'd never thought of her as *inhuman* until now.

She looked weird.

She hauled me to my feet. I tried to fight her, but she was stronger. She dragged me through the camp. I'd wanted to see the Blood Moon up close, but certainly not like this.

"Solange, what the hell?" I snapped, trying to make myself as heavy as possible. My parents taught me to go limp if I was ever arrested in a protest. "Ow!"

"Walk or get thrown."

We passed rows of ornate tents, vampires talking, arguing, some even packing up to go home. Everyone's gaze was drawn to her, like a magnet. She preened.

"Where's your mom? The others?"

"Banned." I halted in shock, and she hauled me along roughly, impatiently. "I don't have time for this."

"You kicked them out?"

"I had to."

"You really are crazy."

"This way I can find Nicholas," she said smoothly. "Isn't that what you want?"

I stumbled along beside her, trying to find my best friend in the lithe, hard girl with the sickly sweet smile. She may as well have been a different person. No one stopped us as she took me past guards and rows of motorcycles, past more guards and over a stream. I couldn't keep up. I was panting, sweat burning into my eyes. When she stopped I felt a trickle of fear. She just smiled again, like a little girl.

"What are you going to do?" I asked, looking around frantically for a makeshift weapon.

"Get rid of yet another problem."

She was reaching for me when the voice speared between us.

"Get the hell away from her."

"Nicholas!" I was so happy to hear his rough, angry voice, I could have cried. "You're alive!" I wanted to throw myself at him, but Solange had me by the throat. I struggled even though I knew it was useless. Nicholas's eyes looked like a winter storm, all fog and black ice. He stalked toward us.

"Ah, the prodigal son returns."

"I mean it, Solange," he said, his jaw clenching. "Get off her. *Now*." He moved so fast I just saw a blur of pale skin and furious eyes, and then he was right in front of us. He was covered in blood and gashes, his shirt torn, ugly burns on the side of his neck. He reached for me.

Solange tightened her grip.

I would have squeaked but I had no breath left to make even the smallest sound.

Nicholas froze. It would be easy for her to snap my neck. I knew it, Solange knew it, Nicholas knew it.

Instead, she lowered her head and licked the blood trickling from the cut on my hairline.

"Solange, gross!" I flinched and tried to kick her since my legs were about the only thing I could move.

"She'll die if I so much as get a splinter," Solange warned him calmly, almost sadly. "I don't want to, Nicholas, so don't force my hand."

"Let her go," Nicholas ground out. "Solange, she's your best friend. More than that, she's like your sister."

She shifted so I was held up against a tree by the pale spear of her arm. "A lot's changed since you've been gone," she said. "I just need you to listen for a moment."

He jerked a hand through his muddy, dirty hair. I ached to touch him, to kiss him. He wouldn't even look at me. "I'm listening. Christ."

"I'm the queen now, Nicholas."

"Which explains why you're wearing a crown." He sounded

exhausted. His hands were trembling. When he finally looked at me, he could only stare at the blood on my forehead.

"I need to know that you're loyal to me."

"My loyalties?" he shot back. There was a stake in his hand and a kind of mad serenity in his expression. "Are you kidding? After everything that's happened? After what I just went through?"

"What *did* you go through?" I asked.

He still wouldn't look me in the eye. "I got away, that's what matters. They thought they broke me."

"I need to know," Solange insisted. "I need to be sure you're on my side."

"Then be sure."

"I'm not just a princess anymore."

"You're an assh—" I managed to hiss out before she pushed harder with her thumb, and my trachea threatened to explode. I struggled not to pass out as black spots danced at the edges of my vision, then faded. My eyes rolled back in my head.

And then Nicholas was all fangs and fury. He attacked so fast I had no warning, wasn't even sure my eyes could register motion that quickly.

But he still wasn't quicker than Solange.

"Stop!"

A stake bit into the tree beside me, so close that a splinter grazed my cheek. It was a small scratch barely noticeable, but it bled. And the coppery scent of blood made the battle all the more fierce, all the more vicious. I could barely make out what was going on, and couldn't jump in with a stake of my own since I might accidentally stake my own boyfriend. Or my best friend. And every time I moved, even an inch, Solange was there, shoving me back.

And then Nicholas brought his arm down with enough force to break her wrist. I heard the snap of the bones even as she released me so abruptly I choked and dropped to my knees. I hauled air into my bruised throat. My lungs felt as if they'd turned to paper.

Solange hissed in pain, cracking her wrist back into position. It might hurt but it wasn't enough to stop her. I was pushing to my knees and Nicholas was reaching for me when she struck again. She kicked Nicholas in the chest with her boot. He staggered just out of reach, for barely a moment. She yanked my arm behind my back, hard enough that I yelled.

"An eye for an eye," she said. "I'll snap her bones and call it justice."

Nicholas shrugged.

He *shrugged*.

I gaped at him.

"She's mine, broken or not," he said darkly.

I felt like throwing up.

Solange was silent for a long moment. My elbow was bending the wrong way, shooting pain up my arm like rusty iron nails. Her fingers were so tight around my wrist that there were bruises already forming. It hurt enough that tears burned my eyelids if I so much as breathed too deeply against her hold. Rocks and tree roots dug into my knees.

Then she smiled. "Yes, I can smell the darkness in you," she murmured.

"Can you?" His expression, his stance, the leashed violence in his smile; it was all wrong.

"Yes, and if you give into it, prove yourself to me, then you can come back to the camp. Lucy goes free."

I really wanted to poke her in the eye with a sharp stick. Better yet, right in the heart, the undead cow.

She raised an eyebrow at Nicholas. "She's your bloodslave, and yet I don't smell her blood on you."

Nicholas just folded his arms, as if the fight had never happened, as if this were all very normal, as if he weren't bruised and battered. As if it didn't hurt me just to look at him. "Yeah. So?"

Suddenly I didn't know who I wanted to poke more.

"So, I believe you'll drink her blood, right here and right now if you want to keep your claim on her. Otherwise, I'll think you're playing me, brother."

I went cold. "You're not serious." I tried to jerk away again, but it was no use. Every muscle in my arm screeched. I tried to catch Nicholas's eye, but he still wouldn't look at me. He stepped closer. "Nicholas, *don't.*"

When he finally looked at me, fear whispered through me, insidious and soft, making my bones watery.

We'd lost Solange. And now Nicholas wasn't acting like himself. Was he drugged on her pheromones? Had she compelled him? Where had he been all this time? What had happened to him? He'd just broken her bones to protect me, but now I had to wonder, for the first time, if it was vampire possessiveness playing out, not love. Nothing made sense anymore.

Nicholas had never drunk my blood before. He'd never had to. He was the one who was always worried about what it might mean. But it had never really bothered me. I wasn't lying when I told Jenna it was like donating at the blood bank.

But now I wasn't so sure.

No needle or antiseptic or plastic blood bag held such menace, such hunger.

Solange shoved my frock coat off my shoulder, revealing my slip dress, which was really meant to be a nightgown. It was sleeveless, and goosebumps marched from wrist to collarbone as the snow began to fall again. It caught in my eyelashes, making prisms of colors when I looked at Nicholas's pale skin, his gleaming fangs. I shivered, from cold or fear, I couldn't say. Likely both.

He lifted my arm gently to his mouth, and for a brief moment I thought he'd use the leverage of our position to somehow free me from Solange's grasp.

He didn't.

He just ran his lips over the vulnerable crook of my elbow, back and forth, soft as moth wings, until I felt every snowflake sizzle on my exposed skin, every tree root and acorn under my knees, even the smell of cedars as it tickled my nostrils. I was exposed, like a bare electrical wire. My teeth chattered.

Nicholas's eyes were like gray fog on the ocean, the kind that sinks ships and leads people off cliff sides. It wasn't pretty or magical; it was deadly.

But he was still Nicholas; he had to be.

He licked at the blood pebbling over the numerous scratches and scrapes I'd already sustained. His mouth was gentle, completely at odds with the burning angle of my shoulder and the smug sinister shadow of Solange falling over me. The snow was starting to stick, making the forest too soft and too bright.

When the bite of fangs sunk sharply into my skin, I couldn't help but make a small strangled sound. It hurt, but only briefly. Nicholas ran his tongue over the cut, then sucked gently until blood welled into his mouth. I felt him swallow, felt the brush of cold air on the small cuts, the pressure of his mouth when he bent to drink again.

I felt lightheaded even though I knew, logically, that he'd barely drunk enough to notice the loss. I'd bled more the time my grandma's psychotic cat bit me.

"There," he said to Solange, wiping a small drop off his lower lip. "I'm with you, but Lucy?" He sounded dark, and baleful. "Lucy's *mine*."

EPILOGUE

Kieran

Saturday night, 11:00 p.m.

If Solange wasn't trying to get herself killed, Lucy was.

I was beginning to think that all of my training wasn't actually about killing vampires anymore, it was about saving my girlfriend and her best friend from themselves. And it was a full-time job.

Though technically, Solange was my ex-girlfriend now.

But that didn't sound right, and it sure as hell didn't feel right either, even if it had seemed inevitable that night on my front porch. I could still feel the shape of her under my hands, see the look on her face and the delicate treachery of her fangs when I kissed her.

I didn't know what my dad would think about Solange and me. Treaty or not, hunters and vampires didn't date. And they sure as hell didn't fall in love.

Until the Drakes.

Now even Hunter had fallen, for Quinn, of all vampires. It effectively made us both traitors or revolutionary heroes, depending on who you asked. I didn't want to be a traitor; I didn't even want to be a hero.

I just wanted Solange back.

But first I had to find Lucy and rescue her, despite the fact that I knew damned well she'd hate the term "rescue." The GPS flashed another warning, and I checked my position one last time before slipping it into my pocket. I headed deeper into the woods. Thank God she wasn't in the Blood Moon camp. I'd never get her out of there. As it was, I should probably call Hunter for backup. Eric wouldn't come, not for a vampire. He was better about my new friends than the others, but he wasn't quite to the point of helping me save one.

It didn't matter. There wasn't any time anyway.

Because if the GPS tag was activated, it meant only one thing: Lucy was in trouble. And so was Nicholas. Because the only reason he wouldn't save her himself was if he couldn't.

I had no idea what kind of situation I was heading into. I had stakes on my belt, Hypnos powder secured up my sleeve, and nose plugs around my neck. I always had nose plugs with me, ever since I'd realized I couldn't fully trust Solange anymore. I put them on and kept off the trail, trying not to crack twigs under my boots and give myself away. Vampire hearing had me at a disadvantage, but I was used to that. I was used to a lot of things now.

I cleared my head and concentrated on where I was going. A

distracted hunter didn't last long. And at least, despite everything, I was still a hunter. I could rely on that, on the training a hundred years of tradition had afforded me. Even if I did use it for rather less than traditional reasons.

The forest was cold, hung with frost and a thin dusting of snow. Thick pine boughs muffled the last moments of the night into an eerie silence. Dawn wasn't far off; there was already a slight pink tinge to the light. Another weapon at my disposal, even if I couldn't hang it off my belt. I ran for nearly twenty minutes before I saw signs of habitation: a scrap of lace caught on a thorny branch, a lantern half-buried in snow, and finally an empty wine bottle in a decorative metal cage hung with rubies.

Also, a vampire.

She dropped out of the tree above me, landing quietly. She didn't say a word, didn't even bother with the trademark vampiric smirk upon finding a lone hunter in the woods. She just attacked, launched into a feral deadly dance that blurred the colors of her dress and shook the bare branches around us. I didn't have time to fight.

And I didn't have time to lose either.

She cracked her elbow into my stomach before I could dodge her. I doubled over, cursing on a strangled gasp. I used the momentum of my stumble to drop to the ground and roll to the side. I came up, kicking out to catch her ankles with my steel-toe boots. She hissed in pain. It was the only moment I was likely to get. As she staggered, I released the Hypnos from the casing under my cuff. White powder exploded in a cloud right in her face. Before she could react, the hypnotic powder was entering her bloodstream, seeping into her pores. Her pale eyes dilated, her lips lifted off angry fangs.

"Stop," I ordered, pushing to my feet. Dried leaves and pine needles clung to my clothes. "Go home."

She snarled at me, the violence of it contradicting her blond curls and angelic face. I'd long ago stopped believing angelic faces, since the small and pretty Hope killed my father.

I could have ordered this vampire to do anything at all and she would have obeyed. She would have fallen on a stake for me, or even lain down to suntan if I'd asked it of her. But I had no idea who she was. She could be under the protection of a treaty, or belong to some foreign vampire dignitary. A Huntsman would have killed her regardless and wouldn't have considered any other option. I wasn't a Huntsman.

She tumbled away and I pushed between cedar trees, emerging in a strange sort of outdoor living room hung with lanterns and crowded with velvet sofas. A river glittered between Persian rugs. And under a willow tree hung with candles and ribbons, Lucy knelt on the frost-encrusted ground between Solange and Nicholas.

Even at a distance, something wasn't right.

As I ran toward them, Solange glanced up. When she saw me, she jerked once, as if she'd been stabbed. She shoved Lucy forward so that she sprawled over the roots. Then she turned and vanished between the trees, her hair streaming behind her, her skin moon-pale.

"Sol, wait!" Ice and frozen mud cracked under my boots.

"What's going on?" I asked Nicholas. He shouldn't be here, not if Lucy's GPS tag had been activated.

Unless he was the problem.

I stopped, stake in my hand. I catalogued what little information I could in the second it took for Lucy to stand up, looking befuddled. Blood trickled down her bare arm, and there were leaves in her hair. Solange had taken off toward the encampment. There were vampires in the woods, closing in. Nicholas looked as if he'd had the crap kicked out of him.

And he was wiping blood off his lip.

Shit.

I grabbed Lucy's hand and yanked her away, even as I shot the last of my Hypnos at Nicholas. He was already leaping up into the tree, out of range. He hissed down at us, candlelight flashing off his fangs and pale eyes. Lucy stared up at him.

"Nicholas?"

I tugged harder on her hand. "Lucy, we need to get out of here."

She tripped over a root and then dug in her heels. "Nicholas Drake," she whispered. "Stop it. Stop it now." It was as close to begging as I'd ever heard her. "Please."

The light changed quality, burned from pink to gold. Nicholas swung into the next tree, and then we heard him land on the ground and take off, running away from the dawn, away from Lucy. She tried to follow, but I wouldn't let her.

She was shivering, shrugging back into her frock coat as I forced her to move. We ran between the trees without talking as the sun rose, throwing darts of light between the branches. Ice gleamed.

Birds sang from the canopy. I wouldn't let us stop until we were well away from the encampment and any surrounding underground safe houses. We could almost see the road from here and my car parked haphazardly in the bushes. Lucy braced her hands on her knees and bent over, panting.

"Kieran, how did you find us?" she finally asked.

"You were tagged."

She blinked at me, confused. "What? I know my dad threatened to microchip me, but I think I would have noticed if he'd actually done it."

"Nicholas tagged you."

She straightened slowly. "How do you know that?"

"We worked it out as a fail-safe." I checked her coat and found the small tag under her collar. I pulled it out and showed it to her. "He activated it about a half hour ago." I watched her reaction warily, assuming she'd be furious. Lucy tended to punch people in the face when she was furious. Instead she beamed at me.

"That's sneaky and awesome," she said, wiping a tear out of one eye even as she giggled. "And it means Nicholas never really meant to hurt me. He was saving me from Solange."

"Yeah, about that," I said as we pushed through the last of the undergrowth and climbed into my car. "What the hell happened to him?"

"I don't know," she said bleakly.

"He didn't look good."

"I know. Shit!" She interrupted herself, eyes wide. "Jenna! We have to find Jenna!" She scrambled to get out of the car. "She was with me when Solange's guard ambushed us. They left her in the woods. Spencer said he'd go after her."

"Spencer?" I echoed. "Hunter's friend?"

She nodded. "Yeah."

"Okay, hold on, before you go charging back out there." I flipped open my cell phone and hit speed dial. Hunter answered on the first ring.

"I've got Jenna," she said in lieu of a greeting.

"Is she all right?"

"She's embarrassed, and she'll have a hell of a headache for the next few days, but she's fine." I nodded at Lucy so she'd know Jenna was safe. She slid back into the car, looking relieved and exhausted. "Spencer called me to come get her at the gate," Hunter was saying. "I think Lucy's in trouble," she added. "Jenna said they were chasing vampires. We can't get ahold of her."

"Lucy's with me; she's fine," I assured her.

Hunter gave a loud sigh of relief. "Okay. Good. Damn, tonight sucked."

"Talked to Quinn?"

"Yeah. Nicholas is back and Solange just made herself queen."

"Shit," I said, before hanging up. The Solange I fell in love with had shoved a tiara through a vampire's chest rather than claim it as her own.

"There's something wrong with her, Kieran," Lucy said quietly.

"We knew that already."

"No, this is different. It's like she's not really herself. I can't explain it." She rubbed her stomach as if it hurt. "I can just feel it, you know? I could barely recognize her."

"So what do we do?"

"We save her," she said, as if I were an idiot. "We save them both."

She wasn't wrong. Nicholas might not be missing any longer, but he didn't look safe either. "And how exactly are we going to do that?" I scrubbed my face wearily. Lucy always had ideas, even if they were generally dangerous and reckless.

"I have no idea."

And that scared me most of all.

ACKNOWLEDGMENTS

As always I want to thank everyone at Walker & Company and Bloomsbury Books for all of their hard work and their incredible support of the Drake Chronicles. I am truly grateful.

Thanks to Marlene Stringer of the Stringer Literary Agency.

Thanks to Jessica Kelly for all the book photography and to Adam Simpson for indispensable Web help.

Thanks to my husband, who brings me dinner when I'm on a deadline and knows what to do when confronted with Crazy Face (cue *Pride and Prejudice*, back away slowly).

And as always, thanks to my readers, without whom none of this would be possible!

The fight between Drakes and
vampires starts here!

Read on for the thrilling story of how
Liam Drake met his perfect match

Lost Girls

Alyxandra Harvey

1983

Elisabet rattled the cage, pursing her mouth in distaste. "Is that all?"

The three girls behind the bars huddled together. One wept and one was silent, eyes wide and wary. She was covered in bloody bites at her throat, elbow, and wrist. The third girl spat on the iron bars.

"She'll do," Elisabet approved, waving at one of the raven-feathered guards. "Bring her. Lady Natasha's in a mood."

◆

Violet Hill was a dangerous place.

It hadn't taken long for Helena to scratch beneath the veneer of laid-back hippie to the jagged underbelly, where each step was more treacherous than the last. All towns had a unique personality, one she could have drawn like a storybook character, and Violet Hill was a cranky old woman who could as easily offer you gingerbread as stuff you in the oven and cook you for the main course.

Helena happened to like that in a town.

And she liked the mountains eating up the sky and casting long shadows over everything. She might climb up to the top and live in one of the abandoned hunter camps once she figured out how not to get eaten by a bear. Tripped-out junkies and drunken frat boys she could handle, but she was pretty sure kicking a bear in the balls wouldn't be nearly as effective. But it might have been good practice.

If she'd thought of it earlier.

Before a fist to the face knocked her back and had her nearly biting off her tongue.

Cursing and spitting blood, she held up her gloves to protect her face while the spots cleared out of her vision. She knew better than to get distracted. It was sloppy and could get you killed: at home, in back alleys, and in underground clubs like this one.

Sofia grinned at her, blood smeared on her teeth. Her hair was teased into spikes, like needles. Helena's own long and straight dark hair was currently tied back so it wouldn't interfere with the fight. She wore tight shredded jeans and her faded Clash T-shirt. It wasn't much of a costume, like the spectators preferred, but it was her first fight. If she won she'd have money to get proper sparring gear, which would offer more protection than the tulle and leather *Mad Max* outfit Sofia was currently wearing. Helena wasn't into dressing up like a superhero. Blood was a bitch to wash out of spandex.

She'd started coming to The Vortex because the manager didn't look too closely at who was buying drinks or washing up at the bathroom sink. And in the back room, affectionately nicknamed the Thunderdome, girls fought in a makeshift ring for a 20 percent cut of the gambling profits.

Girls without any other options, angry girls, poor girls, lost girls.

Girls like her.

Helena waited until Sofia got closer before retaliating with an uppercut. Her jaws clacked together with a vicious snap and she reeled back. Helena would pay for that later.

The audience clapped and shouted, the hum of violent sound shaking Helena's bones until she felt disoriented. She stayed light on her toes, always evaluating her exit strategies. It was both instinct and a long habit that had served her well at thirteen and still served her well now at sixteen. People always underestimated you when you were young, even when they knew you. Being underestimated was as effective a weapon as a knife or a fist. And Sofia really ought to know better.

Helena pretended to be more tired than she was, slumping weakly as if dizzy. She tried to look like the scared sixteen-year-old girl they expected to see, and waited. Sofia preened, tossing her head back with a smug grin at the crowd. She wasn't much older but she was used to this, knew how to play them, knew how to get them stomping their feet and shouting her name.

Besides, she and Helena were always butting heads. When Helena had first arrived in town, Sofia had offered her a place in the lost-girls tribe. Helena had only joined them when girls started disappearing, when having a gang at your back was no longer a luxury. Leadership gradually shifted from Sofia to Helena, even though she didn't want it. Now they made sure the back alleys were safe for the others. Two girls went missing in the last month alone and though the newspapers claimed fatal drug overdoses, Helena knew the truth.

Vampires.

So she patrolled with the lost girls. They watched one another's backs. Helena could turn almost anything into a weapon. Billie was brilliant with a blade, Sofia was naturally vicious, and Portia could run faster than anyone. Iphigenia was too frail to fight, but she was smart and she saw everything.

Like the vampire circling the ring right now.

Helena followed Iphigenia's telling gaze, and swore. "Vamp at two o'clock," she muttered at Sofia.

Sofia didn't look. "Let the others handle it."

Ordinarily, Helena would have done just that. She was kind of busy, after all.

But then she saw the familiar face.

He was different from the others. There was a stillness inside him that made her think of the girls outside the yoga studio down the street or a cat waiting for a pigeon to land. Money passed hands, men whistled, girls laughed. And he just slipped between them, so softly they barely saw him.

But she saw him.

Liam Drake.

The rat bastard.

He was pale, not the kind of pale of her underfed brethren who huddled under bridges for warmth, but the kind of pale that reminded her of moonlight or winter fog. He looked to be in his twenties, with dark hair and wicked cheekbones. He circled the fight, glancing at her again when he got close. She could have sworn she could smell him, even through the fumes of smoke and the deep fryer in the kitchen. He was cool night air, rain, and copper. She felt light-headed and couldn't help but stare at him as if he was pulling her right out of her body.

She almost forgot to react when Sofia suddenly ran at her.

Her eye was nearly poked out by hair spray–stiffened hair. She straight-armed Sofia, ramming the heel of her hand into her chest. She let the momentum of the hit pull her forward and swept her leg behind the other girl's knees. Breathless, Sofia fell backward, landing hard. Her head struck the floor. She blinked dizzily and didn't even try to sit up.

The crowd hesitated, then erupted into cheers and insults. Sofia cursed her viciously and the girls waiting to fight on the other side of the ropes glared at her, but Helena didn't care. No rules. Grady, the ref, was clear about that before they'd climbed into the ring. She wanted to lean on her knees to catch her breath and steady her shaking arms, but she wouldn't give anyone the satisfaction of seeing even a moment of weakness. Billie caught her eye and grinned. Behind her, Liam paused in the audience. He winked at her before melting into the shadows toward the exit. Warmth flooded Helena's belly and made her cheeks red and she wasn't entirely sure why.

"Good job, kid." Grady held her arm up for a victory lap. She barely heard him. She didn't want drunken accolades or threats, she just wanted to follow Liam Drake.

And kick his ass.

She yanked her arm free and jumped the ropes, shoving through the grumbling until she was able to push through the back door and dart up the grimy concrete steps to the alley behind the club. A group of guys smoked in a huddle. A girl was throwing up behind a Dumpster, and an older man gave her an oily smile. She considered kneecapping him on principle but she didn't want to lose Liam. He was already down the alley and turning the corner. She knew from experience that he moved faster than lightning when he wanted to.

There was something between them, a recognition she hadn't felt since before her brother died in that car crash. It was annoying. Even back then her mother hadn't cared what happened to Helena, but Sebastian had cared. He had always been there to play peace-maker, to see that Helena got enough to eat and new clothes for school. And then he drank too much beer and drove his car into a tree. She didn't let the memory slow her down; she never did. It didn't do any good.

And it would let her quarry get away.

She hurried down the alley, mice dodging under the Dumpsters and the wind pushing litter against her ankles. The music from The Vortex thrummed faintly through the cool night air. Her cheek throbbed, a bruise already forming. There'd be another bruise on her left elbow, and her right wrist would hurt for the rest of the week. Sofia was stronger than she looked.

She popped around the corner, stopping at a dead end, full of pop cans and cigarette butts. There were brick walls and a startled cat.

But no gray-eyed Liam.

"Bloody coward," she muttered. He thought he could ditch her. While she hadn't thought they'd get married and have lots of fat babies together, they'd fought feral *Hel-Blar* together near one of the abandoned factories. Before that he'd been kind, watching her with a glint in his eye that made her toes curl. Afterward, a scorching kiss in the darkness.

And now nothing.

She raised her voice. "I know you're out there, Liam Drake."

No response. The alley stretched back to The Vortex, and went off to the right into a rabbit warren of narrow, unlit passageways. Inexplicable disappointment made her mouth taste like lemons.

"Stupid," she muttered at herself. There was no one waiting for her, no moment with a devastatingly handsome young man. And she didn't want that kind of thing from Liam anyway. She knew better. Girls like her didn't hear poetry and compliments.

Girls like her heard screams in the dark.

Typically their own.

◆

Cass was so grounded even her grandchildren would be grounded.

She and her grandmother went into the rougher parts of Violet Hill, which was really only a single downtown block near the warehouses, and handed out coffee and sandwiches to the homeless.

Everyone knew Posy Macalister. She clomped around in denim overalls and construction boots and terrified everyone but the street kids. They understood she was the one to go to when they were too wary to try the shelters or Children's Aid. Posy believed in people taking care of one another, even though she claimed that people in general were dumb as dirt.

Cass believed in it too; she loved helping her cantankerous grandmother, even on those bitter winter nights when she thought her nose might actually fall off her face. It felt good to help. Even though she technically knew better than to stray alone in any part of Violet Hill at night. It probably served her right that she was lying on the ground, feeling her own blood seeping into her hair.

Screaming seemed like a really good idea about now.

If only she could remember how.

She felt funny, foggy. Fear rocketed through her but she just couldn't seem to make herself move. The woman who lifted her off the ground looked too slender to be able to support her weight but Cass hung bonelessly off one arm, as if made of feathers. Blood dripped from the ends of her hair. The woman licked her lips.

Inside her head, Cass screamed but her throat would only make a small mewing sound. Her grandmother taught her better than this. She had Wolfgang train Cass to defend herself. He'd tell her stories, family secrets, and rhymes to help her remember how to keep vampires at bay. But the rhymes fell right out of her head the minute she met a real vampire. She was embarrassed. It was one thing to believe in nonviolence and quite another to die horribly drained of blood because you couldn't even muster enough will to protect yourself.

She flopped like a dead fish, her arm dangling uncomfortably. She felt the tip of those teeth sink into her neck, felt the sharp jab of skin breaking, the uncomfortable pull of blood being sucked out of her veins. Her neck burned, then tingled. It didn't hurt after a moment; pain was too simple a feeling for the complicated sensations rolling her about like a paper boat on a stormy sea.

The woman pulled back slightly, sighing with disappointment. "This one's a vegetarian," she said distastefully. "I thought the hippies were finally extinct. They never taste as good."

"Then give her to me, Elisabet." A man, equally slender and pale and with Elisabet's same curious amber-colored eyes and blond hair, stepped out of the shadows. "You're too picky."

She sniffed. "I have standards, Lyle."

"And I have an appetite." The man smiled hungrily at Cass. "So pass her over."

"No." Elisabet tightened her hold petulantly, her long blond hair swinging to curtain Cass's face. "She's mine. Get your own."

"Technically she belongs to Lady Natasha."

Elisabet's eyes glittered. "Are you threatening me, little brother?"

"Just hurry up."

She wiped blood off her lower lip with her thumb. "I hate Violet Hill. I wish Lady Natasha didn't insist on visiting this backwoods village. Everyone tastes . . . green. Like spinach." She grimaced. "I miss Texas."

Cass continued to hang limply, feeling smug triumph mix with the fear and confusion. Her grandmother rolled her eyes when Cass picked the bacon off her breakfast plate or refused to eat the turkey at Thanksgiving. The slight reprieve gave her time to fill her lungs with air. She gathered every last bit of energy inside her and then opened her mouth.

If Elisabet had been human, Cass's scream would have shattered her eyeballs.

Instead, Cass's grandmother would have to finish the job.

"Get the hell away from my granddaughter!"

◆

Helena reached the alley just in time to see Posy Macalister swing a heavy flashlight across the back of a vampire's head. Posy's granddaughter, Cass, the one who was always handing out baked-tofu sandwiches no one wanted to eat but took anyway because they didn't want to hurt her feelings, tumbled to the ground. There was blood in her hair and on her shirt but she pushed to her feet. The blond vampire girl staggered against the wall. A guy who could only be her brother swore viciously and attacked.

Helena didn't think. She didn't have to. Leaping into fights was what she did best.

She'd been busted for fighting at school more times than she could remember. She didn't get busted anymore, because she'd dropped out. She'd been on her own since the day she turned thirteen and her mom shoved her down the front steps and changed the locks. She learned how to poach stale bread from behind bakeries and barely wilted vegetables from behind the grocers, how to slip past bouncers at the clubs, how to make a passable fake ID, and how to find clean public bathrooms.

But she still hadn't learned how to avoid a fight.

To be fair, it wasn't exactly a skill she was eager to learn.

"Hey! Back off the old lady," she shouted, swinging her already bruised and bloody fist at the blond vampire who was snarling. She reached for the stake tucked into her left boot. Billie had whittled the stakes to killing points from branches they gathered in the park near their bridge. Hers was plain but sturdy. The weight of it was a comfort in her hand.

"Who are you calling an old lady?" Posy muttered, throwing the flashlight with the force of the old farm wife she was. It caught the guy under the eye, snapping his head back.

"Oh, Elisabet, now we're going to have some fun," he promised silkily. Helena couldn't believe he was still standing after that blow. Something about the two of them made her shiver, and she hadn't been afraid of a fight since before her brother died.

Elisabet backhanded Posy into the wall. She hit it hard and slid into a pile, groaning. Cass didn't waste time with more screaming. She leaped to stand protectively over Posy. Helena grabbed a handful of Elisabet's long hair and yanked savagely, spinning her away. Elisabet screeched and before she'd finished twirling, her brother was on Helena.

"Lyle, I want first blood," she spat.

Helena punched Lyle in the face. He punched her back. She flew backward, dropping her stake, her shoulder slamming hard into a Dumpster. The bin creaked in protest. Elisabet and Lyle closed in, smiling. Helena scrabbled back, searching for anything else she could use as a weapon. She kicked out with her boots to give her some time. Elisabet reached down and grabbed her arm, hauling Helena to her feet. Her wristbones crunched. Elisabet bent her head and licked the blood off Helena's battered knuckles. Disgusted and infuriated, Helena struggled.

Posy blew a high-pitched whistle as her granddaughter helped her to her feet.

Lyle was reaching out to grab her other arm when a hand closed over his shoulder and spun him away. He crashed into the metal fire escape. It rattled like iron rain, the sound shivering through everyone's teeth.

Liam Drake suddenly appeared and flicked Helena an inscrutable glance before blocking Lyle's counterattack. He moved like water, water deep enough to drown in.

Helena tried not to let herself get distracted by his lean, charming face or his wicked right hook. Instead, she concentrated on keeping Elisabet away from her neck. She smashed her elbow into the vampire's face. Her nose cracked, spurting blood. Being this close to Elisabet was making her feel fuzzy and tired. She was way off her game. But if there was one thing she knew, it was fighting despite insurmountable odds. She didn't recognize defeat as an option.

Still, it certainly helped when Liam knocked Lyle into Elisabet with such force they both tumbled away from Helena. When Lyle leaped to his feet, hissing, Elisabet yanked on his arm. "Wait," she said. "We don't have time." All three of them tensed, as if they heard something Helena didn't, under the sound of Posy's ear-searing whistle. She blew three short bursts that sounded like a code. "We have to go," Elisabet insisted.

They vanished into the darkness. Liam closed in on Posy and her granddaughter, nostrils flaring.

"Cass, behind me." Posy put a protective arm across her granddaughter. Cass was pale, but her jaw was set.

"I'm not going to hurt you," he murmured. His voice was like brandy cream. Helena wasn't actually sure what brandy cream was, but she'd read about it once and imagined it was like his voice, dark and sweet, and laced with fire.

He touched his fingertips to Cass's chin to tilt her head back and look at her wound. His back teeth clenched but his hold stayed gentle. "You'll be all right," he said. "You won't need stitches and you're not infected." He looked straight at Posy. "So don't worry. And don't let your guard down."

She snorted. "Like I ever would, boy."

He turned back to leave, passing so close to Helena that she could see the peculiar pale glint of his gray eyes. He paused beside her. The way he looked at her, when he finally deigned to acknowledge her presence was as if she were a rose where everyone else, including herself, saw only thorns.

"What?" she asked belligerently.

The sound of motorcycles roaring down the alleys from all directions interrupted whatever reply he might have made. Instead, he vanished up the nearest fire escape.

Posy limped over, supported by Cass's arm. "Are you hurt, girl?"

Helena shook her head, buzzing with adrenaline that suddenly had no place to go. It flooded her bloodstream, making her feel jittery and angry. "I really hate vampires."

"We have to get out of here," Posy said as the motorcycles rode into view. Three tattooed, leather-and-jean-clad men looked grimly at them.

"How many?" one of them demanded.

"Already gone." Posy waved her hand. "Cass needs some bandages and I need some gin. Get us home, boys."

Helena gaped as the old woman swung her leg over the bike, climbing on behind a grizzled man who looked like he might eat kittens for breakfast. Even Cass perched on the seat as comfortably as if she was sitting cross-legged and meditating, or whatever it was flower children did in their spare time.

Posy pointed at Helena. "She saved Cass's life. She comes home with me."

They sped away, leaving Helena blinking at the last biker. He grinned. "Get on. No one argues with Posy."

Helena crossed her arms, eyes narrowed. "I'm not going anywhere with you. Do you think I'm stupid?"

"No, I think you're a smart lass." He had a Scottish accent and bruises on his knuckles. "And maybe a little scared."

Helena sputtered, "I am not!"

"Posy won't hurt you. Unless you eat her chili. I'd steer clear of that if I were you. Name's Bruno," he added. His hair was long under his bandanna, and tattoos poked out from under his collar and cuffs. "Are you coming or what, little girl?"

He was barely twenty, despite his attitude and the crinkles at the corner of his eyes. And she wasn't scared. She didn't do scared.

"Fine," she said, sliding onto the bike behind him.

"Atta girl," he approved, taking off the minute her fingers hooked into the back of his belt. Like hell she was going to wrap her arms around him. "Mind the exhaust there, it gets hot."

She rolled her eyes even though he couldn't see her. "I've been on a bike before."

"You haven't been on a bike until you've been on mine," he said as they came out of the narrow alleys and onto the deserted road. "What's your name, sweetheart?" he shouted over the rush of the wind.

"Helena," she shouted back. "And if you call me sweetheart again, I'll knife your tires."

His laugh trailed behind them.

◆

"You like her," Geoffrey said quietly as they watched Helena take off on the back of a motorcycle. They stood at the corner of the highest roof in the Warren, with a view of the lights and the humans scurrying below.

Liam stared at the taillight of the bike until it winked out of sight. "You know the rules."

"Yes, but she's not like Deirdre."

Liam clenched his back teeth. "I know that."

"This one's strong."

He sighed. "Does it matter?"

Geoffrey looked thoughtful, sad. "Yes," he replied finally. "I think it does."

"Even if Natasha's noticed?"

"Especially then."

◆

"I thought I was clear about staying, young lady."

They were in Posy's kitchen: a wounded girl, a street girl, and three tough-looking bikers—Bruno, Mason, and Wolfgang—gathered around a scarred harvest table. Between the blood, the bruises, and the tattoos of laughing skulls, everyone knew the old lady was the scary one.

Cass winced. She was holding a striped dishtowel to the now-clean wound on her neck as Posy rifled through a worn first-aid kit for bandages. "Sorry, Nana. She was all huddled in the corner. I thought she was hungry."

Bruno snorted. "She was, lass."

After assessing all the exits (sliding glass door, two windows, front door, and a mud room), Helena sniffed at the herbal tea Cass had given her, longing for the black coffee everyone else was drinking. Who wanted to drink boiled flowers? But Cass was so earnest that she kept the cup, feeling like the street kids who ate baked tofu just to see her smile. Bruno caught her eye and winked, sliding his coffee to her and taking her tea. There was something sweet about someone so tough-looking drinking mint and rose petals.

"Jan, sit down before you bleed on my floor."

"Nana, I told you, it's Cass now."

Posy rolled her eyes. "Last week it was Star. I can't keep up."

"Cassiopeia is a star constellation, Nana."

"I'm calling you Beth from now on."

Cass sat in a chair. "That's not even my name."

"No, but it's easy to remember." Posy might be acting calm and composed, but her hands trembled when she pulled the towel away from her granddaughter's throat. She let out a shaky breath. "It's not so bad. But don't tell your mother what happened."

They exchanged knowing, slightly ironic glances. Mason stood up and went to have a closer look. He smelled like smoke and beer.

He grunted. "No stitches, she'll be fine." Then he left without another word. The grizzled old biker Wolfgang sat back, relieved.

Posy gently taped a white bandage to Cass's throat. "He was right," she said thoughtfully. "The man in the alley."

"Liam Drake," Helena spat.

Posy raised her eyebrows. "Know him, do you? The Drakes don't share their names with just anyone."

Aside from being someone she'd considered kissing a lot, Liam was also the first vampire Helena had ever met. At first, she'd thought she was talking to a cute boy in the park. When she found out otherwise, she'd tripped over her own foot and fallen in the river. "Yeah," she sneered. "I'm so lucky."

"And now you've really annoyed them."

Helena smiled, showing a lot of teeth. "Good. Too many damn vampires in Violet Hill lately."

"Don't forget the witches," Cass interjected pleasantly. "And maybe werewolves, but I can't seem to get an eyewitness confirmation of them. And someone at school claims his uncle's girlfriend's cousin saw a Sasquatch last year."

Helena crossed her arms. "I know all this."

"You know about the Sasquatch?"

"Okay, maybe not that part."

"Definitely a spike in disappearances," Wolfgang agreed. "And there's new activity at an old school outside of town I think might be mixed up in all of this, but I'm not sure how. No one can get close enough to find out, not even Posy, and she's been here the longest."

"I grew up here," she confirmed to Helena. "I was born in the mountains, at the start of the Depression. We didn't even have running water up in our cabin. We ate fish and trapped rabbits." Posy pulled food out of the fridge. "Anyone who grows up in those mountains can tell you strange creatures are there." She slapped meat onto fresh bread, then added cheese. "After my brother got bit, we learned not to go too far alone at night, and to always carry a knife or a sharp stake. A girl died not too long after but then it all seemed to go away, like a bad dream. Until about four years ago when they found a girl drained of blood outside of town. She was the first."

"My sister was the second," Bruno added quietly. "I only came here because they found her body in the lake after she ran away. I'd never even heard of this place before then." Bruno's jaw clenched and there was a glint of something dark in his eyes. Something Helena recognized. "Posy had me pegged practically the second my boots hit the sidewalk at the bus station. I was going to kill them all, you see." His accent was even thicker now, and bitter. Helena sat down without really realizing it. She knew what he felt. She'd have done the same thing if Sebastian had died that way. As it was, she'd broken into the junkyard and set the wreck of his car on fire the night of the funeral.

"Not that it would have brought her back," Bruno said, sounding tired. Cass reached over to hug him. He patted her arm awkwardly. "Fell in with a rough crowd, and when I got out of juvie, Posy took me in for a week until I got my bearings again. I was one of her first strays."

"And still my favorite." Posy smiled at him affectionately. "The whistle was Bruno's idea," she explained to Helena. It was a good idea, Helena thought, one she'd mention to the lost girls. "He's always looking out for us."

"Someone has to." Wolfgang snorted. "Especially now that the disappearances have started again."

"I know," Helena said grimly. "My friends and I are doing our best to stop them. But it's not working as well as we'd like."

Cass shivered, touching her bandage. "I, for one, think your best is pretty damn good."

"The thing about vampires," Wolfgang said, looking at Helena, "is that they tend to be creatures of habit. And vengeance. You need to be careful."

"I can take care of myself," she said. "I should go." The others would be looking for her. And if she stayed away too long Grady would keep her cut of the profits from the fight.

"Sit down," Posy ordered, interrupting. "You won't be sleeping behind a Dumpster tonight."

Helena could have pointed out that she never slept near the

Dumpsters. They stank. And the lost girls had rules: no handouts, no social workers, no shelters. "I'm not going to one of those shelters," she stated. "So save your breath."

"At least eat something." Posy slid a plate piled high with sandwiches onto the table.

Helena was hungry enough to stay for a meal. She reached for a sandwich and took a huge bite, even though her leg muscles twitched with the urge to take off. "So, what, you guys just go around killing vampires? I thought you fed the homeless." Crumbs landed on her shirt.

"I do," Posy said. "And I do what needs doing."

"Not all vampires are evil," Cass said firmly. "Some of them are good."

Helena honestly didn't know which category Liam fell into. Even after he'd kissed her that one time.

Maybe especially because of that kiss.

"One of them saved Wolf once," Cass added.

Liam had saved her too, damn it.

Wolfgang nodded. "Back in my drinking days," he said crisply. "Drank myself stupid and nearly got bit for the pleasure. Some woman wearing the strangest dress, like Queen Victoria herself, saved me. Never saw her again."

"You saved Cass's life tonight. I can't ever repay that," Posy said softly.

Helena squirmed, embarrassed. "It's fine." If the old woman offered her money she'd walk out. She wouldn't take pity or charity. Even though her stomach grumbled just seeing the bowl of fruit on the counter, and that was after she had eaten two-and-a-half sandwiches. She wondered if she could steal a few for the girls and sneak out before dawn. Iphigenia loved oranges.

"What do you know about Liam Drake?" she asked. She may as well get information while she was here.

"Not much," Posy admitted. "He keeps to himself. Haven't seen him since I was a girl, and that was only because I snuck out to meet a boy. Your granddad," she added as an aside to Cass. "I saw Liam first. Looks exactly the same, even now." She looked at her wrinkled hands. "Hell of a thing."

"Wait, so he's really old?" Helena asked. Posy speared her with a look. Cass giggled. "I mean . . ."

"I know what you meant, young lady," she said, disgruntled. "But yes, he's older than I am."

It was totally wrong that someone so old could be that hot. He should have dentures and a comb-over. It made her head hurt.

"Drakes keep to themselves," Wolfgang confirmed. "Probably for the best."

"I hope you'll stay the night," Posy offered, even though Helena still had a hundred questions about Liam. "I still have the bunk beds from when my granddaughters were little. It's just Cass now that Lucinda's away at university. Or you can take the couch." She ran a hand over Cass's hair, as if checking to make sure she was still okay. "Those vampires saw your face, Helena, and they have long memories. They might come back. I hope you'll let us help you."

"I'll take the couch," she said reluctantly, mentally kissing her prize money good-bye. "But just for tonight."

Besides, she knew in the primal, hidden corners of herself—the parts that recognized the electric smell of an approaching storm— that someone was out there in the darkness.

Watching her.

◆

The girl was going to be a problem.

◆

Helena snuck out of Posy's house as dawn turned the sky the color of tangerines. She took some food but left the handful of dollar bills crumpled on the coffee table. It took her twenty minutes to walk to their squat under the bridge. The wild tiger lilies masked most of her movements, though no one was likely to be about that early. Even the crazy joggers with their sweatbands and matching leg warmers waited until there was a little more light.

She found the others sleeping under their sleeping bags, except for Iphigenia, who was huddled with her knees to her chest. Her lower lip trembled when she saw Helena crawl under the ivy they'd pulled down as a screen. Only one of the candles stuck into the craggy wall was lit. The light made her look even younger and thinner. "You're back!" she exclaimed. "We thought you'd be taken."

"I'm fine," she said, tossing Iphigenia one of the stolen oranges.

Portia sat up, her hair tilting dramatically to the left. Her eyes were red and worried but the kick she aimed at Helena's ankle was vicious. "Where the hell have you been?"

Helena jerked back, ankle throbbing. "I ran into some trouble."

"Good." Sofia scowled, opening one eye. Billie kept on snoring, oblivious. "You punched me in the face, you bitch."

Helena wasn't remotely sorry. "You punched me first."

"Grady wants you to fight again tonight. Wear something pretty."

"Kiss my ass."

Helena grabbed a few hours' sleep, ignoring the girls as they devoured the fruit she'd left for them. When she woke up there was only a banana left, on which Sofia had written rude things with a marker. Helena ate it anyway, then rinsed her mouth out with the mouthwash they hoarded like candy. It was their single prized possession and the first thing they bought with any scrounged money, before hot dogs, before coffee when they were able to find a decent cup, even before chocolate.

Iphigenia watched her rinse the dried blood from her hair in the river. The water was getting cold as summer faded. "What happened to you?"

"Nothing," Helena assured her. Iphigenia was such a worrier, she didn't need to know. "Just don't go anywhere alone at night," she said. "You still have that knife?"

She nodded. "Yes, I put it in my bag. Portia said someone was following her last night."

And Helena had been sure she was being watched. She slipped her own hunting knife into the side of her boot and started to climb out from under the bridge.

Iphigenia scrambled after her. "Where are you going?"

"To get my money off Grady before Sofia sweet-talks my share off him."

"I'm coming too."

They'd found Sofia, predictably batting her eyelashes at Grady. He was sprawled at a table near the empty ring, smoking and drinking bottled water. He claimed it kept him pretty. There was glitter in his hair. "My favorite girls," he said. "All together."

Helena's smile was brittle. "Hi, Sofia."

Sofia narrowed her eyes. "What?"

Helena ignored her, looking at Grady. She didn't smile or flirt. "Where's my money?"

Grady looked wounded. "Would I cheat you, darling? You ran off so fast I thought you were leaving it for me to reinvest in the Thunderdome."

Helena held out her hand. "Like hell."

He shook his head, blowing smoke rings. "You could be a little nicer, like your friend here."

Sofia smirked. Helena just raised an eyebrow. "I don't do nice," she said. "That's why I won the fight."

Grady laughed and passed her a stack of folded dollar bills. He knew the lost girls preferred small bills that attracted less attention. His gaze roamed appreciatively over Iphigenia's thin body, her huge blue eyes, and translucent skin. "When are you going to join the fun, beautiful?"

Helena stepped in front of her. "Try never."

His eyes went hard. "All the girls fight for me eventually, Helena. Even your precious lost girls."

"Yeah, about that. You said you wouldn't pit us against each other."

He grinned. "I lied." He leered at Iphigenia. "You're kind of skinny, but put you in a short skirt and no one will care if you punch like a girl."

Helena slammed her boot on the chair, right between his legs. He froze, gulping. If she pressed any harder he'd walk with a limp for the rest of his life. "Leave her out of this."

He swallowed audibly. "Sure."

Sofia walked lazily around Helena, sighing. "You're such a drama queen."

Helena pressed down a little harder just to prove her point. When Grady went cross-eyed, she backed off. "Let's go," she told the others.

Sofia followed more out of a show of solidarity than any real desire to go anywhere with Helena. Iphigenia followed them quietly.

"You have to stop being such a bitch," Sofia muttered.

"Why?" Helena asked. "He's sleazy."

"He also pays the bills, such as they are."

"Whatever." She shrugged the bills off. "I have things to do. Look after Iphi."

"Yeah, yeah."

"Sof?"

"What?"

"Do you think vampires can be the good guys?"

"Are you high?" Sofia asked. "Vampires are picking us off, remember? They're not our friends."

She'd have thought the same thing before Liam found her in the alley last night.

"Never mind." She waited until they'd wandered off before heading deeper into the Warren. The alleys were deceptively welcoming at this time of the day, even with the afternoon sun cooking the garbage under clouds of flies. The sounds from the back doors of restaurants were cheerfully boisterous, and someone was blaring Billy Idol out of a fire escape window. Everything here made sense. Survive. Don't be a victim. Avoid Scrawny Johnny at all costs, if you wanted to get out of the Warren with all your limbs intact. He was the meanest drunk Helena had ever seen and she'd heard the other street girls whisper about him.

What happened last night didn't make sense.

Starting with the fact that she'd let her head be turned by a pretty set of cheekbones.

Glowering, she stopped at the spot where Elisabet and Lyle had attacked her. It looked like any other alley: Dumpster, skids, litter in the groove of the pavement by the sewer. Cheerful light glinted off the peeling fire escapes, the broken windows at the top of the building on her right. Most of the storefronts were abandoned on this corner.

She stood over a dark stain on the ground, where Cass's blood had fallen. They'd intended her to be the next missing girl. The gash under her hairline would leave a scar. Helena intended to leave a few scars of her own.

She investigated the entire area, even the broken skids that she'd knocked over. She didn't find anything that might help her track down Elisabet and Lyle. If they were the ones taking all the girls, she wanted them. She wanted them dusting the end of her stake. She spent several pleasant moments envisioning her revenge.

Until there was the soft scuff of a boot behind her.

She'd stayed too long. The sun had set behind the buildings, casting long violet shadows. It was too dark now. Not the kind of darkness in which she could hide but the kind that hid things from her. She whirled, using her elbow like a mace. She hit a hard chest and kicked a little lower. A hand blocked the strike, held her immobile. She spun out, kicking.

And then she was pressed against a brick wall, fingers over her mouth, gray eyes staring a warning into hers.

"We're not alone," Liam mouthed. "Don't move."

His hand dropped away and she drew in a shallow breath. He was even more beautiful up close. His gray irises were flecked with black and silver, his mouth inches from hers. His teeth were sharp, faintly pointed but not particularly vampiric. His body touched her from shoulder to ankle, shielding her. She didn't know what to think. She wasn't used to being shielded and she wasn't entirely certain she liked it.

But she liked it better than being caught by Elisabet and her psychotic brother.

"I can smell her," Elisabet murmured. "I want payback, Lyle."

"I know," he replied. "Haven't you said so a dozen times since we left the caves? She's a street rat, she could be anywhere."

"No, she's close. Can't you smell her?" she asked again, sounding as if Helena was a pastry fresh from the oven.

Liam eased away from her and she felt inexplicably cold. He motioned to the Dumpster beside them. Helena blinked at him. He pointed. She shook her head. He shoved her gently toward it. She dug in her heels. She was not going to hide in a pile of garbage. She had her pride. Not to mention her sense of smell.

When she refused to move, he just picked her up and tossed her into it. She landed on old Chinese food and rotten cabbage and watched as the lid closed down over her head.

Vampire or not, she was going to kill him.

Twice.

It felt like forever until the lid lifted again, letting in blessedly fresh air. His pale face came into view. "They've gone," he said. He had a faint accent, almost British but not quite. She couldn't place it. "You can come out now."

"That," Helena stated, leaping over the side of the bin, "was disgusting."

"But necessary."

"Easy for you to say."

"Elisabet caught your scent, love, and she knows the taste of you now. She'd have tracked you to your bed and killed you there."

Helena shuddered, both from the wet noodles clinging to her arm and the thought of Elisabet finding the lost girls. "Don't call me love," she said, just because she thought she should.

"Come with me," he said gently.

"Where? Your place?" she asked acerbically.

"The dojo at the end of the edge of the Warren has showers. I can get us inside," he said, amused. "No offense, but you smell horrid."

Of course he wasn't hitting on her. She had moldy lettuce in her hair. Feeling like an idiot, she scowled. "Fine."

They didn't speak as he led her there, using the side alley next to the dojo to pick the side door lock. She watched him curiously. He flashed her a brief smile, but it was enough to make her breath catch in her throat. "I know the owner."

She wasn't sure she believed him, but she didn't care. She didn't want to smell like garbage. And she didn't want him to smell her like this either. She slipped past him and headed across the studio to the back. She went through the door marked "Ladies" and took the fastest shower she could, watching the door the entire time. Helena washed her clothes too and slipped into a white dojo T-shirt she found in one of the lockers, along with black *gi* pants. She stepped back out into the studio feeling strangely vulnerable.

Liam was silhouetted against the window, hands in his pockets. He turned to look at her. When he took a step toward her, she moved back, grabbing one of the practice staffs from the wall and holding it horizontally in front of her. "Bar's closed, pal."

"I didn't bring you here to feed on you."

"Then why did you?"

"To keep you safe."

She snorted. "Yeah, right."

He studied her for a quiet charged moment before moving. He was so fast he bled colors and light. He tossed the staff aside. It may as well have been a matchstick for all the good it did her. He spun her around, his arm around her neck. His voice was raw, lips brushing her ear. "If I wanted to hurt you, I could," he said. "You're safe with me."

"You have a hell of a way of proving that." She kicked back, clipping his knee with her boot. Then she slammed her head back into his face. He stumbled, loosening his hold. She swung a fist at his pretty face but he dodged it easily. She went for a kidney punch and he caught her hand. It was like punching a wall. "Ouch."

Liam let her go so quickly her shoulder muscles twanged. "I'm sorry. I've been away from people too long. I forget how fragile they are."

"I'm not fragile," she said, insulted. "I can look after myself." She was tired of having to remind everybody of that. None of the lost girls had been captured, had they? She thought they were doing pretty well, all things considered.

Eyes narrowing, she kicked out, leaning until she was parallel to the floor. He bent sideways, defying gravity and basic physics.

"I really hate vampires," she muttered again. She kicked at his knee and he sprawled on the ground. "Ha!" She probably shouldn't gloat. Hell with that, she was totally going to gloat. She deserved it. Especially since one of the cuts on her arm from her sparring match with Sofia yesterday had opened up. Blood trickled hot and slow down her bare arm. "Think you can—"

His face changed, eyes silver, teeth sharpening. She felt like she had that day when she'd watched him through a veil of freezing river water. She tingled and shivered. Helena lifted both her fists protectively, turned sideways. She'd barely pivoted when he was on her. He should have looked silly in his dark pin-striped suit; instead he just looked elegant, deadly. He closed in like a panther, all sleek muscles and intensity.

There was clearly something twisted inside her that she could find that kind of animal stealth so hot.

Helena reached for the discarded staff but it was barely in her hand when he twisted her wrist and it clattered to the floor. She backed up. He followed.

"Don't run." He sounded like he was pleading. She froze, inches away from the wall. "Too late," he said, desperately.

She should be afraid.

She wasn't.

It was the weirdest thing. She felt free, powerful. As if this deadly dance was as romantic as holding hands at the drive-in. He sparked something in her, or they sparked it off each other. It didn't matter. He was leashing his hunger, struggling to stay human. It was noble, difficult.

Liam wasn't like the others.

Neither was she.

She flashed him a crooked grin, catching him utterly off guard. Then she hooked her leg behind his knee and shoved him. When he fell, she followed him. He landed on the cold hardwood floor and she landed on him, still grinning.

"I'm not afraid of you," she whispered. "I wonder why that is."

"Because you're a fool." His voice was harsh but his fingers were gentle as they slid through her hair. He traced the line of her jaw with his thumb. His other hand flattened against her lower back, brushing her skin where the edge of the T-shirt rode up. He looked at her mouth. She almost forgot how much she wanted to punch him. Her lips tingled and he hadn't even touched her. He drew her head down to his, paused just before his mouth could claim hers.

He let her go abruptly. "This is a bad idea." He shoved her away and got to his feet slowly, painfully, as if he didn't trust himself. His fists were clenched, knuckles white. "I'm sorry. I came to warn you," he continued hoarsely. "Those two from the alley are reapers."

It took her a minute to get her brain off the feel of his cool muscled body under hers. Damn him for making her feel that way. Damn him for pulling away.

And damn her for not wanting him to.

"What the hell's a reaper?" she asked as a cover for the question she was embarrassed to admit she wanted to ask: Why didn't you kiss me?

"The Domokos siblings—the blonds from last night. They're the reason all those girls are disappearing, the reason that girl was bitten."

"Cass? Do they know her?"

"No, but now they know you. And you're interfering in their games, Helena," he said. "Lady Natasha doesn't take kindly to that."

"Lady Natasha can kiss my ass." She paused. "Who's Lady Natasha?"

He smiled briefly. "Natasha fancies herself the queen of the vampires."

Helena rolled her eyes. "Lame."

"Perhaps. But she enjoys her little harvests."

She paused for a heartbeat, feeling sick. "Harvest? As in . . ."

He nodded. "As in she likes to feed on them, yes."

"How do we stop her?"

"You don't."

She gathered her wet clothes, the staff. "I do too."

"Helena, this is my problem. I'll deal with it."

"Because I'm a girl?" She threw a wet sock at his head.

"No," he replied softly. "Because it's my fault."

◆

The moment shattered when they left the dojo. She stepped out into the alley and was once again a hungry street girl with damp hair and a suspicious nature. He was a vampire, cloaked in mystery and solitude, and as moody as a fourteen-year-old girl with PMS.

But she couldn't forget the glimpses she'd seen.

She shoved her hands in her pockets. It was later than she'd thought. "I guess I'll see you around."

His profile was chiseled, flawless. It kind of made her want to mess him up. "I'm not leaving your side," he said quietly.

She frowned. "What?"

"I have to keep you safe."

"This again." She rolled her eyes. "I'm fine. Go away."

"You're sixteen."

She went cold. He thought of her as a little girl. She'd imagined everything in the dojo. He'd been acting as a vampire, not as a man. It shouldn't matter.

It mattered.

"Liam," she said as calmly as she could. "I'm not your responsibility."

He put a hand on her arm, stopping just outside the glow of

a streetlight. His expression was stark as he drew her behind the concealing bulk of a parked van. "Do you know why my family is so reclusive?"

She shook her head mutely. When wild animals ventured out of the forest you didn't speak to them, you didn't move. You just waited.

"Because five hundred years ago a woman spoke a riddle and named a Drake daughter not even born yet as the next vampire queen."

"Is that even possible? Having a child? Aren't you undead?"

"It's possible in our family."

If there was one thing Helena knew about, it was girl fights. "Let me guess, this Natasha chick isn't too happy about that."

"Not happy and slightly insane."

"I know a lot of girls like that." She offered him a small smile. "Maybe you shouldn't hide," she said. "You should fight. You have friends." She was startled to realize she'd fight with him if he asked her. When exactly had she lost her mind?

"I thought so too, once," he said.

"What happened?"

"I fell for a girl."

Helena decided she wasn't the least bit jealous. Really. "So?"

"So Lady Natasha killed her." He glanced up to make sure they weren't being watched. The shadows were busy lately. "Do you know why Cass was bitten?" Helena shook her head. "Because I talked to her grandmother once. Her pregnancy probably saved her."

"That was like fifty years ago." She paused. "How old are you anyway?"

"Old enough."

"You look twenty-six, twenty-seven, max." And that was because of the eyes, not because of any lines on his face. He would have looked younger without all the sorrow and guilt.

"I'm not. My brother and I have seen a lot of innocent girls destroyed by Lady Natasha. The last girl who disappeared? She ran out in front of my car when she was drunk. I took her to the hospital. She was gone the next night."

She stared, horrified. "So Lady Natasha is targeting us on purpose. Killing street girls because there's no one to protect them."

He didn't smile but his eyes crinkled with dry amusement. "Until you."

"That's why you took off after I fell in the river and drew a crowd," she realized slowly. "And why you wouldn't talk to me anymore, even after we killed that *Hel-Blar* vampire."

"Now, you understand." He touched her arm, a quick moth-soft touch. "So, please. Please let me stay and make sure you're safe."

◆

He followed her to the club, staying in the shadows where no one would see him. She had to force herself not to look over her shoulder. It felt strange to know there were friendly eyes in the dark. The bouncer at the side door of the club nodded at her when she skirted the lineup.

"You're late. Grady's mad."

"Grady's always mad." Helena pushed past him into the smoky darkness of The Vortex. She felt Liam behind her but he didn't say a word, just broke away and lost himself in the crowd and strobe lights. Helena went down the hall to the cramped changing room with the tiny attached washroom. Sofia lounged on the only chair, Portia leaned against the wall eating Pixy Stix, and Billie crouched in the corner whittling stakes.

"Nice of you to finally show up," Sofia drawled. "Give the girl one win and she thinks she's a rock star."

"Oh, shut up," Helena muttered. "I've got fifteen minutes until the fight."

"And that's what you're wearing?" Sofia asked dubiously.

Helena glanced down. She'd forgotten she was wearing the clothes she'd taken from the dojo. Hers were in a sodden mess in her backpack. "Shit."

Sofia sighed theatrically. "I've got something you can wear."

"Hell no. I'm not wearing a tutu."

Portia wiped sugar off her shirt. "You can wear this tank top," she offered, pulling it off from under her fishnet top. She contorted impressively. Grady would have put her in the ring on the spot if he'd seen her.

"Thanks." Helena caught the black top and switched her T-shirt out. Her baggy black pants were hardly inspiring. She didn't really care. She couldn't stop thinking of Liam's mouth so near to hers. *Focus, Helena.*

"Trade me these pants for your skirt?" she asked Billie. "Just for the fight." Her denim miniskirt was shorter than anything Helena would ordinarily have worn but at least she could move freely in it.

"Still needs something," Portia said.

"Are you going to help?" Billie kicked Sofia's swinging foot.

Sofia snapped her gum loudly. "I already offered a tutu."

"Never mind, I have an idea." Portia reached for the can of spray paint she always carried in her knapsack. Half the art on the alley walls was hers. She shook the can with a grin. "To the lost girls."

Helena closed her eyes so she wouldn't get paint splattered into them. The chemical scent floated in the cramped space. Sofia coughed. Portia chewed on her lip, the way she always did when she drew. It didn't take her long. "There."

Billie chuckled. "Awesome."

Helena looked down. Portia had spray painted, in pink no less, a circle with a stylized face, elongated fangs, and a slash across it.

NO VAMPIRES ALLOWED.

For the first time, the thought made Helena uncomfortable. She wondered what Liam would think when he saw it. Never mind that he wore elegant suits and she wore spray paint; he'd saved her life.

"You don't like it." Portia sounded disappointed.

"Of course I do," Helena rushed to assure her. "I need some makeup, don't you think?" She hurried into the bathroom where she could be alone to wonder why she was suddenly concerned about delicate vampire sensibilities. The whole thing was ridiculous.

"Get your head in the game," she snapped at herself. She grabbed one of the black eyeliners in the plastic cup on the back of the sink. She was lining her eyes like an Egyptian queen when she saw it.

Iphigenia's favorite striped scarf.

Stuck to the wall on the tip of a knife.

She turned slowly, her stomach dropping. There was a piece of paper stuck between the blade and the scarf. It was a charcoal sketch of Helena. Calligraphy curved around the edges:

Your presence is required by
Lady Natasha in Crofter's Woods.

She stumbled out of the bathroom. Sofia and Portia were bickering as usual. Their voices sounded thin, distant. The floor shook from the crowds shouting and stomping their feet in the Thunderdome. Billie frowned at her. It took a moment to realize the other girl had spoken to her. "Helena, what's wrong?"

Reality slammed into her like a wave breaking over the shore. She fought the undertow, lifted her chin. "Iphi's missing."

Sofia waved that away. "She's probably in one of her hiding spots."

Helena shook her head, lifting the scarf. "It's got blood on it." Silence fell like an icicle, cold and deadly. She flung the paper out at them. It floated like delicate pollen, before landing faceup on the dirty glitter-strewn floor. "Let's go."

They darted down the hall. Grady stopped them before they reached the back door, motioning to Angelo, one of the bouncers. He was built like a bull and took his job very seriously.

"Where do you think you're going?" Grady asked silkily. The blue eye shadow he wore didn't make him look any less threatening.

"We have to go," Helena said. "Iphi's in trouble."

"You owe me a fight."

"Later." She shoved past him. He caught her by the hair even as Angelo pushed her down the step, away from the door. Helena hissed.

"You can go after the fight," Grady said. "Not before."

Portia and Billie bristled. Sofia was the only one who didn't look particularly concerned, but Helena read the tension in her brittle hair flip.

"Grady," she purred. "Can't you cut us a break? This is important."

"No."

She ran a hand up his arm, the one still clutching Helena's hair. "What if I fight for you?"

"You're not on tonight's list, sweetheart."

"I'll fight for free," she offered. "Just tonight."

He considered it. Sofia pouted invitingly. Helena reached for the pocket knife she knew was in Billie's skirt pocket. She always had a knife.

"Deal," Grady finally said. "Because I'm feeling generous." Helena snorted. He pulled savagely on her hair. "What was that, sweetheart?"

Sofia glared at her warningly. For Iphigenia, Helena didn't punch him in the crotch. "Nothing."

"That's what I thought." He waited another heartbeat before releasing her. He nodded to Angelo. Helena, Portia, and Billie were through the door before it was even halfway open.

She could have called for Liam. God knew they could use the backup. But Lady Natasha hated him, was targeting him. She wouldn't add to his troubles. And the lost girls were her responsibility anyway, not his.

She had enough blood on her hands.

◆

Something was wrong.

Liam felt it, smelled it in the thick club air. He searched the crowd for a threat. He was about to head to the back to find Helena when Grady stepped out to the microphone hanging from the ceiling. A girl in a sequined bikini pranced behind him, smiling the smile of a thousand toothpaste ads.

"Ladies and gents," Grady boomed. "Welcome to the Thunderdome!"

The audience reacted so loudly Liam wondered if there was blood in his ears. Sensitive hearing wasn't always an asset. He kept his gaze moving quickly, checking the entrances. He still felt it, some secret pull of danger.

"Tonight for your entertainment we have the feral and very fine Finnegan, battling the delectable and sexy Sofia!"

Liam had to fight to keep his fangs retracted.

Helena was gone.

◆

Portia hotwired a car parked on the edge of the Warren. It took them half an hour, at top speed, to race to the edge of the forest that led to Crofter's Woods. They left the car under a canopy of branches and went on foot the rest of the way. Billie handed out stakes. Portia bit her nails. Helena wanted to scream.

As the path narrowed to a trail, a branch cracked. Helena whirled just as a shadow broke away from the trees. She threw a stake before she fully registered who she was throwing it at. A girl squeaked as a second shadow knocked her to the ground. The stake slammed into an elm tree. Cass pushed Bruno's long hair off her face. "Ow."

"Easy, killer," Bruno said to Helena, helping Cass to her feet.

"What the hell are you doing here?" Helena demanded as they stood. "I nearly staked you!"

"We saw you heading out of town," Cass replied. Blood spotted the bandage on her throat. "And we heard another girl went missing."

"So?" Helena asked.

"So, I'm not an idiot . . . ," Cass pointed out. "You're about to do something stupid. No one heads into the mountains at this time of night without a monumentally stupid plan."

Bruno grinned, flipping his pocket knife between his fingers. "And we want in."

"No way," Helena said automatically, even though they could probably use Bruno. "You can't 'om' your way through this, Cass. What are you two doing out this late anyway?"

Cass blushed. "Don't change the subject." She crossed her arms, crystal necklaces catching the very faint moonlight. "I'm coming with you. Or you can leave me behind and I'll follow alone. By myself. All vulnerable and shit."

"Nice threat." Helena looked impressed despite herself.

"Thank you. Now what's the plan?"

"Iphigenia's down there somewhere," Helena explained darkly. "We get her out. If Lady Natasha's around, I get to shove a stake in her chest." For Iphi. For all the missing girls. For Liam. "They're waiting for us in Crofter's Woods."

"I know that place," Bruno said, all teasing gone from his voice. His accent was suddenly so thick Helena had to concentrate to understand him. "They'll have guards posted. I have a better spot."

They followed him around the bend to a rocky ledge. They crawled on their bellies to the edge, peering through the leaves. The clearing was ringed with torches. In the center, Iphigenia was tied to a red pine. The wind tossed needles over her. She was pale, her short cap of blond hair glinting like gold. She must be terrified.

But she was also alone.

"There," Helena said, rage making her feel hot all over. "We might be able to get her out before they know we're here."

Bruno pulled the shotgun she hadn't seen strapped to his back. "And if not, I'm a really good shot."

"We're dealing with vampires," Helena reminded him.

"Might not kill them but it'll sure as hell slow them down."

"Um, guys?" Cass asked.

"What?"

"Hello? Big fat trap down there?"

Helena scrubbed her face. "I know. But it doesn't matter. Billie, you should stay up here," she suggested, mind racing. "You're better with knives. Find a tree to climb and you'll see them before they see any of us. I'll go in alone." She ignored the requisite protests. "I mean it. They asked for me, they'll get me. Anyway, they won't take me seriously, a single raggedy girl. So we'll use it. It might be the only advantage we have."

"I don't like it," Bruno muttered.

Helena shrugged. "It doesn't matter. It's all we've got."

Cass took a lighter out of her purse. "Maybe not." She smiled softly, looking more like her grandmother than a New Age freak. "If we burn them out, they might not notice you freeing Iphigenia. Vampires like to be stealthy and there's nothing stealthy about a forest fire."

Portia whistled. "Nice, Tofu Girl. There's hope for you yet."

Bruno winced. "You're going to double back and siphon the gas out of my bike, aren't you?" She nodded. "Well, shit." He got up to help her. "Don't move until we're back," he ordered Helena.

"Watch out for the reapers," she told them.

"The reapers? That doesn't sound good," Cass remarked.

"They're the ones that bit you."

"Definitely not good."

Helena smiled at her, sharp and deadly as a fox in a henhouse. "Payback's a bitch."

Cass smiled back.

◆

The forest was on fire.

That could only mean one thing, Liam thought.

Helena.

◆

Helena's heartbeat felt so loud she was sure any vampire within a ten-mile radius could hear it. She breathed slowly, making sure her stakes were secure. She'd already checked them six different times on the climb down to the meadow. There was one in each boot, one in her skirt pocket next to Billie's knife, and one tucked into the small of her back. She was as ready as she was ever going to be.

She crept through the forest, wincing every time a twig snapped underfoot. She could drift through the Warren and never be seen, but put her in the middle of the woods and she was hopeless. She circled a tree and then passed through a bush she sincerely hoped wasn't poison ivy. The wind shivered through the leaves. She crouched at the edge of the trees. It felt like forever before she caught the scent of fire. Smoke curled between the trunks, obscuring even the sharpest of vampire vision.

Now or never.

Helena went low and raced across the open field, her neck prickling nervously. She had a stake in one hand, a knife in the other. She heard a shout in the distance but couldn't be sure if it was vampiric or human. She kept running.

"Hurry," Iphigenia sobbed, pulling against her ropes. "I'm scared."

"It's okay." Helena slid the last few feet toward her. "Are you hurt? Did they bite you?" Iphigenia shook her head. There was dirt on her face and across her shirt and her jeans were ripped, but Helena couldn't see any blood. "I'm going to get you out of here. Just hold on."

She sawed through the thick ropes with the knife until her skin chafed and blistered. Her blood smeared the twine, made her grip slippery.

Iphigenia struggled. "Hurry!"

"Almost got it," Helena assured her. The certainty that the trap was about to close around them made Helena short of breath. Every nerve ending felt jagged. The knife slipped, cutting into her palm. She wiped the cut on her shirt and went back to sawing. The ropes finally frayed apart. Iphigenia stepped out of the pile coiled around her like pale snakes.

And then she screamed as loud as she could.

Helena recoiled, then tried to slap her hand over her mouth. "Iphi," she said, thinking her friend hysterical. "Don't be afraid. I'm here to get you out."

"I'm not afraid," Iphigenia assured her, drawing another breath and jerking free. Her next scream was more specific. "She's here!"

"Iphi?" Helena goggled. "I don't understand."

"They wanted you, Helena. Not me." She shrugged one shoulder. Her waifish pixie face hardened. "It's always you."

"But . . . why?" She could not wrap her head around the betrayal.

"They promised to turn me." Iphigenia looked enthralled, fascinated. It made Helena want to throw up. "So I can be strong, strong like you."

Helena shook her head, as if it could change the truth. She took a step back. "This can't be happening."

Iphigenia's scream called her vampire allies out of hiding. They raced between the trees, pale and deadly. They moved so fast, as if Helena was in slow motion. A knife flew past her head, but it missed its vampire target and landed in the ferns. Billie's knife. Bruno's shotgun went off from the ridge but Helena couldn't see where the bullet had struck. She was too busy fighting off Iphigenia. She finally let go with a right hook, sending the tiny blond girl sprawling in the mud.

"You were a lost girl," she spat.

"And now I'll be immortal," Iphigenia spat back. "No one will ever be able to hurt me again. Not Grady, not my brother, no one."

"Iphi."

Iphigenia folded her arms. "You pissed them off, saving all those girls."

"I thought you were saving them too."

"We both know I was holding you guys back, that I'd be next." She shrugged. "So I had to save myself first."

Helena stayed low in the concealing smoke, kicking out when a vampire woman streaked past her. She rolled through the long grass and jabbed down with her stake. Ash clung to the wildflowers. She crawled away, hoping the fire and the smoke would conceal her.

No such luck.

"Got her!" Three more vampires sprinted in her direction. Bruno shot again but with the fire eating through the leaves and belching thick smoke, he was shooting blind. Helena threw a stake but she missed too. Heat from the encroaching flames hissed at her. Sweat stung as it dripped into her eyes.

She couldn't hide here any longer. Her escapes were being cut off by fire and vampires. She jumped to her feet and ran, flinging stakes behind her. Bruno's shotgun blasted again, and another, closer. She slammed right into a guy with black hair and nose plugs. "Who the hell are you?"

He looked military, in cargo pants with a walkie-talkie strapped to his shoulder. He even had night-vision goggles on his head. But he didn't look that much older than she was. "Roarke Black. Stand down."

"Bite me."

"We have it covered," he insisted. "This is no place for a civilian." He relented enough to incline his head. "We've been keeping an eye on your gang. Good work."

"You were the ones trailing Portia!"

"Yes. Now get out of here. Don't run until you're sure they're chasing us!"

He and three others, also armed to the teeth, launched themselves into the melee. Crossbow bolts whipped through the air. They burst through the clearing and spread out in all directions. The vampires followed, unable to resist. Iphigenia had already gone to ground. One of Billie's knives shot past Helena, nearly slicing the tip off her nose. She jerked back, swearing.

There were a lot of the commandos.

But there were a lot more vampires.

She let out an ear-piercing whistle. Three of the other vampires snapped around to look her way. She waved her fingers teasingly. "Hello, boys."

Then she ran.

She pushed her legs until they felt like they'd crumble, ran until her chest tightened and her breath was like hot sandpaper at the back of her throat. She could hear them behind her, closing in. She tried to stay out of the shelter of the ridge, hoping Billie and Bruno could see her pursuers. One of them fell back, knife in his eye. Helena leaped over a log and kept running. Bruno's gun took out a second, so Helena had just enough time to turn and stake her through her rib cage, as the vampire clutched her leg. There was only one vampire left and he halted. "Screw this," he muttered, taking off.

Helena leaned against a tree, panting. The light from the fire pierced the smoke, dancing cheerfully. It was surreal. She forced herself to stumble back toward the clearing.

"I told you these backwoods hicks would make a mess of it."

Helena froze, recognizing the musical sing-songy voice.

Elisabet.

"Lady Natasha won't be pleased," Lyle agreed. "But she can hardly blame us."

"We're her reapers, idiot. Of course she can blame us. We're meant to be reaping. Now even that blond twit of a girl is gone."

Helena didn't dare move, didn't dare even exhale. Somewhere, very faintly, fire-truck sirens sounded. The only reason the Domokoses hadn't seen her or caught her scent yet was because of the smoke and the general mayhem. Shadows shifted, veiled in curtains of gray fog and ash.

"There are two girls left in the cage," Lyle reminded his sister.

"Leftovers." Elisabet sighed. "She won't be impressed with that."

"Better than nothing. Let's bring them to her as a peace offering."

There were two girls left. Helena held onto that thought, punched on it like a hungry cat. Two girls who weren't dead. Yet.

She followed the reapers, hoping the sounds of the fire and the fighting would cover her footsteps. Portia and Cass intercepted her.

"I can't believe Iphi's a traitor," Portia said, disgusted. Blood ran down her leg from a deep gash. "That little weasel."

"Helena?" Cass frowned at her. "You're going the wrong way. That way's full of fire and fangs."

"There are more girls that way," she said, straining to see where Elisabet and Lyle had gone. If she waited much longer, she'd lose them altogether.

"We're coming too," Portia said, gritting her teeth against the pain of her leg.

Helena shook her head. "You're wounded. Cass, take her back to Bruno and Billie. I have to go."

"It's like you do it on purpose," Portia muttered. She leaned on Cass, shooting a glare at Helena. "If you die you're really going to piss me off."

◆

Finding two vampires in the dark smoky woods wasn't easy.

If it wasn't for a pair of sleepy doves startled into the sky at their passing, Helena might have wandered for hours. She followed the commotion, staying well back when she caught a glimpse of moonlight on pale skin and gold hair. The Domokoses moved quickly, eyes glowing even from a distance. They were scared.

Good.

They crossed a valley to a small cave nestled among rocks and roots. It was really more of a weed-choked hollow created by a long-ago avalanche. Inside, Helena caught a glint of iron.

The cage.

Lyle pulled out two bony girls in tattered clothing, wearing necklaces of dried blood. They were alive, though, and able to walk. She stayed far back enough that she couldn't hear what they were saying. One of the girls was trembling so violently she looked like an aspen leaf falling from a tree. Helena scurried after them, picking her way around twigs and branches, praying she wouldn't get caught.

She paused on a crest of rocks, staying hidden in a scraggly bush. Elisabet and Lyle were coming around the crest, toward another set of caves ringed with torchlight and guarded by fierce vampires. A woman came to the opening and looked out impatiently. Helena fell back, holding her breath. She had straight white-blond hair in a perfect waterfall down her back. She wore an old-fashioned dress and a ransom in diamonds. She glittered and preened, deadly as ice breaking on a winter lake.

Helena knew she had to head them off at the pass, had to get the girls free before they reached the caves and reinforcements. It had to be now.

She had no weapons left except a single stake. She scrounged on the ground for rocks, scrambling back around to the other side of the hill. She aimed the first rock at Elisabet's head. She nearly took out one of the girls instead. The second rock caught Elisabet's ear. The third was snatched out of midair.

It wasn't enough.

Helena crouched down, jamming her back against a boulder. She dug with her feet, kicking and shoving dirt, pebbles, rocks, anything she could reach. The rockslide wasn't enough to bury Lyle and Elisabet, but it was enough to distract them. The girls scurried like rats to safety. Helena kept kicking rocks. When there was nothing left but dry dirt she hurried to the ledge, helping them up.

"Run," she gasped, not caring that running was generally a bad idea around vampires. There were no choices left. They had to get out of there.

Fear outweighed starvation and fatigue and pushed them down the rocky hill and through the trees. Helena whistled around her thumb and forefinger, three short blasts, hoping Bruno was close enough to hear. She looked over her shoulder, saw fangs and furious eyes.

She cut right, away from the girls running on bleeding bare feet. The Domokoses followed her. She knew she couldn't keep up this pace much longer. And it didn't matter. Vampires were faster, always. She tried to stay within view of the glow of the fire, but she was getting turned around. She was lost and exhausted.

She stopped running when she was gagging on her own breath. She turned warily, not saying a word. Elisabet and Lyle smiled at each other.

Helena raised her chin. If she was going to die here, she'd die with curses on her lips and their blood under her fingernails.

She only just barely saw someone standing behind them.

Liam.

He paced them like a sleek vengeful panther, dark hair blending into the night. Only his eyes gave him away—and the flash of his fangs.

Shock made Helena laugh. Elisabet turned her head.

Liam attacked.

Helena leaped at Lyle, last stake in her hand.

He deflected, sending her crashing into a tree. She slumped, using the same tactic she'd used in the Thunderdome: look more wounded than you are. She waited, gasping. Lyle approached her slowly, even as his sister blocked Liam's stake.

"Liam Drake." Elisabet laughed. "Protecting this one, are you? Won't Lady Natasha be interested to hear that." She smirked. "She so enjoyed Deirdre."

Helena was the one who hissed at that.

Lyle grabbed her by her tank top and hauled her up. Her feet dangled. She let herself go boneless. His fangs lengthened. She staked him. Unfortunately, she wasn't strong enough at that angle to pierce his heart. The stake ricocheted off his ribs. He snarled. She tried to gouge his eyes out but he had her pinned. His fangs brushed her neck.

And then she was falling, ash drifting around her.

Liam's stake finished the job, piercing Lyle's heart, ripping her tank top, and landing in a maple tree. Elisabet whirled, too shocked to scream for a moment, before rage made her insane. She howled like a rabid animal, pupils ringed with red. She went for Liam's throat with her teeth, her nails, every part of her a weapon. Liam fought back but there was already a gash on his upper arm. His shirt was ripped. Elisabet slammed a stake into his chest, just under his collarbone, missing his heart. He pulled it out, blood dripping into the grass.

Elisabet continued to howl. She was strong, snapping Liam's shoulder out of its socket with a single blow. He snapped it back, blocking the tip of her boot as it jabbed at his kneecap. It wasn't enough.

Helena yanked at Liam's stake embedded in the tree, trying to work it free. Sweat made her hands slick.

Liam went down, blood on his face.

Elisabet grinned savagely. She retrieved her stake in the grass and pierced Liam's shirt, skin, flesh.

Helena finally got the stake out, tears of frustration stinging her eyes. The end was broken. She didn't care.

She leaped on Elisabet's back, jamming it toward her heart as hard as she could. Elisabet screeched, releasing her own stake as she flung Helena off. Helena managed to turn over, hands and knees bloodied from her landing, just in time to see Liam pluck the stake from his own chest and drive it into Elisabet.

She turned to ash, drifting like gray snow between the trees.

Helena sat up, wincing in pain. Three short whistles sounded from the woods near the fire. Bruno. Everyone was okay. Helena whistled back as Liam crawled to her, gathering her up in his arms. "You just took years off my life."

She smiled. "Good thing you're immortal."

◆

Liam took her to the lake. It was cold but Helena didn't care. She stripped down to her bra and underwear and jumped into the water, rinsing the blood and mud and ashes off. Liam followed, pale and perfect.

"Anyone ever tell you you're insane?" he asked.

She pushed her wet hair off her face. "Once or twice." Maybe it was shock, but she felt good. Happy. The girls were safe, she was safe. Liam was at her side. There were a million stars above them and the blood was out of her hair. She drew her fingertips around the gash the stake had left under his collarbone and over his shoulder. "Does it hurt?"

He shook his head, drawing her close. "I don't feel anything but you."

His mouth took hers or hers took his, she wasn't sure. She only knew that his claim on her seared through her and burned all the way to her toes. He tasted her, his tongue touching hers, his hands stroking her bare spine. She wrapped her legs around him. The cold water held them up as they finally gave into the longing and the need between them.

"We have to stop," he murmured against her lips.

She looked at him as if he'd proposed tea with Lady Natasha. "Why?"

He groaned. "Because I'm way too old for you."

She rolled her eyes. "You're undead and you're worried about a little thing like age?" Her tongue touched his lower lip.

He swallowed and pulled back, jaw clenched. "You're turning me into a dirty old man."

She tilted her head. "How old are you, really?"

"Eighty-one."

She blinked. "Oh." She ran her hands up his muscular arms. "You look good for a decrepit old perv."

He laughed despite himself. "I've never known anyone like you." He kissed her again, quickly, too quickly. "I'll wait for you."

"Where am I going?"

"Not you. Me. I'm leaving Violet Hill."

"Forever?" The water was suddenly cold, freezing her to the bone. She swam to shore. "Then why bother with all this? You should have let Lady Natasha kill you, since you're letting her win anyway." She pulled her clothes on angrily, teeth chattering.

Liam was suddenly behind her, arms around her waist. "I'm not leaving you," he murmured in her ear. "Never. But you're sixteen. I'll come back for you in two years. After I've had some time to draw Lady Natasha away from this town. She doesn't know to fear you yet, not with Elisabet and Lyle gone."

"Are two years really going to make that big of a difference? You'll be eighty-three instead of eighty-one. Big deal."

"But you'll be legal. And you'll have a chance to find a sense of yourself, a sense of who you could be. You might not want this life."

"I want you," she said softly. Admitting it took as much courage as facing down a vampire queen and all of her minions. "And I'm going to take those two years to learn how to really kick your sorry undead ass."

He turned her around, kissing her tenderly. "Promise?"

She nodded solemnly. "I promise."

"Good." He kissed her again and it flared so hot and so desperate it was physically painful to pull away. "I have to go," he said. "But I'll find you."

She dug her fingers into his hair and pulled his mouth back to hers. "If you don't find me, Liam Drake," she vowed, "I'll find you."

Fall for Alyxandra Harvey all over again

Violet Willoughby doesn't believe in ghosts . . .
but they believe in her

www.alyxandraharvey.com

A magical world, a wicked ruler, a forbidden love. Enter a world of faery romance . . .

Catch up with the latest news and giveaways
from Alyxandra Harvey at
www.facebook.com/myloveliesbleeding

To order direct from Bloomsbury Publishing visit www.bloomsbury.com
or call 01256 302 692

Seven handsome brothers, two best friends and one captivating story

The Drake Chronicles

OUT NOW!

Visit facebook.com/myloveliesbleeding for extracts and more